THE AMARNA AGE:BOOK 5

LADY OF THE
TWO LANDS

KYLIE QUILLINAN

First published in Australia in 2021.

ABN 34 112 708 734

kyliequillinan.com

A catalogue record for this book is available from the National Library of Australia.

Ebook ISBN: 9780648903901

Paperback ISBN: 9780645180046

Large print ISBN: 9780645180053

Hardback ISBN: 9780645180060

Audiobook ISBN: 9780645377170

This is a work of fiction. Any similarity between the characters and situations within its pages and places or persons, living or dead, is unintentional and coincidental.

Cover art by Deranged Doctor Design.

Edited by MS Novak.

This work uses Australian spelling and grammar.

LP02062023

ONE

Our arrival into the Egyptian harbour city of Rhakotis was nothing like I anticipated. I had pictured the five of us standing triumphantly at the prow as the ship drew into port. Intef on one side of me, Istnofret on the other. Renni and Behenu behind them, Mau perhaps already tucked into her basket and slung over Behenu's shoulder. My babe still secure in my belly or, at the very least, cradled in my arms.

Instead, I had only my shadow for company. I glanced down to where it stretched along the deck, attached as always to my soles.

"I suppose it is not what you pictured either, Shadow," I said. "Do you feel his loss as keenly as I do?"

But my shadow didn't respond and although I had not expected it to, I felt all the more lonely. Did it blame me for the loss of both Intef and his shadow? Did it hate me now? We had built some level of trust in the hours we were separated while in the underworld. No doubt that was ruined. Istnofret disturbed my lonely thoughts as she came up behind me, accompanied by Renni.

"Samun?"

"I am well."

"Renni thinks it best we hide your face, so I brought you a shawl."

"Why? It is unlikely anyone here would recognise me and, besides, I look nothing like I used to."

"There were many images of your face in Memphis," Renni said. "Murals, statues. Plenty of opportunities for someone to recognise you. Possibly lots of motive too. There might be a reward for information on you."

"Surely not after all this time. We have been gone for, what, two years?"

"Must be close to that," Renni said. "Still, I think we cannot afford to risk it until we know what the situation here is. We have heard little from Egypt for some time now."

Intef would want me to do whatever Renni said, so I took the shawl and draped it over my head.

"How do you feel?" Istnofret asked as she fussed over the shawl, positioning it just so.

"A little tired but well enough."

I didn't miss the concerned look that flashed between them.

"Renni-" Istnofret started, but he already nodded.

"As soon as the ship docks, you and Behenu find somewhere she can rest while I go secure lodgings."

"I really am only a little tired," I said.

"We cannot risk it," Renni said. "You know what happens when you get too tired."

The times the Eye had twisted my mind had all been when I was tired. We didn't know for certain that fatigue was what allowed the Eye to influence me, but it was our best guess. The Eye made me crave power. When I was under its spell, I would forget that my friends were no longer my servants and would expect them to carry out my orders. I would believe I was queen again. We all feared what I might do if I sank too far under the Eye's control.

We left the ship as soon as we were permitted to disembark, carrying our various bags and packs. We had only brought as much food as we would need for the eight-day journey from Crete to Rhakotis, but we had accumulated an unwieldy number of other items on our travels, including cooking pots, blankets, warm clothes and our hide shelter.

"Wait over there in the shade," Renni said. "Try not to engage with anyone. We don't want any rumours spreading, especially not before we know whether anyone is watching for Samun."

"Shall I come with you?" Behenu asked.

"No, wait here with the others. Your face might be recognised just as easily as Samun or Istnofret. It would only take one person who worked in the palace, or who had reason to go there at some point, for word to get out."

"Nobody will remember me," Behenu said. "I was just a slave. Nobody ever even saw me."

"Or me," Istnofret added. "It is only Samun we need worry about."

"You might be surprised at how a particular face sticks in someone's memory," Renni said. "Perhaps you were kind to them once, or got in their way when they were in a hurry. The smallest thing could make them remember you. I will be back as soon as I can."

We sat together in the shade and pretended to be immersed in conversation. The heat was both shocking and familiar at the same time. At least a steady breeze blew in over the ocean to cool us somewhat. I tried to stay alert to who was around us and how close they came, but it was difficult to watch without being obvious about it. This wasn't something Intef had taught me.

My eyes filled with tears at the thought and I blinked hard before they could spill over. Why did Intef have to be the one who stayed? Why couldn't it have been someone else? But who? Renni? Would I take him away from Istnofret so that I could keep Intef with me? Behenu? Would I deny her the chance to go home after this was all over? Istnofret even? My loyal lady and the only one of my three serving women who still lived. She had travelled all the way across the civilised world with me. There were no good answers to my question.

"Here comes Renni," Istnofret said.

I turned to look and the shawl slid off my head.

"Don't look up," she hissed.

She grabbed the shawl and managed to stop it from falling off completely, although I ended up with it mashed against my face. She quickly draped it back over my head again.

"Keep your head down. Behenu, did anyone see?"

"I don't think so."

"I have found somewhere for us to stay," Renni said as he reached us. "It is just for a couple of nights, but it will give us time to seek out news and make a plan."

I started to ask a question, but he quickly shook his head.

"Not here. Wait until we can be assured of privacy."

I snapped my mouth closed. It was a good reminder that no matter how much Intef had taught me, there was still much to learn. I had no idea how he and Renni constantly remembered all these things.

Renni led us to our accommodation. It was a small cottage comprising no more than a single chamber which felt rather cramped once we were all inside, but it had four walls and a roof and a door which locked.

"We don't have many supplies left." Behenu was already

digging through our packs. "I suppose there is enough for tonight but that is all."

"I am going out for a while," Renni said. "See if I can hear some news. I will get supplies."

"Where will you go?" Istnofret asked. "I am not sure it is any safer for you than for us."

"Someone has to go," he said. "We all know that. Yes, it could be you or it could be Behenu, but it may as well be me."

"But if something happens to you-"

"Then you will have to protect Samun." He touched her cheek gently. "It is a risk we must take."

At length she gave him a reluctant nod. "Be careful."

"I will. I will be back as soon as I can."

He disappeared out the door. I didn't miss the fact that he took his pack. The one that had the Eye stashed at the bottom. We had agreed it would be best if I didn't have access to the Eye until the time came to use it.

I paced around the chamber for a while.

"Samun, you should lie down and rest," Istnofret said.

"I am not tired anymore."

"Well, I am, so I should think everyone else is too. You know you need to be careful when you are tired."

I swallowed my irritation. I had promised I would pay heed any time one of them said I was too tired or acted irrationally. We had been afraid that such proximity to the Eye might make its effect on me stronger, but it didn't seem to be the case. Fortunately, when the Eye twisted my thoughts with images of power and glory, I usually said something odd, which would alert the others. They would encourage me to rest, but even just being aware of it seemed to nullify the Eye's effect somewhat.

Renni was gone for hours. Istnofret grew increasingly anxious, although she did her best to hide it. But she kept slipping over to peek out through the shuttered windows and even when she sat, she was still in motion, tapping her foot or fiddling with a loose thread on her skirt.

"Don't worry about him," Behenu said to her at one point. "You know Renni can look after himself."

"Yes, but he is one man," Istnofret said. "At least when he had Intef with him…"

Her voice trailed away and I tried to pretend I didn't notice them both shooting me anxious looks. We hadn't really talked about what had happened. How we needed to leave one of us behind as a companion to Keeper of the Lake in order for the rest to be allowed to pass through the gate they guarded. Intef had insisted on being the one to stay. He was so furious that I gave our daughter to Osiris as payment for the Eye that he hadn't even been able to look at me afterwards. He hated me so much that he would prefer to live in the underworld with whatever manner of creature Keeper of the Lake was. He was rarely far from my mind and I supposed the same was true for the others, given the number of times they mentioned him, then quickly changed the subject. Footsteps on the path outside distracted me from my miserable thoughts.

"Renni?"

Istnofret opened the door before I even had time to wonder whether it was him. Renni rushed inside, pushing her back in, and quickly shut the door.

"What did I tell you about staying out of sight?" he asked. "That means you do not open the door and you most definitely do not go outside."

"But I was sure it was you," Istnofret said.

"I probably would have done the same thing if Istnofret had not gotten there first," Behenu said.

"Promise me you won't do that again," Renni said. "No matter what you hear outside."

She hesitated and he gave her a stern look.

"Please, Ist. With the news I have, it is more important than ever that you do as I say."

"Fine," she said, a little sulkily. "I was just anxious to see that you were well."

"As you can see, I am fine, but we have trouble. I ran into someone we all know... Khay."

TWO

M y heart stuttered a little at Renni's words. This was bad news indeed.

"Who?" Behenu asked.

"He used to be one of my guards," I said. "In fact, he was Intef's second until he betrayed me."

"What did he do?" she asked.

I shook my head, suddenly so filled with rage that I couldn't even speak. I hadn't thought about Khay in a long time. I had certainly never expected to see him again.

"Have we never mentioned him?" Istnofret asked, when it became clear that I wasn't going to respond. "Ay sent a spy to pose as a serving lady. She was supposed to watch Samun and report back to Ay on everything she did. Khay knew about it and had promised to protect her if she was caught. Well, she did get caught and he couldn't decide quickly enough whether to help her and it all came out. We didn't know he was a traitor until then."

"What happened to him?"

"Samun sent him to labour in the Nubian gold mines for

three years, along with the spy."

"Tentopet." Was this the first time I had said her name since those events? Quite possibly. "I doubt she survived, but I knew Khay would."

"Why did you not give him a harsher sentence then?" Behenu asked. "Unless you wanted him to survive?"

I could only sigh. My chin wobbled and I suddenly found myself on the verge of tears.

"He and Intef were close," Renni said. "I was Intef's third at the time, but he and Khay managed most things between themselves. I don't think Intef quite trusted me back then. I am not sure he ever really trusted me until the night we left Memphis."

"You should not take it personally," I said. "He never trusted anyone other than Khay and when he realised he had been wrong about him..."

I couldn't say any more without crying. Everything Intef had ever done had been to protect me. And look at how I repaid him.

"Renni, tell us what happened," Istnofret said.

I was thankful when they all turned their attention to him. I wiped my eyes and tried to sniffle quietly.

"There is a market down by the dock. Apparently they set up there every evening. Food, fabrics, household items. There is a spot where the dock workers gather to have a drink at the end of their shifts. I got myself a mug of beer and sat down. Just wanted to listen really. Get a feel for what is happening, see if there was any mention of Ay or of war with the Hittites. I hadn't been sitting there more than a few minutes before someone sits down beside me. Renni, he says, I thought that was you."

"What did he want?" I asked, having gathered myself sufficiently to be able to talk without crying.

"To know where you were. He hedged around it for a good while, asking what I had been doing and why I left Memphis. He knew Ay had sent you to the mines. Said he heard that Intef and I both disappeared around the same time and wondered if we went after you."

"What did you tell him?" Istnofret asked.

"That with the queen gone, I figured I was about to be out of work so thought I would go see the world. Got a job as ship's crew and just kept moving, going wherever the work took me."

"Did you tell him you went to Crete?" I asked.

"Of course not. I doubt your sisters are still there, but I didn't want to give anyone reason to go looking. I didn't mention Babylon either. Said I was in Syria for a while. Figured I could talk about that enough to be convincing if he asked. Told him I had some savings now and was getting tired. Decided to come home and see if I can find myself a wife."

Istnofret pretended to glare at him and he shrugged, unapologetic.

"Keep as close to the truth as you can. That is how they train us. Make the lies as small as possible so they are easier to remember."

"Do you think he believed you?" Behenu asked.

"Couldn't really tell. He asked a lot of questions, pretended to be casual, but kept circling back around to how Samun disappeared on her way to Nubia. Said he figured someone knew what had happened and he just had to find that person."

"What did you say to that?" I asked.

"Not much. Muttered about how it left me out of work. Good job it was too. Steady pay, decent captain. I am not certain he believed me, but he started boasting about how he had easy work now. Got some labouring job and apparently he is friends with the overseer, so the fellow looks the other way while Khay lazes around. He offered to get me work there too."

"I hope you told him you didn't need a job," Istnofret said swiftly.

"I kind of said yes." Renni looked abashed. "Couldn't think of a way to get out of it quickly enough. If Intef had been here..."

His voice trailed away and I could feel them all concentrating on not looking at me.

"Well, anyway, I already told him I had been here for a week or two. Said I had a fever and had been lying low but needed to find work now. So I could hardly say no when he offered me this easy job, could I?"

"Renni!" Istnofret glared at him.

"A couple of days, Ist," he said. "That is all I need. Just enough time to put him at ease, convince him I really don't know anything. He will lose interest soon enough and we can slip away."

"Can we not leave now?" Behenu asked. "Tonight? Khay is the only one who knows who you are."

"I agree," Istnofret said. "Samun, what do you think?"

I hesitated. Behenu's plan was sensible, but this could be a chance to get reliable information before we headed to Memphis.

"I think you should do it," I said to Renni. "Just for a couple of days and then we disappear."

"Samun, that is a terrible idea." Istnofret put her hand on Renni's arm. "Please, Renni, it is too dangerous. We need to leave tonight."

"He is already suspicious, love," Renni said. "Don't worry about me. I will be careful. I will work for a couple of days, then we can slip away. If I don't, we will be looking over our shoulders the whole time and wondering when he will find us."

"Would it really matter if he knew?" I asked. "What can he

do? He is an outlaw. I banished him. He should not even be in Egypt."

"He is an outlaw, yes," Renni said. "And that means he is looking to legitimise himself again. If he figures out you are here, he will go straight to the palace."

"He won't get an audience," I said. "Ay won't see a criminal who was banished."

"He doesn't need to get to him," Renni said. "Not directly anyway. He only needs to get to someone who can pass a message to him, and you and I both know there are plenty of people willing to tell tales to Pharaoh."

"Did he tell you anything about the mines?" Istnofret asked.

"Just that it was an experience he would rather not have had. I suppose it is old news for him these days. It must be, what, at least ten years since Samun sent him away. He served his three years and was released years ago. I didn't push him. In fact, I would rather not have asked, but it would have seemed strange if I didn't."

"Did he mention Tentopet?"

I almost didn't ask, unsure whether I wanted to know her fate. I wasn't surprised Khay had survived. He had been the best of the best — Intef wouldn't have chosen him for my personal squad otherwise. I knew when I sent them both away that if it was possible for anyone to survive, Khay would. I had done that for Intef. Because he had loved Khay like a brother before he found out he was a spy.

"Not by name," Renni said. "He hinted he had a woman with him, but I was not sure exactly what the relationship was and thought he might get suspicious if I asked too many questions."

"He might have helped Tentopet," Istnofret said. "That would not surprise me. Khay was always kind to me."

I shot her a look. "You would defend a traitor?"

"I am not saying he is not a traitor, only that he was kind to me. He may have felt responsible for Tentopet, especially since he didn't protect her as he promised to. He might have helped her. Made sure she had food. Perhaps done some of the worst of her labouring. With someone like him to help her, Tentopet could have lasted three years."

It was no more than I had been thinking myself.

"He asked about you, Ist," Renni said.

"Me?" Her voice was high. "Why me?"

"People noticed that you disappeared at the same time as Intef and I. There was a rumour you had run off with one of us, or maybe even both."

"People are disgusting." She gave him a dark look. "What did you say?"

"You don't want to know, love. I said what he would expect to hear and it is nothing I would repeat in the company of a woman."

I thought she would press him to tell her, but she only shook her head.

"Men are disgusting."

"Sometimes," he said cheerfully. "Now, I need to get some sleep if I am to work tomorrow."

"And what are we three to do while you are off working?" Istnofret asked.

"Someone will need to go out for supplies," Behenu said. "It looks like Renni didn't get any."

"You will have to wait until I finish work," Renni said. "I will pick up supplies on my way home. I am sorry I could not do it tonight. I didn't want to linger once I was able to get away from Khay and he would be suspicious if he saw me getting more than I needed for myself."

"It will be a very long day with nothing to do and not even

bread to eat," Istnofret said. "I will go for supplies in the morning. I will wear a shawl over my face," she added quickly when Renni started to object.

"Maybe I should go," Behenu said. "It is less likely that anyone would remember my face. You went everywhere with Samun, Ist. People are more likely to have seen you. Envied you even."

Istnofret snorted, which was most unlike her.

"Envied me? What a ridiculous thing to say."

"You were the queen's attendant," Behenu said. "You had her ear. You wore beautiful gowns and ate the same food as she did. I used to watch you sweep down the hallway, completely confident that you were entitled to be there. I envied you and I doubt I was the only one."

Istnofret stared at her for a long moment, as if wondering whether Behenu was joking.

"You never told me that before," she said eventually and her voice was a little wobbly. "I am just a servant. I am nobody important."

"You are not a servant anymore, Ist," I said. "None of you are. You are my friends."

"Does that mean I could leave if I wanted to?" she asked.

"Of course you could. I have told you that before."

I brushed away the tear that unexpectedly spilled from my eye. Was that what they really wanted? To go off and live their own lives and leave me by myself? If I still had Intef, maybe it wouldn't have bothered me quite so much, but they were all I had now.

"Well, hasn't this suddenly gotten morose." Istnofret's voice was determinedly cheerful. "I did not mean I was actually planning to leave. You know perfectly well that we are going to see this through with you. We will all be there when you confront Ay."

My dream came back to me, the one in which I either faced Ay alone or watched the Egyptian army be slaughtered by the Hittites. They wouldn't be there with me at the end. They might not know it yet, but I did.

THREE

Renni left early the next morning, taking with him the pack in which the Eye was hidden. I was torn between relief that it would be out of my grasp for the day and worry that he might have to leave his pack somewhere while he worked. What if someone went through it, looking for valuables to steal?

We women spent a long and hungry morning waiting for Renni's return. We had two strips of dried meat, which we shared between the three of us. Istnofret found a broom and a cloth, and busied herself with cleaning, even though the chamber looked clean enough to my eye. Behenu waited at the window, her face pressed to the closed shutters.

"Come away from there," Istnofret said to her. "Someone will see you."

"Even if they do, they will see only an eye peering out through the gaps between the shutters," she said. "And maybe I will see something useful."

"I wish we could open the window." I wiped the sweat from the back of my neck. With both door and window closed, the cottage was stifling.

Sometime around the middle of the day, Istnofret finally put away her cleaning equipment.

"I am too hungry to wait any longer," she said. "I will go out and get us something to eat."

"Renni said to stay here," I said.

"He cannot stay angry with me forever. Besides, I swear I will eat my boots if I don't get something better to eat soon."

"I would like to see that," Behenu said, although even the promise of Istnofret eating her boots wasn't enough to draw her away from the window. "Let me go. I will wear a shawl and keep my head down."

"It is too dangerous," Istnofret said, although she sounded less sure now. It seemed the prospect of Behenu bringing back food was wearing her down.

"We need proper clothes," I said. "Sandals, kohl."

"I could say that my mistress and I have recently arrived by sea and she wants to dress like an Egyptian woman," Behenu said.

"You would pretend to be a slave?" Istnofret asked. "Are you sure you want to do that?"

Behenu shrugged. "Telling a few strangers that I am a slave does not make me one again."

They both looked to me for approval. Once it would have been Intef who made such decisions.

"Go," I said. "But be careful, and come straight back if anyone asks too many questions."

"Well, not *straight* back," Istnofret said. "Take a winding path. Pretend you are going somewhere else and double back. Make sure you are not followed."

"I know. Renni taught me the same things he taught you."

Behenu slipped out the door without another word, likely hurrying away before either of us could change our minds.

Then it was just Istnofret and I left in the stuffy chamber. We looked at each other.

"She will be fine." Istnofret sounded like she was trying to convince herself as much as me.

"I hope so. Renni is going to be really mad at both of us if something happens to her."

We sat and waited.

Eventually, Istnofret got up to pace around the chamber.

She sat and I paced.

Still we waited.

"We should not have let her go," she said. "Maybe we should go out and look for her?"

"What good would that do? As angry as Renni will be if something happens to her, he is going to be even angrier if we all go out."

"We made a mistake. We can find her and get her back before he returns."

"You know he would tell you to wait. That just because you cannot see what is happening, it doesn't mean something is wrong."

"Ugh. You sound just like him," she said with a groan.

Soft footsteps came from just outside the cottage.

"Do you hear that?" Istnofret asked.

"Ssh."

I eased my dagger out of its pouch and quietly got up. We should have already been on our feet, keeping ourselves limber and ready to move, instead of sitting around on cushions. There was a soft knock on the door.

"It is me," Behenu whispered.

"Oh, thank Isis." Istnofret rushed forward to unlock the door. Behenu slipped inside and Istnofret quickly closed the door behind her. "Did anyone recognise you?"

"Let her put down her packages first, Ist," I said, taking a basket from Behenu's hand.

Behenu set the rest of her packs on the floor.

"Nobody noticed me," she said. "I kept my face covered and acted the part of a docile slave. I took the long way back and made sure nobody followed."

"Are you very certain?" I asked.

"You brought back a lot of stuff." Istnofret eyed the packages with a frown. "Renni will notice. Maybe we should hide some of it."

"I got clothes for all three of us, some kohl like Samun wanted, and food for a couple of days. Maybe I did get a bit much, but I only had the gem to trade with. I didn't want to be seen to be accepting too poor a trade, given that I was supposed to be shopping for my mistress. She would have surely told me how much to get for the gem she gave me."

"How long until Renni returns do you think?" Istnofret asked. "Do we have time to eat or should we hide it all away now?"

I had been rummaging through the packs as they spoke and my fingers came across something silky. I pulled it out, revealing a diaphanous white gown. I hadn't worn something like this since we left Egypt.

"I got that for you," Behenu said. "It reminded me of that pale green one you used to have."

"It is beautiful, but Renni will know someone went out if I wear it."

"Oh." Behenu looked crestfallen. "I thought you would like it though. I can picture you in it."

"I will wear it, I promise, but I think we should hide it away for now. Later, once we have been out a couple of times, it will not seem so odd if I suddenly have a new gown."

Istnofret had been digging through the packages while we spoke and pulled out a white gown with a long skirt and sheer sleeves.

"Oh," she said.

"That one is for you," Behenu said.

"I love it," she said. "It has been so long since I have had a beautiful gown to wear."

"This one is for me." Behenu pulled out another gown in a similar style.

"It will feel rather odd to be dressed like an Egyptian again," I said.

My fingers crept over the silky fabric, even as I reminded myself that we should hide it away.

"Maybe we could quickly try them on?" Istnofret suggested. "Renni won't be back for ages yet. They won't send the labourers home until the sun starts to set."

"What if he leaves early?" I asked. "If Khay gets suspicious, he might come straight back. We should pack everything up and be ready to go, just in case."

Istnofret sighed and carefully folded her gown.

"It is beautiful. I cannot wait to dress like a proper Egyptian again."

As I set my gown back in the pack, I noticed a pretty little clay container painted to look like a palm tree.

"I used to spend so much time having my face made up." I opened the container to inspect the kohl inside. It was a deep shade of green. "It feels like such a waste of time now. I am not sure I want to go back to that."

"Oh, but your eyes look so beautiful with kohl." Istnofret took the container from me. "Let me make up your eyes. Just a tiny bit. Renni won't even notice."

"I don't know."

"Go on," Behenu said. "We could all put a little bit on. I am sure that men don't notice such things."

I refrained from reminding them that most Egyptian men wore just as much kohl as the women did.

"Only a little bit," I said. "You know how mad he will be if he realises someone went out."

Istnofret applied the kohl around my eyes. Her touch was so light, I could barely feel it.

"That looks lovely." She stepped back to view her handiwork. "Behenu, your turn now and then you can do me."

I felt different once I had kohl around my eyes. More like myself. Like a part of me that had been missing was suddenly restored. Much like how I had felt when I was reunited with my shadow.

We packed away the new clothes and hid them beneath the pile of bags and blankets in the corner.

"We really should see if we can trade some of those blankets for something more useful," Istnofret said. "We are not likely to need them again."

"They are useful for now, though," Behenu said. "I don't know what we would cover those packs with if we didn't have them. And we don't know whether this is really the end of our travels yet."

"What do you mean?" Surprise made my tone sharper than I had intended. "I am sorry, I didn't mean for that to sound so…"

"I know," Behenu said. "I only meant that until you have done what you came to do, we don't know that there will not be another journey ahead of us yet."

"But we have the Eye," I said. "Where else would we go?"

Behenu shrugged. "I am sorry. I didn't mean to upset you."

"I am not upset. I just don't understand where else you think we might go."

"I am starving," Istnofret said. "Can we hurry up and eat?"

"I got dried fish," Behenu said. "And some of those little onions that Samun likes, and this." She beamed as she retrieved a jar from one of the packs. "I know you have missed this."

I unstoppered the jar and my mouth watered at the scent that arose from it.

"Melon juice," I said. "Behenu, you are a goddess."

Istnofret fetched some mugs and I poured us each an even portion. The taste was sweet and fragrant but not quite as full as I remembered. Perhaps it had been watered down. Still, I savoured my mug, sipping it little by little until it was gone. I almost forgot my hunger, lost as I was in the simple pleasure of something I once thought I would never taste again.

The dried fish was chewy and not as fresh as I might have expected for a harbour town. The onions were indeed the type I favoured, but they weren't as crisp as they should have been. Perhaps they too were old.

"If you are finished eating, we should pack this away," Istnofret said. "In case Renni comes back early."

We wrapped the remains of our meal in a blanket and stashed it under the packages. Then there was nothing else to do but wait for Renni.

FOUR

The last of the light faded from the room and Istnofret lit the lamp. We waited.

The sun was long set and the night must have been half over before we heard footsteps outside.

"Renni?" Istnofret's question was more of a breath than a whisper.

My heart pounded so loudly that I couldn't even hear the footsteps anymore.

The door handle rattled.

Both Istnofret and Behenu had their daggers in their hands and I finally realised that mine wasn't in my pouch. I must have stashed it away with the remains of our meal.

"It is me," came Renni's voice a moment before he eased the door open. "Why is the door not locked?"

"You didn't need to sneak up on us like that," Istnofret said, crossly. "And where have you been? You should have been back hours ago."

"They all go out for a drink or two after work," Renni said. "I could hardly refuse given that I supposedly had nobody waiting for me."

He gave us all a careful look and set down the sack he carried.

"Who went out?"

We women looked at each other.

"Out?" Istnofret's voice was high. "Whatever do you mean?"

"Don't lie to me, Ist. You are all wearing kohl and I can smell fish. Someone went out after I explicitly told you not to."

"It was me," Istnofret said, quickly. "I was starving and I could not possibly wait until you came back. I went out to get food."

"And some kohl?" His voice was sceptical.

It wasn't fair that Istnofret took the blame since we had all agreed Behenu should go out.

"You don't have to protect me, Ist," I said. "Renni, it was me."

"Neither of them went out," Behenu said. "It was me. I went alone."

Renni looked at each of us and shook his head. His anger seemed to have disappeared and now he just looked tired.

"I told you to stay inside. That was for your own safety. I cannot believe you did that, whoever it was. It was risky and it was foolish."

"We were hungry," I said.

"You knew I would bring food back with me," Renni said. "You were in no danger of starving to death."

"Do you have any idea how long the day can be when you have nothing in your stomach?" Istnofret asked, tartly. "And no idea when the person who is supposed to bring you food will bother to make his way home? It must be near midnight. You have been out drinking when you knew we were waiting here, half starved."

"And yet you were not starving," he said. "You went out. Or someone did. Or maybe you all did. What am I supposed to do? How can I keep you safe if you won't do what I say?"

"Don't be mad at her, Renni," I said. "It was my idea."

"No, it wasn't," Behenu said. "It was my idea."

"Actually-" Istnofret began, but Renni threw up his hands and shook his head.

"Forget it. I don't care who it was. I just want to know that it won't happen again."

"Maybe if you don't leave us alone all day with no food, it won't," Istnofret said. "But if you do, we will be forced to take matters into our own hands again."

Renni turned to me. "What do you think Intef would say about this?"

"Does it matter?" I asked. "Intef is not here and he is never going to be here again."

Tears filled my eyes and I blinked quickly, but not before Renni noticed.

"I am sorry," he said. "I am being unfair. Of course you were hungry and you had no idea when I would be back. I really did not mean to be gone for so long."

"We could slip away now," Istnofret said. "Tonight. We could be a long way from here before dawn."

"And what would Khay think if I did that?" he asked. "He would be suspicious and would likely come looking for me to find out why I left. I know how his mind works. We were trained together, after all."

"How long do we need to stay here?" she asked. "One day was bad enough. I cannot bear to think of being here for weeks on end."

"A while," Renni said. "A few days at least."

"Three?" she asked. "Four? Give me a number. I need to know."

"I don't know, Ist. Long enough that Khay doesn't get suspicious when I leave. The work is not terribly hard and the pay is decent. It will look odd if I leave too soon."

"Maybe you could get yourself fired?" Behenu suggested.

"Yes." Istnofret was quick to agree. "You could... I don't know. Pick a fight with somebody. They will tell you not to come back and we can leave straight away."

Renni looked like he was actually considering it. He cocked his head towards me.

"What do you think, Samun?"

"I suppose it is not a bad plan. Just don't hurt anyone too badly or you might get arrested."

"It would not look suspicious if I left after that," Renni said. "After all, if word gets out that I am argumentative, nobody in Rhakotis will hire me. I would have to leave to find work elsewhere."

"Maybe you should drop some hints about where you might go next," Istnofret suggested. "So that if Khay gets suspicious when you leave, he will go looking in the wrong direction."

"Won't he be even more suspicious when nobody can find Renni?" Behenu asked.

"Not if Renni is vague enough," Istnofret said. "Khay will think he misunderstood."

"Can you do that?" I asked Renni.

"I have told worse lies in your service."

"You are not in my service anymore."

He shook his head, but whether he disagreed or shook away an unwelcome thought, I wasn't sure.

"Is anyone hungry?" he asked.

"Depends on what you brought," Istnofret said.

We shared a quick meal, although Renni was probably the only one who was really hungry. I ate so that he wouldn't be reminded that someone had gone out and I figured Istnofret and Behenu did the same.

When Renni left the next morning, we packed up our belongings. Even though we had been here for only two nights and a day, there seemed to be things strewn from one side of the cottage to the other. We were supposed to be ready to leave as soon as Renni returned. As the day wore on, Istnofret began to pace.

"Sit down, Ist," I said eventually. "He will be back soon."

"It is taking too long." She wrung her hands. "Something is wrong."

"He probably just hasn't had a chance to do it yet," Behenu said, although her tone suggested she was more worried than she sounded.

We waited all day and still Renni didn't come back.

"I will go and find him," Istnofret said eventually.

"You know we should wait here," I said. "He will come back when he can."

"It didn't work," she said. "Something went wrong. I can feel it."

"What you are feeling is nerves," I said. "Not a prediction."

She shot me a dark look.

"Where is he then? How long does it take a man to pick a fight with someone?"

I shrugged, reluctant to be drawn into an argument. In truth, I was beginning to worry too. Renni really had been gone much longer than I expected.

"Maybe he was not able to get himself fired," Behenu

suggested. "He might have had to work all day. He will be home soon."

"Unless they all go out drinking again," Istnofret said.

"The sun will be starting to set soon," Behenu said. "Even if he has not gotten himself fired, they won't keep working once the light fades. I will make some dinner, something we can eat as we walk if we need to leave in a hurry. He will be hungry after working all day."

But although we sat up and waited until long into the night, Renni still didn't return. Eventually we ate without him.

"I am going to sleep," I said. "If he comes home this late, he might want to leave straight away. Best that we rest while we can."

"Something really is wrong," Istnofret said. "He was home much earlier last night."

"He has probably just had a long day of work and is out drinking," I said. "I am sure he is fine. He will come crawling back some time before dawn, filled with far too much drink and feeling sorry for himself."

"When has Renni ever done such a thing?" Istnofret said. "He would not do that and I cannot believe you even suggested it."

"I am just trying to give you a reason not to worry." In truth, I felt rather awful about what I had said. "I didn't really believe it."

Istnofret sighed. "I know. I am just so worried. I really do think something went wrong. He picked a fight with the wrong person and he is lying somewhere, injured and bleeding and-"

"Don't think like that," I said, quickly. "You will go out of your mind if you spend all night imagining the things that might have gone wrong. We should try to rest and if he has not come back by dawn, we will go looking for him."

But dawn arrived and Renni still hadn't returned. Istnofret didn't even wait long enough to break her fast.

"I cannot sit here any longer," she said as she slid her feet into her sandals. "I am going to find him."

"Maybe I should go," Behenu said.

Istnofret shook her head. "I know you mean well, but it only takes one look to tell that you are not Egyptian. I will go play the worried wife who is furious that her husband went out drinking after work and never came home."

"I could be your slave, sent by you to find your wretched husband," Behenu said.

Istnofret gave her a long look as if she actually considered it but shook her head.

"I must go myself. If you went, I would go out of my mind waiting for news. Even if I learn nothing, it will give me something to do."

I should offer to go with her. After all, that is what a friend would do. But even as I opened my mouth, Istnofret shot me a look.

"I know what you are thinking," she said. "And no, you cannot come either. You are the most at risk of being recognised."

"Be careful," I said. "Stay safe."

"I will. I will be back as soon as I have news."

She slipped out the door, leaving Behenu and I to stare at each other.

"I suppose we may as well have breakfast," Behenu said.

FIVE

I forced myself to eat some bread. Behenu's appetite seemed unaffected and although she must have noticed that I ate little, she didn't comment. We cleared away the remains of our meal and waited.

Several hours passed before Istnofret finally returned. She closed the door firmly behind her, set her hands on her hips, and shook her head.

I could barely breathe as I waited to hear what she had learned. She hadn't been crying, so it couldn't be too bad. It wasn't until she spoke that I realised she had been so furious, she could barely force out any words.

"He has gotten himself arrested," she said.

"What in Isis's name did he do?" I asked.

Behenu put her hand over her mouth and shook her head. She looked more upset than Istnofret.

"He picked a fight with the overseer," Istnofret said. "The man had him arrested on the spot and he has been locked up to await trial."

"Trial?" My voice was weak. I hadn't expected something so

serious. "Why in the name of the goddess did he fight with the overseer?"

"Nobody told me directly, but from what I pieced together it seems the man might have said something insulting to Renni, so Renni punched him in the face." She huffed and shook her head. "Stupid man."

"Maybe he had not had a chance to pick a fight with anyone else and was getting desperate," I said. "He would surely have known he would not walk away from a fight with the overseer."

"What do we do now?" Behenu asked. "Do we wait for the trial and hope he is declared innocent?"

"He won't be," Istnofret said. "There were too many witnesses."

"Will Khay speak for him, do you think?" After all, they had worked closely together in my personal squad and as far as Khay knew, Renni was here in Rhakotis alone.

"I don't know," Istnofret said. "I believe Khay has spoken to the magistrate, but whether it was for Renni or against nobody seems to know."

"What will happen if he is found guilty?" I asked.

A tear spilled down Istnofret's cheek. "I don't know. He might be kept in prison. He might be whipped."

"He could be sent to the slave mines." Behenu's voice was little more than a whisper, but we all heard her clearly enough.

"We have to intervene," I said. "I wonder whether my word is any good? If I speak to the magistrate, perhaps I could get him released?"

"That might just make things worse," Istnofret said. "You were declared a slave. Unless Ay revokes that, I suppose you are technically still a slave here. You could be arrested yourself if anyone recognises you."

"So what then?" Behenu asked. "We cannot just leave him there."

"We will have to break him out of prison," Istnofret said.

Behenu and I stared at her.

"What?" I asked eventually. "I thought you said…"

"I did." She glared at us both. "He would do the same for any of us and you well know it. We are going to rescue him."

"But how?" I asked.

"I have no idea," she said. "But we need to figure it out quickly."

We spent the rest of the afternoon coming up with plans and discarding them just as quickly. They were all unsuitable for various reasons. Too likely to expose us. Too risky. Too uncertain.

"These streets will be filled with pickpockets," Behenu said. "If we can find out which guard holds the keys to Renni's chamber, we can send a pickpocket to steal them. Then we just have to wait until the guards are not watching, slip in, and unlock the door."

"They would not be so stupid as to have nobody watching the prison," Istnofret said. "And the guard with the keys likely changes with each shift. By the time we figure out who he is, he will have handed the keys off to someone else."

"Perhaps we could get one of the jailers drunk," I suggested. "We could convince him to show us the prison, then lock him in a chamber, steal the keys, and let Renni out."

"If the guards are professionals, they won't be so daft," Istnofret said. "A man would lose his job by taking a woman on a drunken tour of the prison and good jobs are not so easy to come by that anyone would risk that."

"Could we find some cattle, maybe make them go stampeding through the prison?" I suggested.

"That will make a lot of noise," Behenu said. "Surely the guards would hear them coming."

"Whatever we do is going to make a lot of noise," I said.

"I will go find the magistrate first thing in the morning," Istnofret said. "See if I can convince him to release Renni. Let's try the official path first."

"Take some gems," I said. "He might be open to bribery."

"Maybe we should all go," Behenu said. "If you are able to get Renni, we should leave immediately before the magistrate changes his mind."

"No, wait here," Istnofret said. "But be ready to leave, just in case. I think it would be best if I go to the magistrate by myself. I can play the distraught wife who will be left homeless and destitute if her husband is convicted."

"Maybe you shouldn't try to bribe him." I already regretted my suggestion. "What if you get arrested as well?"

"Well, then at least Renni and I will be together," Istnofret said bitterly. "And it will be up to the two of you to save us both. That cattle stampede idea of yours might be useful yet."

I slept restlessly that night, my dreams filled with confusing images. At one point I walked beside someone whose face I never saw. The sand and water and sky that surrounded us looked strange and I understood that this was not my own world. I sank deep down into water and knew I was drowning. I stood on the edge of the Lake of Fire, staring into its depths, its heat blasting against me.

Then the dream changed and I saw Khay looming over me. He smiled. "I have waited a long time for this day," he said. I saw myself shackled in a dark place. Men came to grab hold of my arms and lift me to my feet. My legs buckled beneath me and when I couldn't stand on my own, they simply dragged me between them.

The dream shifted and again Khay stood over me. He smiled and said the same words, but this time someone sliced through the ropes that bound me. I walked out of the dark place and hurried away.

I woke feeling unsettled and confused. At some stage I would encounter Khay, that much was clear. But it seemed I would be a prisoner at that point. Was he responsible for that or was it just a lucky coincidence for him? If only I knew what it was that would make the difference between me leaving that place as a prisoner or walking out on my own feet.

SIX

Istnofret left early the next morning to try to meet with the magistrate. She had only been gone for a few minutes before I changed my mind.

"We should have gone with her," I said. "We could help her."

"It is too late now," Behenu said. "We don't know where the magistrate is and if we go looking for Ist now, we might miss her when she comes back for us. And it will take us too long to pack everything up anyway. I don't know how we made such a mess again already."

"We will take only what we cannot afford to leave. We will come back for the rest if we can. But we should go after her and be ready to leave Rhakotis immediately if we must."

"We cannot. We have to wait now."

We lapsed into uneasy silence. I couldn't bear to sit still, so I walked lap after lap of the chamber. Behenu sat with her legs tucked under her and stared down at her hands. If my excessive motion irritated her, she hid it well.

"It was a mistake to let her go alone," I said.

"Remember the time she got you all out of prison?"

The memory of Istnofret smacking the guard in the face with a chamber pot never failed to make me laugh. Istnofret had single handedly gotten Intef, Renni and me out of a Theban prison. If she had done it once, she could do it again.

Barely more than an hour had passed before Istnofret returned. Even as she slipped in through the doorway, I could tell by the look on her face that she hadn't been successful.

"The magistrate will not be bribed," she said, before anyone could ask. "I didn't ask outright, but I hinted at it and he immediately said he hoped I was not trying to bribe him or I would find myself in prison beside Renni."

"Oh dear." I gave her a sympathetic pat on the shoulder. "I am sorry."

"Maybe I should have let him lock me up," Istnofret said. "At least then we would be together."

"We are not giving Renni enough credit," Behenu said. "He is probably working on a plan to get out of there right now. I am sure he will be back soon."

"And how long do we wait before deciding that he cannot get himself out?" Istnofret asked. "The magistrate said he will consider Renni's case tomorrow. We need to get him out before then."

"So tonight," I said. "Whatever we are going to do must happen tonight."

We stared at each other. Did they feel as helpless as I did? We needed Intef. He would know what to do.

"I wish Intef was here." Istnofret shot me a guilty look. "I mean…"

"I know."

"He would expect us to use our wits and get Renni out," Behenu said.

"The first thing he would do is inspect the prison," I said. "Ist, you have seen it. What can you tell us?"

"A large mud brick building. Bigger than I might have expected for a town this size, but I suppose with all the sea traffic, maybe they need extra space for sailors who commit some crime at sea."

"What else?" I asked. "Intef would say to tell us everything you remember and not make any assumptions about what is or is not relevant."

"Whitewashed walls. I was hoping for a thatch roof, but it is solid. Guards at the front entrance."

"How many?" Behenu asked.

"Two that I saw," Istnofret said. "There would be more inside."

"But maybe we only need to worry about the ones who can see us," Behenu said. "Were any guards patrolling the back of the building?"

"I didn't go around behind," Istnofret said.

"Could we make a hole in the back wall?" I asked. "We could do it at night when they have fewer guards on duty."

"We just need to figure out where Renni is," Behenu said. "So we go through the right part of the wall. Otherwise we might end up in someone else's cell and still not be able to get to him."

"And how exactly would we get through the wall?" Istnofret sounded a little more hopeful now.

"A battering ram of some sort," I said. "Maybe a couple of strong men."

"I think we need to do this by ourselves," Istnofret said. "We don't know who we can trust here and if we say the wrong thing to the wrong person, we might end up in prison ourselves."

"So something that the three of us can wield," I said. "We

only need to damage the wall enough for Renni to break through from the other side."

"What if we accidentally let out the other prisoners?" Istnofret asked.

"The more confusion the better," I said. "Then they won't know who we were trying to get."

"But what if we let out someone really bad?" she asked. "A murderer maybe."

"We need to get Renni." I made my tone as firm and confident as I could and pretended I didn't share her concern. "Anything else that happens is of no consequence to us."

"I will go out and look around the prison some more then," Istnofret said. "I will check the back. See if I can find something we can use as a battering ram."

When Istnofret returned a couple of hours later, she didn't look at all convinced about our plan.

"There are houses behind the prison," she said. "We are going to make a lot of noise if we try to break through the wall and someone will definitely hear us."

"We will just have to hope they are not inclined to get involved," I said. "Unless either of you has come up with a better idea in the meantime."

"The good news is that there are windows," she said. "They are small and barred, but at least we will be able to talk with Renni through them."

"Did you speak to him while you were there?" I asked.

"I didn't try. There was a man in the front yard of one of the houses. He gave me a funny look and I thought it better not to linger."

"Did you find a battering ram?" Behenu asked.

"There is a blacksmith," Istnofret said. "He has a long piece of bronze and two heavy mallets. He will leave them outside his shop when he closes up tonight. I thought we could use the bronze bar to break through the wall. And if we can find Renni's cell, I think the mallets will be small enough to pass through the bars. Once we damage the wall, he can help from the inside."

It wasn't much of a plan, but it would have to be good enough. The afternoon passed slowly and I tried not to think about all the ways it might go wrong. We waited until the moon was high before we left, figuring the middle of the night gave us the best chance of fewer guards. We took only what we could carry easily, mostly just our own small packs with a change of clothes, the stash of gems and some food for tomorrow. As long as we had the gems, everything else could be replaced. I looked longingly at the silky white gown Behenu had bought me and reluctantly left it behind.

"I hope Renni has his pack," I said. "He has the Eye."

"He will have it," Istnofret said. "You know he would not let it out of his sight."

We went first to the blacksmith's shop. True to his word, he had left a long bronze rod and two mallets in front of the door, covered with a heavy cloth. I lifted one of the mallets. It was too heavy for me to wield comfortably, but surely Renni would manage. I took both mallets while Istnofret and Behenu carried the length of bronze between them.

The prison looked just as Istnofret had described. A long, low mud brick building. Whitewashed walls. There seemed to be only one guard at the front entrance as we slipped through the shadows to the back of the prison. He never even noticed us.

We set down our items beneath a dom palm tree, where we could blend into the shadow of its trunk if necessary, and studied our surroundings. The back wall of the prison was long and interspersed with small, barred windows. Not far behind us stood three cottages. Lamp light shone around the shutters in two of them.

"You wait here," Istnofret said. "I will go find Renni."

She went to the first of the cell windows.

"Renni, are you in there?" she whispered.

"Who is it?" came a voice from within.

"Never mind." She went to the next window.

"Who are you?" called the voice from the first chamber. "What are you doing?"

Istnofret hurried down the length of the wall. Voices followed in her wake, men who had been woken by her calls. At length she turned and waved us over. Between us, Behenu and I carried the bronze rod over and dropped it in the dirt. She went back for the mallets.

"What are you doing, Ist?" I heard Renni say. "You should not be here."

"Neither should you, you great fool," she said, a little tearfully. "We have come to get you out of here."

"Don't be ridiculous." His voice was alarmed. "You will get yourself arrested. Go home. I am to see the magistrate tomorrow and I am sure I can make the man see reason."

"Give me a mallet," Istnofret said and Behenu handed one over. Istnofret held it up to the bars. "Renni, take this. Can you use it to break through if we can weaken the wall?"

The mallet disappeared into the cell.

"What on earth do you have planned, Ist?" His voice was admiring now.

"Do you have another of those?" came someone else's voice.

Istnofret quickly passed the second mallet in.

"We have a battering ram," she said. "We thought to crack the wall and then you can break through from your side."

"We are going to need some cover noise, fellows," the

stranger said. "Have at it."

An enormous racket rang out. Men shouted and howled, banging things against the bars of their windows. It was a gleeful noise and I supposed the chaos was a welcome break in their routine. Surely the guards already ran through the prison hallways to see what was happening, but I couldn't hear them over the prisoners' noise.

We picked up the bronze between the three of us and readied ourselves. If either Istnofret or Behenu spoke, I couldn't hear them but at Istnofret's nod, we slammed the end of the bronze into the wall as hard as we could. It bounced off, sending us flying backwards.

When I picked myself up off the ground, I saw we had done little more than dent the mud bricks. We hit the wall again. On the third try, a crack appeared. Encouraged, we hit it again and the crack lengthened.

A hand appeared through the bars, waving at us to step back. We moved away and over the howls of the prisoners, I could just faintly hear rhythmic thuds as Renni and his cell mate pounded at the wall. It began to crumble and soon a hole appeared. Not long after, Renni was able to squeeze through. He turned back to help his cell mate, who turned out to be a wiry little Egyptian man.

We rushed back to the dom palm and snatched up our packs. Faces watched us from the cottage windows, but nobody seemed inclined to come outside.

"It will take them a while to get the men under control again," Renni's cell mate said. "We should go now though."

He set off into the shadows and Renni waved at us to follow him. I wanted to ask who the man was and whether Renni was sure we could trust him, but there was no time. We followed the stranger through the dark streets of Rhakotis.

SEVEN

The stranger set a swift pace and I was quickly exhausted. It had only been a couple of weeks since I had given birth to Meketaten and my strength was still not what it had been. Behenu was first to notice my struggle.

"We have to stop," she said. "Samun needs to rest."

"I can go on," I lied.

"Behenu is right," Renni said. "Mahu, stop a minute."

His cell mate didn't even slow down. "They will have realised we are gone by now. They are almost certainly searching for us."

My foot caught on a rock and I tripped, landing on my knees in the dirt. I huffed, more annoyed than hurt. If my servants would only slow down a little, I wouldn't be tripping over things.

"Mahu, stop." Renni grabbed my arms and helped me up. "Samun, are you hurt?"

"I am fine," I said. "Although I have dirt all over me now. I will require a hot bath when we reach our destination."

"We really need to stop," Renni said. "Mahu, she has to rest."

"We cannot afford to." Mahu finally turned to eye me, although the moonlight might not have been bright enough for him to see the dirt on my skirt. "Surely she can push on a little longer?"

"It is complicated," Renni said.

"Samun, it is happening again," Istnofret said to me, very quietly. "Fight it off. You know it will recede once you are aware of it."

I gave her a dark look. "I am tired."

"We all are, and you know what happens when you get too tired. Listen to me with your heart, like you promised. Intef would want you to listen to me."

She was impertinent for a servant and felt far too free to speak her mind. I started to reply but stopped as her words sank in. Listen with your heart. She had said that to me before. My mind started to clear as soon as I realised I had been letting the Eye twist my thoughts.

"I am sorry," I said. "I will try harder."

"Does that mean we can keep going?" Mahu asked.

"Even if they see us, they aren't likely to take much notice," Renni said. "They will be looking for a group of men. They won't expect it to have been women who helped us escape."

"We cannot afford to test that theory," Mahu said. "If she says she can walk, we should go."

We walked through the rest of the night and as dawn broke, we were well past the outskirts of Rhakotis. Eventually we reached a stand of dom palm trees.

"I think we can rest for a while," Renni said. "I have seen no signs of pursuit."

I dropped my pack and followed it to the ground with a sigh.

I had barely been able to keep myself on my feet for the last hour and it was only by constantly focusing on what I knew about how the Eye corrupted me that I had managed to resist it. Behenu sank down beside me.

Mahu gave us a brief bow. "I thank you. I was due to be sentenced today and I am most pleased to avoid that."

Istnofret gave him a steady look. "What did you do?"

"Excuse me?" Mahu puffed out his chest a little, seemingly affronted at her question.

"It seems you are expecting to travel with us. I want to know what manner of person you are before we decide whether we will permit it."

"Permit it?" Mahu barked out a laugh. "Surely, it is not your decision."

"We make decisions between us, Mahu," Renni said, a little awkwardly. "This is Istnofret and I would suggest you answer her question. She is not likely to let it go until you do. This here is Samun and that is Behenu."

Mahu nodded at each of us in turn as Renni introduced us, then turned back to Istnofret. He considered her, as if wondering whether to take her as seriously as Renni suggested.

"I was caught stealing," he said at last. "I have an illness. Some days I am well and others I do not have the strength to even rise from my bed. It makes holding down a job impossible and I must steal to survive. It is not an honourable profession, I know, but no man will hire someone who only shows up at work a couple of times a week. It seems my luck finally ran out. I have been caught before but have always been able to talk my way out of it. This time they arrested me."

I was only half listening, too busy with checking the packs.

"Renni, where is your pack?" I asked. "The one with… my special thing in it."

Renni shook his head.

"The guards took it from me when they locked me up. Don't worry, I will go back for it. I wanted to get you all away safely first."

"What?" I asked. "You let them take it?"

"Renni!" Istnofret said. "You cannot go back. You will not, and that is final. We didn't go to all that effort to break you out of there for you to go back and get yourself arrested again."

"He has to go back," I said. "After everything, we cannot go on without the Eye. We need it."

Istnofret and Renni were too busy glaring at each other to pay any attention to me.

"I did not exactly expect you to come and break me out," he said. "Had I thought you might, I would have been working on a way to get my pack back."

"You did not think to get it before we left the prison?"

"It was the furthest thing from my mind. My only thought was getting you women away from there before you all got arrested."

"We came to help you," she yelled at him.

"I did not need your help," he yelled back. "I was working on my own plan."

"Well, you were not working on it fast enough."

They glared at each other and Mahu spoke into the silence.

"What is this Eye you are all so worked up about?" he asked.

Renni and Istnofret both shot me guilty looks, but I held up my hand to fend off any apology.

"It is my fault," I said. "I am the one who mentioned it."

Nobody else spoke. It seemed they were waiting for me to decide how much to tell him.

"Can we trust him?" I asked Renni, trying to ignore the fact that Mahu could obviously hear me.

Renni gave Mahu a considering look. "I think we can trust him with the truth of who you are, at least."

"Go on then," Mahu said. "I am thinking this is going to be good after all this fuss."

I took a deep breath. I wanted to trust Renni's instincts, but my own said we should be cautious about Mahu. A man who lied for a living was unlikely to be honourable. I staggered to my feet. This felt like an announcement I should be standing for.

"I am Ankhesenamun," I said, finally.

Mahu's face didn't change. It seemed my name meant nothing to him. I sighed. Once I wouldn't have felt at all uncomfortable about saying this, but I had been just Samun for so long, that I could barely remember Ankhesenamun. I was no longer she. Before I could speak, Istnofret stepped forward.

"My lady is the rightful Queen of Egypt. Lady of the Two Lands, Great Royal Wife, Mistress of Upper and Lower Egypt. Great of Praises, Sweet of Love, Lady of Grace."

Mahu laughed a little and turned to Renni, as if expecting him to contradict her. The look on Renni's face seemed to make him pause.

"Are you serious?" Mahu asked. "She…" He gestured vaguely towards me.

"I am the daughter of the pharaoh Akhenaten, may he live for millions of years. I am the sister-wife of the pharaoh Tutankhamun, may he live for millions of years. I was forced to marry Ay, may the gods destroy his house. He stole the throne and he stole my country."

Mahu's mouth opened and closed. He shook his head and walked a little way from us. I let him go without comment. Let him process this news in his own time and see how he reacts. Then I might decide whether to trust him. At length he returned to us.

"Your majesty," he said and prostrated himself in front of me in the dirt.

"That is not necessary," I said. "You may rise."

"So why are you here?" he asked as he got to his feet and dusted himself off. "Have you come to take back the throne?"

I tried to ignore the twinge of unease that flashed through me. Renni trusted this man. I should too. But still, I didn't like anyone outside of our little group knowing of my plan to remove Ay from the throne. I didn't want the throne for myself, but so far I had no good plan for what I would do with it once Ay was gone. The other big problem we were here to solve was the ongoing conflict with the Hittites. Ay had been the one to order the murder of the Hittite prince, Zannanza, who had been on his way to marry me. I didn't know how I was going to resolve either problem.

"And Renni's pack has something important in it," Mahu continued. "Something you need in order to do this."

"Yes."

I had thought he might ask more questions, but he seemed satisfied with this much.

"I should go back now," Renni said. "Before they remember my pack and dispose of it, or perhaps split up the contents amongst the guards. It may be difficult to track the Eye down again once it disappears into someone's pocket."

"I will come with you," Mahu said. "If we are caught, I will distract them. I can better afford to be caught again. You, it seems, have an important mission. You need to see the queen back to Memphis."

Renni held his hand out to Mahu and they clasped each other's wrists briefly.

I felt like I should say something queenly.

"I thank you for your service," was all I could think of.

It had been so long since I had been that person. Did I really want to go back to the pomp and ceremony and idleness of my previous life? I pushed away the thought. Egypt was my responsibility, whether I wanted it or not. Once I had put things right again, perhaps I might leave Memphis. Make a new life for myself somewhere else. But for now, I must be queen again.

EIGHT

Renni, Mahu and Behenu went back into the city, leaving Istnofret and I to wait under the dom palm trees. I wasn't very happy about Behenu going with them, but Renni said they might need a face that wasn't known to anyone in Rhakotis. Obviously, I couldn't go, even if I wasn't so fatigued, so it had to be either Istnofret or Behenu. Istnofret wanted to be the one to go, but Renni pulled her aside for a quiet discussion. They shot a few looks my way and when they returned, Istnofret announced that she would stay with me.

"What was that about?" I asked, after the others had left.

"Renni says it is important that you and I not be separated. If someone finds us, he thinks we will have a better chance together."

Likely Renni was just trying to keep Istnofret away from danger. After all, she could hardly defend me in the way he could.

As the sun crept through the sky, the shade we sat in eventually disappeared. Sweat dripped down my face and rolled between my shoulder blades.

"I think I had forgotten just how hot it gets during *shemu*." Istnofret wiped her forehead on the hem of her skirt. "How did we ever bear it?"

"I expect it is even hotter in Memphis. Here we are still close to the coast. I can feel the faintest gasp of sea breeze every now and then. Remember what Memphis was like, with not the slightest breeze and the heat bouncing off the walls and the paths?"

"If we were on Crete, we would have refreshing sea breezes all the time."

"Do you really intend to go back there? To live, when this is all over?"

She shot me a surprised look.

"Of course. I have told you that."

"I was not sure you were serious."

"Oh yes. Now that I have seen Crete, I cannot imagine myself living anywhere else."

I swallowed down my response. Her words filled me with sadness and I had nothing but bitterness with which to reply.

"And you?" she asked. "Could you bear to be away from Egypt? I know you and Intef had planned to live near us…"

Her voice trailed away, likely hit as was I with the painful reminder that Intef was gone. Anything he and I had planned for our future would never happen now.

"I am sorry," she said. "I am sure you have not had time to think about such things yet."

I exhaled and tried to find the right words to explain my conflicted feelings. That I had never thought I would live somewhere other than Egypt, but I didn't know if I could bear to stay here alone. Once Istnofret and Renni returned to Crete, and Behenu went home to Syria, there was nothing left for me here. They were my only friends and I had no family left. My two sisters had been on Crete, although I had not seen them with my own eyes. They were guarded by Intef's sister, Tey, and she intended to remove them from Crete the very day she saw us. They would be long gone by now.

I couldn't find the right way to tell Istnofret any of this, so I said nothing and eventually she spoke of something else. Her question stayed on my mind as we waited for the others to return. I should have been frantic with worry about the Eye, but all I could think about was Istnofret's question. We were silent for most of the afternoon. After all, when people have spent as much time together as we have, there is often nothing left to be said between them.

"Maybe I will try to find my sisters," I said into one of our lengthy silences.

"Tey could have taken them anywhere."

"I know, but surely I can follow their trail. They cannot have disappeared. Someone must have noticed three women leaving Crete together and without any men. Someone will remember something. Maybe I will come back with you, just until I can find their trail. Once I have put things here to rights, of course."

"Of course," she echoed.

"What is it that you don't believe? That I will leave Egypt again or that I will be able to follow my sisters?"

She took a long time to answer.

"Both, I think. I know how much you love this country and you have been so focused on finding the Eye so you can rectify something that is not even your fault. I don't think you will ever feel like the task is finished. You will keep finding something else to blame yourself for. There will always be something else you need to fix."

I felt oddly chastised.

"You are being unfair," I said.

"I don't mean to be. Truly. But you asked and I do you the honour of telling you the truth, rather than what you want to hear, because you are my friend."

"And when I am queen again, will you still tell me the truth?"

She gave me a sideways glance.

"That will be up to you. If you will accept me as your friend still, I will be honoured to always tell you the truth. However, if you want me to be your servant again, I will treat you as my lady, not my friend."

The afternoon passed slowly. Eventually we saw two figures approaching in the distance.

"Is that Renni?" Istnofret asked.

"I think so."

The smaller figure at his side was undoubtedly Behenu. Where was Mahu?

As they drew closer, we could see that Behenu's sleeve was torn and she favoured her left leg. Renni had a black eye and a darkening bruise on his jaw. My gaze fastened on the pack slung over his shoulder and my breath caught in my throat.

They reached us and sat down without a word. Renni leaned over to rest his head on Istnofret's shoulder. Behenu sniffed a little and looked like she was trying not to cry.

"You may as well tell us what happened," Istnofret said, eventually. "Where is Mahu?"

"He was captured," Renni said. "We barely got away and would not have if he had not distracted them. He bought us time to flee."

"You left him there?" she asked.

Renni gave a great sigh and looked off towards the setting sun.

"He told us to go. He was injured. He would not have been able to move fast enough."

"What will happen to him?" I asked.

"I don't know," Renni said. "The guards were pretty rough. I expect they were punished for letting us get away and they will make Mahu pay for that. Once they are done with him, he will probably be charged with escaping custody."

"And the likely sentence?"

He looked at the sunset again and didn't answer.

"Tell me, Renni," I said. "He would not have gone back if not to help you retrieve the Eye. Tell me what will happen to him."

"I don't know and that is the truth," he said, at last. "Likely the penalty for escaping will be worse than what he would have endured to start with."

"Will they send him to the mines?" My voice was no more than a whisper.

"It is possible," he said. "I don't think they will execute him outright, so it might be the mines for him."

"When I am queen again, I shall send for him," I said.

"I hope you will remember," he said.

"Of course I will. Why would you think I wouldn't?"

"Because you will have many very serious and important things to occupy your attention with," he said. "And the fate of one barely-known prisoner might be of little concern."

"If I do not remember, you must remind me. No, better than that, in case I forget, I authorise you now to retrieve him. Send men for him, or go yourself. Have him released in the name of the queen and bring him back to Memphis."

He looked at me for a long moment before he nodded.

"I will. And thank you."

I had been trying not to look at the pack which he had set in his lap, but I glanced at it now, just quickly.

"It is in there," he said.

"How did you get it back?"

He shook his head. "You don't want to know. We got it and that is all that matters."

"Renni." Istnofret's tone was cautious. "What have you done?"

"Nothing, Ist. We got the Eye, Mahu was captured, Behenu and I managed to get away."

"Behenu," she said. "Tell us what happened."

Tears trembled on Behenu's lashes and I shot Renni a hard look as an uncomfortable thought occurred to me.

"Renni-"

"I didn't have to do anything," Behenu said. "I would have, if it was the only way to get the Eye back, but I didn't. I only let them think I would."

"Let who think you would do what?" I asked.

Istnofret poked Renni in the shoulder. "Tell us what happened."

Renni sighed and nodded towards Behenu. "You may as well tell them. They are not going to let it go until they hear it."

"We went to where the guards go to drink," she said, hesitantly. She shot me a look. "Please say you won't be mad."

"I am starting to think I am going to be very mad," I said.

"Hurry up, Behenu," Istnofret said.

"There were two guards there. Off duty for the afternoon." She stopped and buried her face in her hands. "I cannot. Renni, you tell them."

"Yes, Renni." Istnofret's voice was cold. "You had better tell us."

"Behenu went to talk to them," Renni said. "She was the only one who could go. They knew Mahu's face and mine."

"And?" Istnofret asked.

"She struck up a conversation with them. Let them think she was…"

"Renni!" Istnofret put a hand over her mouth. "Tell me you didn't prostitute her."

"She only talked to them," he said, quickly. "But she let them think she was available for a price. They bought her a couple of drinks. She flirted with them a bit. Asked about how the prison came to have a hole in its back last night. It is all boarded over now, of course. We went past to see. But she told them she saw it last night before they boarded it up. And when they said that two men had escaped, she asked if they had the presence of mind to take their belongings with them. One of the guards said they divvied up what we left behind. She asked what exactly that was and they rattled off a few things, some from my pack and others that must have been Mahu's."

"They mentioned a wooden box with an odd-looking amulet in it," Behenu said. "I asked about who got other bits and pieces so they didn't think it was strange when I asked who took the amulet."

"We found the man's home, broke in and took the Eye," Renni said. "He had got my pack as well, and my dagger."

I hadn't noticed the dagger stuck through the waistband of his *shendyt*. I was so accustomed to seeing such a thing that it had escaped my notice when he returned with his dagger.

"Somebody saw us in the street as we were leaving," Renni said. "One of the guards. He recognised Mahu and me. Before we knew it, there were a dozen men chasing after us. They managed to catch up to us and there was a bit of a tussle before Behenu and I were able to get away."

"Did you kill any of them?" Istnofret asked.

"I hope not, for it will be worse for Mahu if we did. A couple were knocked out cold, but I think that is the worst of it. One of them managed to grab Mahu and they fell to the ground together. Mahu was up first but didn't seem to be able to stand on his ankle. He must have twisted it when he fell, or maybe it broke. He told us to go and then he started yelling and throwing punches. He distracted them so we could flee."

I felt bad about Mahu. I hadn't expected him to be captured. I had thought that if he and Renni were together, they would be fine. After all, Intef and Renni always coped with everything together. But Mahu was not Intef, and neither was Renni.

NINE

Renni thought we were no more than a day or two from Memphis by boat. We weren't far from the river, although it wasn't the Great River but rather one of the tributaries that fed into it from the sea.

"Tomorrow we will walk along the river," he said, "and hope to catch a ride with a passing boat."

"Is it safe to stay here tonight?" Istnofret asked. "What if someone comes looking for us?"

There was no cover, apart from the single dom palm tree that had provided meagre shade during the afternoon. We were completely exposed to anyone who might wander out here.

"I don't think anyone will look this far," Renni said. "They might search the town, but how will they know which direction we went?"

"Would Mahu tell them?" she asked. "What if they torture him? Would he keep his silence for people he barely knows?"

I could see that Renni wanted to disagree, to tell her that of course they wouldn't torture Mahu and even if they did, he wouldn't give us up. But he just shook his head.

"Maybe we should walk a little further," he said. "Just in case."

The sun had finished setting by now and the night sky twinkled above us. I looked up as we walked, wondering if my brother and my father watched us. But there were many stars and if they were up there, I couldn't tell. It had always comforted me to know they watched over me, and I felt their absence tonight keenly. The moon appeared, a sliver that gave barely enough light for us to see by.

Intef's loss was particularly sharp tonight. Did he have any kind of normal life in the underworld? Did he and Keeper of the Lake sit down to eat together? What sort of food might a guardian of the underworld eat? Where did Intef sleep? How did he spend his time during the day? Did he miss me during the long hours of the night? Or had he forgotten about me and fallen in love with Keeper?

"Samun?" Istnofret's voice was little more than a whisper. "Are you well?"

I took my time in answering. I didn't want to share my lonely thoughts, but it seemed a disservice to Intef to pretend I wasn't thinking about him.

"I miss him too," she said, before I could respond.

"It seems so unfair. For Intef, of all people, to be stuck there."

"And yet he is probably peculiarly suited to it, is he not? His years of training, of learning to serve and obey. His patience, his dedication. If anyone can live in a place like that, it will be Intef."

"But he should not have to live there."

"It was his choice. Somebody had to stay and he chose for it to be him."

"Only because he hates me."

We were going over old ground, repeating a conversation we

had already had a dozen times or more. She didn't respond further and I didn't blame her.

We walked all through the night, stopping to rest a couple of times, more for my benefit than the others. As the sun crept up over the horizon, Renni finally halted.

"We may as well stop here," he said. "This spot is high enough that anyone on a passing boat will see us."

"We are also visible to anyone looking for us," Behenu said.

It was the first time she had spoken all night.

"We need to rest," I said. "We have seen nowhere more suitable so it may as well be here."

We set down our packs and I laid out my blanket. Renni started clearing some ground for a fire and Behenu began to collect sticks.

"Go sit down, Behenu," he said to her. "I can do this."

She nodded and dropped her sticks at his feet without argument.

"Show me your leg," Istnofret said to her.

It was only then that I remembered she had been limping.

"It is not too bad," Behenu said. "I just need to rest for a while."

She awkwardly lowered herself to her blanket. Her hand rested on her thigh and I could tell she was itching to check her wound but didn't want us to see her do it. She sat with her leg outstretched instead of tucked beneath her like usual.

"What happened?" I asked. "How badly are you hurt?"

Behenu sighed and raised her skirt to show us a strip of linen wrapped around her thigh. It was darkened with blood.

"Renni." Istnofret's voice was horrified. "You let her walk all night like this?"

Renni looked between her and Behenu.

"We needed to move," he said, at last. "And if Behenu thought she could manage…"

"Of course she will say she can manage," Istnofret snapped. "You should have had more sense."

She crouched beside Behenu and unwrapped the bandage. Behenu flinched as Istnofret touched her leg and when the bandage fell away, we saw a long cut that ran nearly the width of her thigh.

"It does not look very deep." Istnofret poked at the wound. "I think the bleeding has stopped. How did your leg get cut like that and yet your skirt was not damaged?"

Behenu shrugged. "I don't really remember what happened. There were people yelling and fighting everywhere. Someone grabbed me and I tried to stab him. I think I might have stabbed myself."

"Beneath your skirt?" Istnofret sounded as skeptical as I felt. "Without tearing it?"

"I fell or tripped or something. I cannot remember. But I was on the ground and I think my skirt had come up."

Istnofret and I glanced at each other. Behenu was looking at her wounded leg, although I couldn't tell whether she was examining the wound or avoiding eye contact with us. I wasn't sure whether she was telling the truth and didn't know whether I should be concerned if she wasn't. Behenu waved Istnofret away and pulled her skirt back down. It could be difficult to remember details later, after the heat of the moment had faded away. Perhaps it didn't matter how she had been injured, only that the bleeding had stopped.

We sat in silence for some time. My stomach began to rumble and I finally realised how long it had been since I had eaten. There must be something wrong with me to be hungry at a time like this. I tried to ignore my stomach, but eventually it growled so loudly that Istnofret heard. She reached for one of the packs and began passing out chunks of bread and a few figs.

"What do we do now?" she asked.

"We wait," Renni said. "We cannot walk all the way to Memphis. A boat will come along soon enough."

"I can walk," Behenu said quickly. "I will not slow us down."

"You cannot walk with a dagger wound in your leg," he said. "Besides, you are not the only one who cannot walk so far."

"I bet if it was just you and Intef, you would walk and be halfway there by now." My tone was a little sour, however much I tried to mask it.

"Maybe not halfway," Renni said. "But yes, if it was just the two of us, we would probably walk rather than spend time waiting for a boat. It would let us stay out of sight more too. Once you are on a boat, there is no way to stop anyone there from seeing you."

"Unless you kill them all." Istnofret's voice was disinterested, as if she only half listened and wasn't really thinking about her words. She stared out at the river as she spoke.

"Why would we do that, Ist?" Renni eyed her carefully as if wondering whether she was about to jump up and start killing people immediately.

Istnofret finally pulled her gaze from the water. She looked at him a little blankly, as if she couldn't remember what she had said. Eventually she shrugged.

"Sometimes you have to do whatever you must to keep the ones you love safe," she said. "It is no more than you have done. Think of the man you killed in the tunnels in Hattusa."

Renni blanched. "You know I didn't mean to kill him. It was an accident."

"The men who attacked us in the middle of the night. You and Intef killed them all, except for the one I killed myself."

"Would you rather we sat by and let them kill us instead?"

"I was just pointing out that you have killed to keep us safe. No doubt you will do it again."

The looks on both Renni and Behenu's faces said quite clearly that they didn't know what to make of her comments. I had told Istnofret once that killing a man would change her. Perhaps she was still figuring out what that meant for her. I too had killed a man. Of all of us, Behenu was the only one who had no blood on her hands. Perhaps Istnofret's words were directed more at herself than at Renni.

"My leg hurts," Behenu said. "A lot. Could someone get me something to put on it?"

It was unlike Behenu to complain about anything so I figured she was trying to distract us.

"Let me see what I can find." I rummaged through our packs. "What should I be looking for? A bottle of herbs? A potion?"

"I think we have some honey and thyme somewhere. It is a paste in a little blue jar. It might help with the pain."

"Should I make you a compress?"

I only had the vaguest idea of how to do such a thing, but we had a fire and we had bandages and herbs. Behenu agreed a compress would be useful and told me how to warm a bandage by soaking it in water we boiled over the fire. Once the bandage had cooled a little, she smeared the honey paste over her wound, covered it with the hot bandage, then wrapped her leg in dry linen. I didn't offer to do it for her, having never applied a bandage to anyone in my life.

When we cut off Intef's arm, Behenu had tended to him and I remembered thinking that it was not the first time she had looked after a dying man. She had mentioned learning from a healer at some point.

"Behenu, tell us about your childhood back in Syria."

My words were impulsive, but I was genuinely curious about her previous life. I knew hardly anything about it because she always shut down questions immediately. This time was no different.

"I don't like to talk about it," she said. "You know that."

"I want to know what it was like," I said. "You obviously know a little bit about healing-"

"I am sure you mean well, Samun," she said. "But that life is over and I don't like to think about it."

"Sorry," I muttered.

If she heard me, she didn't reply.

The night was warm, although a cool breeze drifted across the river and I shivered a little, despite the blanket wrapped around me. Travelling like this without Intef felt strange. We had done it for so long, the five of us, walked all day and slept by a fire under the stars. It was familiar and comfortable, if wearying. But to do it without Intef felt wrong. I was acutely aware of his absence, particularly when I lay alone without his body behind me to shield me from the overnight breeze. A tear trickled down my cheek and I quickly wiped it away, thankful that everyone else was asleep and nobody would notice me crying.

TEN

It was mid-morning the next day when we heard Renni shout. He had been waiting on the riverbank in case a boat happened to pass by. I went to see what was happening. From where I stood behind a clump of tall papyrus, I could peer through it to Renni, but nobody on the water would see me.

Renni stood on the bank, waving at an approaching boat. Its sails billowed as the wind pushed it against the current and it seemed it would sail right past him. Likely the captain was on a schedule and didn't have time to stop for unknown passengers. But then the sails dropped and the boat began to veer towards the bank. The captain appeared at the bow and shaded his eyes with his hand as he inspected Renni.

"Good morning!" Renni called to him. "We are headed to Memphis. Would you have room for some passengers?"

"How many are you there?" the captain called. He didn't sound particularly friendly.

"Just four," Renni said. "Myself and three women. I can work with the crew in exchange for transport and we have our own supplies."

The captain eyed him for a long time. My stomach rolled uneasily. I didn't like the way the man looked at Renni.

"Maybe we should wait for a different boat," I said.

I kept my voice low, although the boat was surely far enough away that the captain wouldn't be able to hear me.

Renni glanced back at me and frowned.

"Why? We cannot walk to Memphis and it might be a day or more before another boat comes along."

"I have a bad feeling about this one."

"It will be fine, Samun. We will be safer on a boat than we are here, sitting by the river. If the captain will have us, we should go with them."

"I don't want any trouble," the captain called.

What a strange thing for him to say, but perhaps he had previously regretted taking on passengers.

"We are not troublemakers," Renni said. "We just need transport. One of our party is injured and another is still weak from childbirth. Give them a place to sit and they will stay out of the way while I help your crew. I am strong and a hard worker."

The captain stepped back out of sight. Presumably he consulted with someone. Eventually he reappeared.

"There is a place a little way ahead where I can bring the boat to shore. You may board there."

We hurried back to the others.

"The boat will wait for us up ahead," Renni said as we picked up our packs. "Behenu, I am not sure how far the walk is."

She already struggled to get to her feet.

"I will manage."

Istnofret helped her up and passed her a pack. I watched Behenu, a little concerned at how stiffly she seemed to be moving. Her leg must be sorer than she admitted.

We walked alongside the river, pushing our way through stands of papyrus that were twice as tall as I was. The vegetation here was dense and I couldn't see the boat. Maybe the captain had changed his mind. I wouldn't be sorry about that. But then the papyrus thinned and I could see the boat some distance ahead of us. It had drawn up to the shore and the sails were down.

"Renni," I said. "Let's wait for the next boat."

He shot me a glance over his shoulder. "What is wrong? Have you dreamed about this?"

"No. Or at least I don't think so. It just doesn't feel right. I would rather we wait."

Renni shrugged. "Ist, what do you think?"

Istnofret gave me an apologetic look. "I think we should go with them if they will have us. I am worried about Behenu's leg. She needs a physician."

"Behenu?" Renni asked.

"I really am rather sore." Indeed, her face was quite pale. "I don't particularly care what we do as long as I don't have to walk for much longer."

"Well, Samun?" Renni prodded.

I sighed. "Fine, we will go with them."

We made our way to the boat. As we approached, the captain stood at the stern. He waved impatiently to us to hurry.

"I will go on ahead," Renni said. "Just follow as quickly as you can."

He jogged off and called to the captain, but the wind blew his words away before I could make out what he said.

By the time we reached the boat, they had laid down a plank for us to cross from the shore. We made our way across with Renni holding Behenu firmly around the waist to steady her. At least she would be able to rest on the boat.

"Perhaps we should ask them to let us off at the next town," Istnofret said softly as we waited for the ship to set sail.

Renni was already off helping the crew and it was just us three women who sat together in a quiet spot on the deck.

"To find a physician?" I asked. "Renni said we are no more than a day or two from Memphis."

"Behenu is in a lot of pain and I think she needs a physician as soon as possible."

On the other side of Istnofret, Behenu leaned back against the bulkhead. Her eyes were closed and if she was listening, she didn't comment. Now that I looked at her carefully, her face seemed rather grey and her breathing was a little too laboured.

"Renni won't be happy about that," I said. "He is in a hurry to get to Memphis."

"I think he wanted to take the opportunity for a ride while we could," she said. "He won't mind if we say we want to get off before Memphis."

I shrugged. "You can tell him then."

"I will wait until he takes a break," she said. "The captain didn't sound very friendly and I don't want to cause any trouble by interrupting while Renni is supposed to be working."

I was about to agree with her when I noticed a woman sitting on the other side of the deck. She leaned against the bulkhead and seemed to be looking at her hands in her lap. The braids of her wig dangled forward, obscuring her face. Something about her figure teased my memory.

"Ist," I whispered. "Look over there."

She glanced at the woman and shrugged.

"Do you know her?"

I stared at the woman carefully.

"I am not sure. I feel like I do, but I need to see her face to be sure."

The woman didn't raise her head and after a while I forgot about her and lost myself in the simple pleasure of the hot Egyptian sun on my skin and the breeze against my face. I didn't mean to make eye contact with the woman, but when my gaze absently wandered in her direction, she was staring straight at me.

"Tentopet," I breathed.

Beside me, Istnofret started.

"Oh no. What do we do?"

"We need to tell Renni," I whispered.

I couldn't take my eyes off her and Tentopet stared back at me. Her gaze flicked over Istnofret and Behenu but returned to me. At length, she smiled.

A chill went through me. Tentopet would have no love for me. She probably hated me. There was no reason for her to smile at me unless she knew something we didn't. The spell bottle hanging on the cord around my neck suddenly burned.

"We need to get off the boat," I said.

"We cannot leave now," Istnofret said. "Unless you mean for us to jump overboard and swim to shore."

"I cannot swim," I murmured, absently.

She knew that, of course. She couldn't swim either. In fact, Behenu was the only one of us who could and she was hardly capable of such a thing right now. A memory teased at my mind. Sinking down into deep water. Holding my breath until my chest hurt. Cradling my belly. A feeling of sorrow. The same memory I had experienced over and over and still didn't understand.

Tentopet continued to smile and stare at me. Goosebumps crept over my skin.

"Renni is just over there," Istnofret murmured. "Perhaps I should go tell him."

Tentopet broke our stare to look pointedly at Renni.

"She knows he is there," I said.

Then there was a shout and the captain pointed at Renni. Men rushed to surround him. Renni had been winding a length of rope, but he stilled and slowly set the rope down on the deck. He held up his hands to show he didn't intend to resist.

Other men came towards us, motioning for us to stand.

"On your feet," one of them said. "Don't do anything stupid or your man over there will suffer for it."

"What exactly are we accused of?" I asked.

The captain pushed his way between the men.

"Treason," he said. "I have been advised that you are all wanted for treason, conspiracy and murder. You will be confined below deck until we arrive in Memphis, at which point you will be handed over to the police."

"The police?" Istnofret said. "That is ludicrous. We have not done anything."

Another man pushed his way between the crew. He stood over us and smiled down at me.

"I have waited a long time for this day," Khay said.

My dream flashed through my mind. Khay standing over me just like this. Being shackled in a dark place. Being dragged away when my legs didn't work.

"Khay."

I tried to keep my face blank. My hands were clammy and I was rooted to the deck.

"There is still a reward on your head," he said, his tone conversational. "Did you know that? I suppose you did not, for surely you would have the sense to not return if you knew. There are a lot of people watching for you. I had a feeling you would not be far from your guard though. When Renni somehow broke out of the prison, I knew that if you were nearby, you would try to get back to Memphis and aren't I lucky? I only figured to try to get there and find you before someone else did and yet I stumble over you on the way. But tell me, where is Intef? I am surprised he is not with you after the way he trailed after you like a lovesick puppy all those years."

I gave him a steady look and kept my mouth shut.

"He has gone to the West?" Khay finally looked surprised. "Well. I suppose he gave his life for you in some dramatic sacrifice?"

I broke our gaze at last. He didn't deserve to know about Intef's sacrifice.

"He did, did he? Well, lucky for me or I would not be fortunate enough to find you here. Not that I expect you will be here for much longer. I doubt Pharaoh will risk sending you to the mines again, not after your friends slaughtered some of his best guards. More likely he will have you killed this time. It is the only sure way to deal with a traitor. You do realise that, do you not? You should never risk leaving a traitor alive. Drawn and quartered would be my guess, but I am happy to take bets on it."

"That is enough," the captain said. "Take them down below. They are to be bound and I want the hatch guarded at all times. There is a pretty reward on offer for their capture from what Khay here says. If we can deliver them safely, I will share the reward with every man on board."

"The reward should be mine," Khay said. "Or the greatest portion at any rate."

"It is my boat and my rules," the captain said.

"You would not know who they were if not for me."

"And that is why you will get a share of the reward. Now help the men take them down below. There is work to be done and you have all been standing around for long enough."

ELEVEN

In remarkably short order, they hurried us down below. They tied our feet and hands and secured the ropes to rings set into the bulkhead. The crew left and soon it was just us four down there. The boat rocked as it pulled away from the bank and for a few moments I felt disorientated. But we had spent many months on boats and the feeling quickly settled.

"They could have at least left a lamp," Istnofret muttered.

"He must have helped her," I said. "Tentopet."

"I did say I thought he might have," Istnofret said. "Was he not supposed to help her if she got caught?"

"I cannot imagine why," I said.

It wasn't like he had felt any loyalty towards Intef, who thought of him like a brother, or to me who had employed him for years. Why would he help a woman he barely knew to survive the mines?

"I told you he was kind to me." Istnofret's voice was very small.

I didn't respond, but I suspected that any kindness he had shown her had some benefit for Khay, just like there must be some benefit to him in helping Tentopet. If we could figure out what it was, it might give us an advantage.

Beside me, Behenu groaned.

"Behenu, are you well?" Istnofret said.

"My leg hurts. Somebody bumped it when they brought us down here and it is much sorer now."

"When we get to Memphis, they will surely let us send for a physician," I said.

We lapsed into silence for a while after that. It was Renni who finally spoke.

"We need a plan," he said.

"They will separate us when we reach Memphis."

Istnofret's voice was steady, but I could hear the pain behind it. She feared she would never see Renni again.

"I wish Intef was here," I whispered.

Renni inhaled sharply but didn't respond. I had hurt him with my thoughtless comment. He would think I didn't trust him to find a way to save us. I wanted to apologise but that would probably only make things worse, so I said nothing.

"Where will they take us?" Istnofret asked eventually. "If we can figure that out, maybe we can make a plan to escape."

"They will likely take you women to an administration centre and keep you there until the trial," Renni said. "When they lock you up, you must convince them to keep you all together."

"What will they do with you?" Istnofret asked.

"A prison pit most likely," Renni said.

"How will you escape?" she asked.

He sighed before he answered.

"There is no escape from a prison pit, Ist. They will let me down on a rope and once they pull the rope up, there is no way out. I will be trapped down there until they decide to bring me back up."

"And when they do, you will need a plan," she said. "They won't leave you down there forever. They will bring you back up to face the magistrate, if nothing else."

"So what do you propose?" he asked. "I will likely have my hands and feet bound and they will surround me with soldiers. Everyone knows of the training Intef's men received. They won't take any chances."

"How many men could you take down yourself?" she asked.

"Maybe three or four if I am not bound."

"And if you are?" I asked.

"It depends on how well they are trained. Against farmers? The same. Soldiers? Maybe two."

"How many are they likely to surround you with?" I asked. "If we had some idea of that, we might be able to figure out a way to deal with the rest."

"Half a squad maybe?" Renni suggested. "I don't really know. It depends how much they know of my training, or how much they think they know. Most soldiers would know we trained with the Medjay. That might well cause them to set a whole squad around me."

"Would they really think it might take a whole squad to subdue one bound man?" I asked.

"If they know I was one of Intef's, yes. It is nonsense, of course, but we were not permitted to talk about our training so folk know nothing other than rumours."

"Then we plan for a whole squad," Istnofret said. "Say Renni can manage two men on his own. How do we deal with the other eight?"

I looked around the dark confines of the hatch, searching for inspiration. If Intef was here, he would have already come up with several plans. How did he think of things like that? My mind was blank. I didn't even know where to start.

"Could we poison them?" Behenu asked eventually. "Put something in their beer maybe?"

"I don't want to kill anyone," Renni said. "Not unless we have no other option. The guards are just doing their jobs. This is not their fault."

"I should have killed him when I had the chance," I muttered.

When Khay was unmasked, Intef had said he would be forced to kill himself in punishment. It was a better fate than risking a trial. If Khay was convicted, they would have killed him anyway and burned his body. There would be no afterlife for him without a body to embalm. It had been my decision to give him a chance to live. It would be ironic if he were now the cause of the failure of my quest.

"Is there a way we could distract them?" Istnofret asked. "Throw rocks at them? Do something to make them chase us?"

"You sure you can outrun them?" Renni asked. "They will be professional guards at the least. Soldiers maybe. They undoubtedly keep themselves fit. They will be able to move fast, and you will tire long before they do."

"Would they lock us up for something like that?" I asked. "Or would we be just an annoyance? Maybe they would not bother to chase us."

"I think it would be obvious that you were trying to distract them," Renni said. "If they have had any decent training, they will not let a whole squad be distracted by such a thing. They might send a couple of men after you, but the rest will stay with me. You won't distract them that easily."

"Could we try to seduce them?" Istnofret asked.

Renni shot her a look. "Ist, no. I will not have you do such a thing."

"I will do whatever I have to." Her tone was somewhat belligerent. "I will not leave you to rot in a prison pit."

"They won't let me rot there," he said. "They will take me out for trial at least. Maybe we should wait and see what my sentence is. It might not be that bad. I can endure it and then they will release me."

"You helped me to escape before I reached the slave mines," I said. "If Ay hears of your arrest, and we know Khay will ensure he does, your sentence will not be light. Ay will surely want revenge on anyone who helped me."

I hadn't thought this through properly. I should never have brought them back to Egypt with me. They should have stayed in Crete, like Istnofret wanted to. Here, they were all in danger.

"We knew the risks, Samun," Renni said. "The situation is what it is. We just need to figure out the best way to deal with it."

I wished Intef was here. The words were on the tip of my tongue again and I swallowed them down. Surely between us all we could come up with a plan that would be as good as anything Intef might think of.

TWELVE

We waited in the dark for a long time and eventually I fell asleep. I slept lightly, disturbed by dreams of a falcon and walking on a sandy shore. I woke, disorientated, and it took me a while to remember where I was. Was that Horus I had dreamed of? Was I remembering what happened in those weeks while I was missing? If I had, though, it was already gone by the time I woke.

I was startled into full wakefulness when someone entered the hatch and came down the ladder. Perhaps the captain coming to release us? Perhaps he had decided we weren't worth the hassle. But my hopes sank when a lamp flared into brightness and I realised it was Khay.

"My, my," he said. "How the mighty are fallen."

"Khay," Renni said. "You are better than this, man."

"I don't owe you anything," Khay said.

"We trained together for years. We were squad brothers."

"And you let them send me to the mines. You could have kept me from that. You and Intef both."

"You made it out of there, though," Renni said. "We knew

your training would get you out and it was better than the alternative."

"You have no idea what it was like. Nothing you have heard can prepare you for it. Forced to work until you drop dead. Overseers standing by to beat you if you pause to catch your breath. We have all heard the stories, but unless you have lived it, you cannot comprehend it. Not truly."

"So tell me then," Renni said.

"You always thought you were better than me," Khay said. "You and Intef both."

"I am sorry if we made you feel that way, but it is not true."

"Always whispering between the two of you. Secrets you didn't share with the rest of us."

"There were things we had to keep confidential from the rest of the squad, but you always knew about them," Renni said. "You were Intef's second, after all. I was only his third. You knew everything I did, and probably more."

Shadows shifted behind Khay. I had been so focused on him that I hadn't even realised Tentopet had followed him through the hatch. She looked us over and gave a haughty sniff.

"Not so much of a queen now, are you?" she said to me with a sneer.

Now that she was closer, I could see the years had not been kind to her. Yes, she was a decade older than when I last saw her, but she looked much older than that. Her hair, as dark as ever, was undoubtedly a wig. Her face was lined and her skin was brittle and covered with scaly patches. Her shoulders were uneven and she seemed to keep reaching for her lower back, then freezing as if she had been caught doing something she shouldn't have. Perhaps it was a lingering injury from her days in the mine.

"If you had told me, I could have protected you," I said.

"Could have maybe, but would you have?" she asked. "You never liked me. Didn't want me. You left me waiting out in the hallway for days."

"I didn't need an additional lady. But I let you into my chambers. I gave you a place to sleep and food to eat. I treated you as one of my ladies."

"Not as one of them. You treated them like free women and me like a servant."

"You were a servant," Istnofret said coldly. "And not a very good one at that."

Tentopet sniffed at Istnofret. "You. One of the favoured ladies. Yet look at you now. I am a free woman and you are a prisoner."

"What did he offer you?" I asked before Istnofret could respond. I doubted anything she said would calm Tentopet's emotions. "What did Ay give you?"

"More than you ever offered," Khay said.

"I would have matched it, whatever it was."

He gave a harsh laugh.

"Intef would have locked me away as soon as he heard I had been talking to Ay. He would not have given you a chance to offer me anything. Where is he, by the way? Has he truly gone to the West?"

I looked away into the dark, struck by sudden longing. He might as well be.

"He is gone," I said.

Khay shrugged, seemingly unconcerned. "He was always a fool. Of course he would have given his life for you."

"Don't talk about him like that," I snapped. "He was a good man and the best captain anyone could have asked for."

Khay shook his head and turned to leave. "You are not worth

it. None of you are. Intef got what he deserved and the rest of you will too."

"Where are they taking us?" I asked.

He hesitated and for a moment I thought he would turn back, but then he kept walking.

"Back to Memphis," he said over his shoulder. "You will face Pharaoh and be judged for your crimes."

He left without another word. Tentopet gave me one last sneer and scurried after him.

We sat in the darkness in silence.

"We knew they would take us to Memphis," Istnofret said, eventually.

"I am not ready," I said. "I haven't figured out what to do. How to use the Eye."

I would either be dragged out of this hold or I would walk out on my own feet. I knew nothing more than that, but it was enough to know that I left as either a prisoner or free. There was still a way I could avoid being hauled before Pharaoh in ropes and I had to trust that if I was able to walk out of here, my friends did too.

"You had better figure it out quickly then," Istnofret said. "We will be in Memphis soon enough."

"Take my pack if you can get to it," Renni said. "You will need to find a way to resist the Eye, but at least you will have a chance to use it."

"I can carry it," Istnofret said. "As long as they keep us women together, we will figure something out, and once we have dealt with Ay, we will come to find you."

"Don't take too long about it," Renni said. "They might decide to try me quickly."

My stomach growled, reminding me it had been hours since we had eaten. The sunlight shining through the hatch had softened, suggesting evening approached. Surely they would bring us some food soon. They would have to untie us to allow us to eat. I looked forward to being able to move my arms. My shoulders were beginning to hurt and I really needed to stretch.

But nobody came. The ship stopped moving, presumably anchored for the night. The light through the hatch brightened as lamps were lit up on the deck. They didn't bring us a lamp, though, nor anything to eat or drink.

"Surely they don't intend to let us starve until we reach Memphis," Istnofret muttered.

"Who knows what Khay has told them," Renni said. "He might well have convinced them that it would be too dangerous to get close enough to bring us food or beer."

Istnofret only sighed in response.

"We had intended to go to Memphis anyway," I said. "At least we will get there quickly."

"It is not going to do us much good if we arrive half-starved and barely able to move from being tied up like this," Istnofret said.

"And without Renni," Behenu added, her voice little more than a whisper.

It was the first time she had spoken in hours. I couldn't see her very well in the dim light, but her face seemed greyer than it had been earlier.

"We will figure it out." Renni's voice was overly cheerful. "We will have to see what the situation is like when we get there. Once we know that, we will be able to come up with a plan."

"But how will we find you?" Istnofret asked. "They will likely separate you from us when we arrive."

"Remember when we left Memphis," he said. "You went out in a load of laundry."

"I remember. It is not exactly something I do every day."

"That is where I will meet you. The place they take the laundry. Find somewhere safe to hide but check for me there at dawn and dusk each day. When I find a way to get away, I will go there."

"What if you cannot?" Istnofret's voice wobbled. "What if I never see you again?"

"We cannot afford to think like that, Ist," Renni said. "Focus on solving the problem, not on what might otherwise happen."

I turned my thoughts back to finding a way we could walk out of here. Renni might still believe we could save ourselves, but I knew it was possible our luck may have finally run out.

THIRTEEN

A little more than a day later, the boat finally began to slow and I suddenly couldn't quite get a full breath of air. This must be Memphis and I still hadn't figured out how to save us.

"Are we there?" Behenu asked.

She had barely spoken the entire time we had been imprisoned here. I had heard Istnofret quietly ask from time to time how she was but could never quite catch Behenu's reply. Nobody had come to bring us food. I felt weak and lightheaded from the lack of food and drink. But however the rest of us felt, Behenu must be so much worse. Her injured leg might even have begun to fester. It brought to mind memories of my brother and how he couldn't be saved once his wound festered.

"Maybe," Renni said. "It is too early for the captain to stop for the night, but he might just be taking on supplies."

We listened to the crew above us. It was impossible to tell whether they prepared to disembark or were merely getting ready to take on supplies or other cargo. At length the boat came to a stop and we heard men calling to each other as they worked.

They sounded jovial, perhaps buoyed by the prospect of time on land.

We waited in the dark in silence. Maybe they would forget about us. If they all went onshore and left us here, even if just for a little while, we could surely find a way out of our bonds. There had been no point trying with the crew present. Even if they were not trained to fight, there were enough of them to over-whelm us, especially as starved and painful as we were. We could escape if we had the boat to ourselves for a short while. This might be how I came to walk out of here.

My hopes were crushed when someone came down through the hatch. With the sunlight behind him, I couldn't tell who it was and I feared it might be Khay come to torment us again. The man lit the lamp which hung near the ladder and it was only then that I realised it was the captain.

"I trust you have been treated well enough." He held the lamp high as he looked us over. "This boat is not made for trans-porting prisoners but we have done the best we could. I hope you will tell Pharaoh you were cared for adequately."

"You think keeping us tied up in the dark without food or drink constitutes adequate care?" I asked. "I hardly think that warrants a mention to Pharaoh."

"He should reward me," the captain said. "I have transported the prisoners he wanted."

"You have only Khay's word for that," I said. "Are you sure you trust him?"

The captain started a little, as if he hadn't considered this.

"Why would he lie? He has no reason to ask that I transport you to Memphis unless Pharaoh is really searching for you."

"He is the one who is a wanted criminal," I said. "Did he tell you that he was exiled from Egypt for life?"

"I find that difficult to believe."

"He was sentenced to work in the Nubian gold mines for the rest of his life." Not entirely true, but I only needed to sow doubt in the man's mind. "So why is he here? Did he escape? Run away? No doubt there are warrants out for his arrest."

"And yet he claims the same of you," the captain said. "So it would seem that one of you is lying."

"And you assume it is me? Did he tell you that I was the one who sentenced him to the mines?"

For the first time the captain seemed to take me seriously.

"He did not."

"He seeks revenge on me for that. He has convinced himself that it was me who was sent to the mines and escaped, when it was really him. He thinks he needs to return me to Pharaoh to be punished."

"The very sad thing about this is that he seems to actually believe it," Istnofret said. "It is such a difficult thing to see someone so caught up in their own lies that they start to believe them."

"I don't think he intended to mislead you," I said. "He truly thinks he is returning a wanted criminal to face Pharaoh's justice."

The captain turned back to look towards the hatch, no doubt wondering whether he should confront Khay about this.

"I understand," I said. "I really do. I will try to convince Pharaoh you thought you were doing the right thing. I just don't know whether he will believe me."

"You know him?" The captain turned back to me. "He will take heed of you?"

"Of course." I tried to convey a confidence I didn't have. "He is my cousin. I know him well."

The last was true, if nothing else. I could hardly tell him that

Pharaoh had been my husband. Might still be even, if he hadn't thought to formally divorce me.

"Show me proof of your words," the captain said.

The conversation had seemed to be going so well that this caught me off guard. What proof could I give the man that I had not worked in the slave mines?

"Your back," Istnofret said. "Show him that your back is unmarked. You heard what Khay said. About how the overseers wait to beat the prisoners. He will have lash marks on his back and you do not."

The captain shot one last look towards the hatch. Perhaps he worried Khay would come down and catch us talking. Finally he turned back to us and hung the lamp on a nearby hook. He pulled a dagger out of the waistband of his *shendyt*.

"I will cut you free so that you can show me your back," he said. "But I warn you, if there is any sign of scarring, I will ensure you are handed over to Pharaoh to face his justice."

He swiftly sliced through my bonds. I tried to unfasten my gown, but my hands were numb and my fingers didn't work.

"Hurry up," he said.

"I am going as fast as I can. My hands have been tied for two days."

He came closer and I sucked in a breath, suddenly deeply afraid. If his intentions were nefarious, there would be nothing my friends could do other than watch. But he merely sliced through the fastenings on the front of my gown. I turned my back to him and lowered the gown to my waist. The light flickered as he held the lamp up again to better inspect my back.

"Your skin is unmarked," he said at last.

I pulled my gown back up over my shoulders and held it closed over my chest.

"Do you have any other proof?" he asked.

"Is that not sufficient? You can see I have never been whipped. Check Khay's back if you want further proof. He was there for three years. He was doubtless whipped many times."

"Check Tentopet's back too," Istnofret said. "She was sent to the mines with him."

"His woman was there too?" the captain asked. "She seems like such a quiet thing."

Istnofret gave a haughty sniff. "She is a spy and a traitor. She deserved every day she spent in the slave mines."

The captain glanced back towards the hold once more and seemed to finally make his decision.

"I will cut you free and you must leave quickly. Go quietly though. If Khay is that certain of the truth of this story he has created, I would rather you were well away from here before he realises you are gone."

"Thank you," I said as he sliced through the ropes around my ankles. "I will be sure to tell Pharaoh how you have aided us today."

"I am only sorry I didn't come down to speak with you earlier. You will ensure he understands it is because I believed Khay, won't you? He was very convincing when he told me about how you were all wanted criminals."

"I am sure Pharaoh will understand."

My legs cramped and protested as I got to my feet, still holding my damaged gown closed. The boat rocked a little as it caught a wave and I stumbled. My feet burned and I hissed in pain. I leaned against the wall, suddenly uncertain whether I could walk after all.

"We should go." Renni managed to sound casual. "As you said, it would be better that we are away from here before Khay realises you have helped us. Another confrontation will likely only send him deeper into his delusion."

"Of course," the captain said. "Let me just check that he isn't in sight before you leave. If he is up there, I will distract him. You should go quickly and quietly."

He put out the lamp and hung it back on its hook by the ladder. As he emerged from the hatch, he spoke.

"Oh, there you are, Khay. I was hoping to have a word with you before we disembark. Let's talk over there."

Khay must have protested, for the captain made a reassuring noise.

"No, no, all is well. The prisoners will be transported as soon as I can make adequate arrangements. But I wanted to discuss with you the possibility…"

His voice trailed off as he led Khay away.

"Wait here." Renni tiptoed over to the hatch and peeked out, then waved us over. "Be quiet. I can still hear the captain but cannot see them. They are not far away."

We grabbed our packs, which had been stacked in a tidy pile nearby, and hurried up the ladder as fast as our stiff legs would allow. Most of the crew had already left and those few still there were too busy with finishing their chores to worry about us. My limbs were starting to loosen although my feet still burned, making walking painful. I held my gown closed as best I could with fingers that seemed to no longer be able to bend.

We crossed the dock and disappeared into the crowd, walking swiftly. Behenu made a couple of quiet whimpers. We would have to see to it that her leg was treated as soon as possible. We wove between various buildings until Renni led us down an empty alley.

"We need somewhere to stay," he said, quietly. "Somewhere we can lie low for a few days. Maybe we should try to get out of Memphis for now."

"But where would we go?" I asked. "We cannot walk far in this condition. We would need another boat."

"We cannot go back to the dock," Istnofret said.

"That is the first place they will look for us," Renni said with a nod. "By now, Khay probably knows we are gone, even if he doesn't realise the captain released us. He may even have convinced the captain he was telling the truth after all. If Khay can get a message to the palace, there might be guards out looking for us within a couple of hours. It would be best if we were out of Memphis by then."

"It was a very clever story, Samun," Istnofret said. "However did you think of that?"

"I don't really know. It just came out. I suppose I thought that Khay could offer no more proof than we could, so it was up to the captain who he chose to believe. I would not have thought to show him my back, though, if you had not suggested it."

"I am sure I could not have come up with such a story," Istnofret said.

"No, you probably would have just smacked him in the head with a chamber pot," I said.

We laughed a little. We had done it. We had escaped. Despite how unlikely it had seemed for a while.

"So what do we do now?" I asked.

"You should all stay here," Renni said. "I will go see if I can find lodgings."

"No, one of us women should go," Istnofret said. "You are too conspicuous. If word gets out that they are looking for a soldier, you will be an obvious target."

"I will go," Behenu said, her voice thready. "I will say I am looking for somewhere for my mistress to stay for a day or two. If they want more information, I will hint that she might be having an illicit affair and is looking for privacy."

I frowned at her. "I don't like that idea."

"It is a good plan," Renni said. "Your mistress can, of course, pay handsomely and will add a little more if she can be assured of discretion and privacy."

"Of course," Behenu said with something that might have been either a wink or a grimace. She fished out the little pouch she wore tucked under her shirt. "Do you think two gems would be enough? One as payment for lodgings and the other for discretion?"

Renni nodded. "No more than that, or they might think we have more wealth than sense and that someone should liberate us of our funds. Go then. Keep to the alleys where you can and watch for anyone who looks like they might be searching for someone."

Istnofret snatched up the gems from Behenu's hand.

"You should stay here. You are in too much pain. I will go."

She hurried away before anyone could object.

Istnofret returned so quickly that I immediately assumed something had gone wrong. However she flashed a smile and motioned for us to follow.

"Come," she said. "I found us somewhere to stay."

"You are certain it is safe?" Renni asked. "And you were not seen by anyone who might recognise you?"

"It could not be safer," she said. "You will see."

She led us to a modest mud brick home just a couple of blocks away. It stood between a tidy vegetable garden and a dom palm tree. My heart ached a little at the sight. This was exactly what Intef had wanted. His own home with a vegetable garden and a dom palm to relax under. And our daughter, of course.

The front door opened and a familiar figure waved us inside.

"Nenwef!" Renni beamed and leaned in to hug him. They

had been guards together in Intef's squad. "What are you doing here? Why are you still in Memphis?"

"Come in first," Nenwef said. "Let's get you out of sight, then I will tell you."

He glanced at me and his eyes widened a little, although surely Istnofret had told him I was here. Perhaps it was my appearance that surprised him, for I wore the gown of an Egyptian peasant. It was not the immaculate and jewel-draped image he would have been accustomed to. He bowed low to me.

"That is not necessary, Nenwef," I said. "Especially not when we are in your home."

"It is good to see you, my lady."

He closed the door behind us and gestured for us to sit. The chamber was of a moderate size and pleasantly appointed with a variety of cushions to sit on and a large window which was thrown open to let in the breeze. A woman came in from the other chamber, carrying a tray of mugs.

"My wife," Nenwef said. "Merti."

Merti set the tray down in the centre of the room and bowed.

"My lady, it is an honour to finally meet you."

"Please call me Samun," I said. "Thank you for your hospitality."

She beamed at me and gestured towards the tray.

"Please sit and drink. Nenwef told me once that you liked melon juice. I hope you still do."

I dropped down onto a cushion and eagerly took a mug. It was much nicer than the juice we had drunk in Rhakotis.

"It tastes wonderful," I said and Merti beamed again.

"Now tell me," Renni said. "Why are you still in Memphis? You were supposed to leave."

"Where is Intef?" Nenwef asked suddenly.

We looked at each other. I didn't know how to explain Intef's absence or even whether we should try. How could anyone who hadn't been there even begin to understand?

"What happened to him?" Nenwef asked. "I thought that Intef, of all people…" His voice trailed away.

Renni cleared his throat and I thought he was going to explain, but he just shook his head.

"It is a long and sad story. Perhaps I will tell you one day, but I think it is too soon for any of us to talk about it."

Nenwef nodded and reached out to clap him on the shoulder.

"I am very sorry to learn of his journey to the West," he said.

Of course he would assume that Intef had died. Nobody corrected him.

"So," Nenwef said eventually. "It is only us still here. Me and Merti. The rest of the squad left Memphis when you did."

"Why didn't you go?" Renni asked. "You told Intef you would only stay long enough to take care of Sadeh."

I had almost forgotten it had been Nenwef who retrieved Sadeh's body and ensured she was embalmed. She would not have had her chance at the afterlife if not for him.

"Thank you for that," I murmured.

Nenwef gave me a brief nod.

"Merti couldn't bear to leave." He shot his wife a fond look. "All of her family is here and she didn't want to go far from them. She was with child at the time and we hoped…"

His voice trailed away and after a moment Merti took up the story.

"The child didn't survive his first year," she said. "And I have been unable to bear another since then. I had wanted to be near my mother so she could help with the children, but I suppose the gods intend other fates for us."

Her voice was calm, but her face betrayed her emotion. Her inability to bear children meant more to her than she said. I wanted to say something sympathetic but couldn't find the right words. I knew something of how she felt, having lost two babes myself. Setau and Meketaten. My son and my daughter.

"Do you still work for the palace?" Renni asked.

"I was reassigned to Bebi's squad," Nenwef said.

Renni shot him a look. "Really?"

"Is that bad?" I asked.

Renni seemed to hesitate, but Nenwef shrugged, apparently nonplussed.

"He is usually assigned the men with the least skills. He is not exactly a captain of Intef's standard, although I suppose nobody is."

"You are too good for his squad," Renni said.

"I needed work and that was where they assigned me. I suppose Djau didn't really trust me after everything that happened."

"Djau?" I asked.

"He assigns positions for those who work in the palace," Renni said.

"You probably know there was tension between him and Intef," Nenwef said.

"No, I know nothing about it," I said.

"Intef always took the best men for his own squad," he explained. "Djau never liked that. He thought he should decide where men were assigned, but it is hard to argue with someone who is selecting for the queen's personal squad. If he says the queen wants a particular man, Djau has no choice but to assign him to her squad."

"I never realised."

What else had Intef done in my name that I knew nothing of? It had all been to protect me, of course, but I still felt a little odd at realising how little I knew of how he had operated.

"So when it became known that the rest of the squad and all the queen's personal attendants had disappeared, Djau took it out on me."

Merti interjected, her voice full of barely contained anger.

"He had Nenwef beaten. He was locked in a dark chamber for more than a week. I thought they would kill him but eventually they let him come home. I told him he shouldn't go back."

"But I did and it meant I got to keep my job," Nenwef said, placidly. He reached out to cover her hand with his own. "I know you were afraid, Merti, but I truly did not think they would kill me. Djau wanted someone to punish for so many men slipping out of his grasp and I was the only one left."

"It was not right," she said.

He squeezed her hand and gave her a small smile. It was clear this was an argument they had had many times.

"I am sorry, man." Renni's voice was filled with regret. "I really am. Everyone was supposed to slip away. Intef would never have left if he had known you would stay."

"And that is why I didn't tell him," Nenwef said. "I already knew we would be staying. Merti and I had talked about what we would do if my lady..." He hesitated and it was clear he searched for a delicate way to express his thought.

"If I was no longer queen?" I asked.

He shot me a grateful look.

"If something happened to you," he said. "We had decided what we would do long before the day you left."

"So what does Bebi's squad do?" I asked.

"Minor things mostly," Nenwef said. "We guard the entrance to the palace, not that there is ever any threat. There are too many guards around for anyone to get to the front doors without being noticed. Sometimes we guard supply wagons as goods are transported up from the boats. That is always a pleasant change from standing at the front doors."

It sounded terribly boring, but I supposed it wasn't much worse than standing at the doors to my chambers. I suddenly remembered something Intef had once said to me, that Nenwef's position in my personal squad gave his family a level of status they wouldn't have otherwise. Looking around their modest home, it was clear it hadn't made him wealthy. I fished in my pouch and pulled out a gem which I offered to Merti.

"This is for all the times that Nenwef had to work late when he was in my squad," I said.

She started to reach for it but stopped.

"I cannot take it, my lady," she said. "He was doing his job and he was paid for it at the time."

"I am sure he is not paid at the same rate in Bebi's squad," I said.

She glanced at Nenwef and hesitated, but eventually she shook her head.

"No, it is harder to make ends meet now. Intef always ensured his men were paid very well for the job they did."

"So take the gem," I said. "If I am able to ensure Nenwef is given a better assignment, I will. But if not, this will help you."

Once I hadn't understood the value of the jewels I wore. Now I knew that this single gem would allow them to live in comfort, even if Nenwef never worked again.

"Take it, Merti," Nenwef said. "I regret that I have made things more difficult for us, but I made the choices I thought were best at the time. Maybe this will make up for it a little."

The look Merti gave him said quite clearly that she didn't think he had anything to make up for, but she took the gem from my hand.

"Thank you, my lady," she said very quietly.

"So why are you here?" Nenwef asked. "I assume you have come to confront Ay? Perhaps take back the throne?"

"Are you sure you want to know?" Renni asked. "Perhaps it would be best if we don't involve you. We can find somewhere else to stay. Leave you and Merti to live your lives without suspicion."

"They already don't trust me," Nenwef said. "Once they know my lady has returned, they will assume I am involved, whether I am or not. So I may as well do what I can to help you." He turned to his wife. "You should keep the gem on you at all times, Merti. If something happens to me, leave Memphis immediately, even if you must go without your family."

"But where would I go?" she asked. "I know nobody anywhere else. At least here, I have my family."

"If I am arrested, they might come for you too. Your family cannot protect you. Promise me you will leave."

"We have friends in Babylon," I said. "Shala and Belasi. It is a long journey — several months by sea — but if you can get to Babylon, find Shala and tell her I sent you to her. She will help you."

"That is a good plan." Nenwef's voice was full of relief. "Will you do that, Merti?"

"Babylon?" She sounded incredulous. "I have never even dreamed of travelling so far."

Unexpected tears filled my eyes. Sadeh had said something similar the time I suggested she go to Babylon. I quickly blinked them away and nodded towards the gem in Merti's hand.

"You have the means to, though, and you will have a friend in Shala when you arrive."

"Please Merti," Nenwef said. "I need to know that you have a sound plan in case something happens to me."

"I never thought I might leave Egypt," she said. "And

certainly not without you. But if you are arrested, I will go to Babylon. If they release you, come and find me."

"I will." He squeezed her hand for a few moments, then turned back to the rest of us. "Now," he said. "Tell me your plan."

FOURTEEN

I stnofret, Behenu and Renni all looked to me. It seemed it would be my decision as to how much we told Nenwef. I made a swift decision. If he was willing to risk helping us, he deserved to know the truth.

"I have come to remove Ay from the throne," I said.

If I had been in any doubt of Nenwef's loyalty, his confident nod would have satisfied me.

"Go on," he said.

Merti started to rise.

"Maybe I should go into the other chamber," she said. "This is obviously confidential."

"Stay, Merti," I said. "You are taking as much risk as Nenwef and you should hear our plans."

"The better you understand what we are doing, the quicker you will realise if things have gone wrong," Nenwef said. "If there is even the slightest hint that the plan has gone awry, you must leave immediately. If it is just a minor hiccup, I will follow after you as soon as I can get away."

Merti gave him a long look, but eventually she nodded and sat back down.

"We have in our possession an artefact of the gods," I said. "It is very powerful and it will help me to take back the throne."

"How?"

Nenwef's question was obvious but it was the one thing I still couldn't answer.

"I don't know," I said. "I don't understand how it works or what it can do, only that it is very old and very powerful."

Nenwef's expression was sceptical, but Merti nodded seriously.

"Tell us what has been happening here," Renni said. "We have heard little and it has been difficult to make a plan without information."

"Pharaoh continues to use fear and cruelty to control the people," Nenwef said. "His sentences are harsh and the magistrates have been directed to punish not just the offender but also their family. There have been too many stories of whole families who have been put to death, or sent to the mines, or left destitute when all their possessions were taken away from them."

"He is a cruel man," Merti said. "Your father had his faults, my lady, but he was never deliberately cruel. I was only a child when he was pharaoh, but I remember my father talking about him."

I didn't know whether to thank her or admonish her. Before I could decide, Nenwef continued.

"We are still free to worship as we choose but many suspect that the temple workers are spying and reporting back to Pharaoh. There is more though. Pharaoh's cruelty has infiltrated every layer of bureaucracy. Fines are larger, wages are smaller. Most of us can barely feed ourselves."

"Does Ay's wife do nothing to try to temper him?" I asked.

"If she does, I have not heard of it," Nenwef said. "But then again, she would probably only do such a thing in private. I have tried to maintain Intef's networks. He had many people who used to pass information to him, but I only ever knew one or two of them for certain. A couple of others I suspected. They don't respect me in the way they did him, though, and it is difficult to get information. I have been reluctant to ask too many questions and draw attention to myself. If I had known you might return, I would have tried harder."

"It would have made folk suspicious," Renni said. "You did the right thing."

Nenwef gave him a grateful smile and I realised for the first time how much he valued Renni's opinion. He looked at Renni the way men used to look at Intef.

"So what exactly is your plan?" Nenwef asked. "I assume you intend to confront Pharaoh?"

"Can you get us into the palace?" Renni asked.

"Considering my usual post is the front doors, that should not be too difficult."

"But how do we do it?" Istnofret asked. "We cannot just stroll in. We will have to be smuggled in somehow."

"Actually," Renni said. "I think we should walk right in. Nobody will expect it and with Nenwef at the door to pretend we are expected, it is unlikely that anyone will look too hard at us."

"But someone will recognise us," she said. "Samun definitely, and probably you and me. Maybe even Behenu."

"We could wear head scarves," Behenu said. "Pretend to be foreign guests."

"The wives of some honoured dignitaries," Nenwef said.

"Come to visit with the queen perhaps?" Renni suggested.

"No," Istnofret said quickly. "That is going too far. Someone will surely be suspicious."

"I don't think so," Renni said. "One thing I know for certain is that if you look like you belong somewhere, people will rarely question it."

Nenwef chuckled. "Do you remember Intef's lectures about that? How many times did he tell us not to assume that someone was supposed to be there just because they looked at ease and nobody else was asking any questions?"

"He was a good captain," Renni said.

"The best," Nenwef added. "I am sorry that he is not here to plan this with us, but between us I think we can come up with a plan that would make him proud."

My stomach growled loudly and Merti quickly got to her feet.

"Please excuse my rudeness in not offering you a meal," she said. "You must all be starving."

"They did not feed us the entire time we were on the boat," I said, a little shamefaced at my obvious hunger.

"I will help you, Merti," Behenu said. "I am more useful in a kitchen than in making plans like these."

She tried to get to her feet but groaned and almost toppled over.

"Stay here," Istnofret said. "I will go. Merti, I wonder if you might have some ribbon? The fasteners on Ankhesenamun's gown have been cut, but if you have a length of ribbon and a needle, I can easily fix it."

They slipped out into the other chamber and we soon heard the sounds of a meal being prepared. Someone else's stomach growled even louder than mine. It must have been at least two days since we had eaten.

"Who else from the palace guards can we trust?" Renni

asked. "I would feel easier if we had a few men in key positions who we knew would look the other way."

"If you can wait a few days, I can get word to two men from our squad," Nenwef said. "Tuta and Woser. They are loyal without doubt. I am not certain of anyone else."

"Where are they?" Renni asked.

"Woser went to Thebes, but Tuta is just a few hours away. If we sent a messenger, they could reach him this evening. He could be here as early as tomorrow morning. It would take a bit longer to get Woser, but it would be worth the wait. The addition of two loyal men is not something to pass up."

"Send word to them," I said. "But I don't want to wait any longer than morning. As soon as Tuta arrives, we make our move."

"I will go find a messenger as soon as we have eaten," Nenwef said as Merti and Istnofret returned, each bearing a tray of food.

There were small, sweet onions and fresh grainy bread. Salad of crisp lettuce and cucumbers, and more melon juice. I eagerly filled my plate with what was probably more food than I needed. With my hunger finally sated, I sipped another mug of melon juice. Only the gods knew what would happen tomorrow. I may as well enjoy melon juice while I could.

FIFTEEN

We slept on blankets on the floor of Nenwef and Merti's house, all of us together in the one chamber. That night I dreamed of Intef. He sat on the floor, cradling a child in his lap. He held the babe securely with his one arm. I didn't see enough to know whether it was a boy or a girl. Intef didn't seem to be doing anything, just holding the child.

Then the dream changed and I saw again the enormous black Gates of Anubis. Intef stood in front of the gates and as they closed, I saw on the other side a girl. She was perhaps five or six years old with tawny eyes and dark hair that fell unrestrained to her shoulders. Her gaze was locked on Intef as the gates closed but her face betrayed no emotion. Intef cried out and tears ran down his face. He leaped forward to try to hold the gates open, but they were too strong for him. As they clanged shut, he fell to his knees in front of them.

SIXTEEN

Tuta arrived shortly after breakfast. He came straight to me and bowed low.

"My lady."

"It is good to see you, Tuta."

"I came as soon as Nenwef's messenger arrived."

"How much do you know?"

"Nothing other than that you were here. It would not be safe to entrust details to a messenger."

"How did you know it was me? Surely Nenwef could have summoned you for any number of reasons."

"Before I left, we agreed that if you came back and needed us — Woser or I — Nenwef would send a messenger to say that Aten had risen. So when a man arrived on my doorstep overnight to tell me exactly that, I took nothing but my dagger and left immediately. Where is Intef?"

His question threw me. Stupidly, I had thought he would already know from Nenwef's message. I hadn't expected to be the one to tell him, but I would probably have to do this many times over. I took so long to answer that Tuta came to his own conclusion.

"How?" he asked.

My eyes filled with tears and my chin wobbled.

"He had to stay behind," I said at last. "But as far as anyone else is concerned, he has gone to the West."

"Will he come back?" Tuta asked.

"No."

He exhaled, a long steadying breath, much the way Intef himself might have reacted.

"And your babe?" he asked. "How long until he is due?"

Another question that caught me by surprise. I looked down at my belly as I tried to find a response. Had it really been less than a month since Meketaten's birth? If I had been unprepared to talk about Intef, I was even less ready to talk about our babe. I had somehow expected that nobody would know. But of course my belly was still swollen and it was a reasonable assumption that the child was yet to be born.

"I am sorry," Tuta said when I didn't reply. "I seem to have nothing to say but that which will upset you."

"You were not to know. I cannot…"

"You don't need to explain anything. Just tell me what you need from me and I will do it. That is why I am here."

"This will be dangerous, Tuta. If we are caught, there will be no light punishments. Ay will make an example of anyone who aids me."

"And if you succeed?"

"If I succeed, there will be a new pharaoh on the throne. I do not yet know who, but it will not be Ay."

"I would like to work in the palace again. Intef worked us hard, but he was always fair. I have not reported to a man of his equal since. Renni would make a good captain though. If you return to the palace and you need your own squad again, I would be very happy to report to him."

"He is a good man," I said. "I hope that when this is over, there will be work for all of you in the palace again. But in case things go bad, take this."

I fished in my pouch and passed Tuta the first gem I retrieved. It turned out to be a russet sapphire. His eyes widened when he saw what I had pressed into his hand.

"I cannot," he said. "I have some funds set aside in a safe place. I will not go hungry."

I closed his fingers around the gem.

"Keep it. If things go bad and you need to run, it will allow you to start a new life anywhere you want. We have friends in Babylon. Shala and Belasi. Tell Shala I sent you and she will help you. Merti will go there too."

Belasi likely wouldn't be pleased about an influx of Egyptians coming to his house, but Shala would be thrilled to meet as many people as I could send her way. New people meant new stories and new things for her to learn. After a long while, Tuta nodded and tucked the gem away.

"Thank you, my lady."

"You don't need to call me that. Nobody does anymore."

"But what would I call you?"

"Samun is fine."

Unease flickered across his face.

"I would prefer my lady."

I remembered how strange my friends had found it when they first called me by name.

"I assume Woser is also on his way?" Tuta asked.

"Nenwef said it would take him a few days to arrive. I cannot wait though. Too many people already know we are here. The sooner we act, the better."

"Tell me what the plan is then."

We spent the next few hours fine-tuning our plan before Nenwef slipped away to make arrangements with a small group of men who were still loyal to me. He took with him promises of extravagant payments and ongoing employment in the palace, both for the men themselves and their children.

"And their brothers and their cousins and anyone else they name," I said. "Agree to anything they want."

"I don't think that will be necessary," Nenwef said. "Assurances of ongoing employment and perhaps a modest reward would be sufficient."

"We cannot afford to have anyone wonder if Ay might make them a better offer," I said.

"I will be very selective about who I speak with. There are only a couple of men who will know and their role will be to do no more than look the other way. You really don't have to promise them riches."

"I want them to be in no doubt that this is their best path."

"Have faith, my lady. These men are loyal to you. Tell Merti I will be home in time for dinner."

I watched with many misgivings as he walked away. Perhaps it would be better if we arrived unexpectedly. If nobody knew we were coming, there could be no possibility of anyone betraying us. But Nenwef was already gone and it was too late to change the plan.

SEVENTEEN

Nenwef didn't return for dinner. Nobody commented although I didn't miss the anxious looks that passed between them. Renni and Tuta kept up a steady commentary, reminiscing about their years in Intef's squad. Every now and then, one of them would slip outside. They would be gone for a few minutes, then return as silently as they had left. Hand signals flashed between them, the secret language that Intef's men used for silent communication.

"What do you do outside?" I asked Renni when I had an opportunity to speak quietly into his ear.

"Just keeping an eye on things. Making sure nobody is hanging around."

"Should we have somebody standing guard out there?"

"If Nenwef does not return before bed, Tuta and I will share watch duties overnight."

"I can help too. We all can."

"I know, but better that you stay indoors and out of sight. Tuta and I can manage between us."

"But then you will be tired tomorrow. I need you both to be at your best."

"We are well trained for that. Don't worry about it."

"But you have not trained in a long time."

He shot me a surprised look.

"There is much a man can do to keep himself fit and alert. I don't need a squad to be able to train."

It seemed I hadn't been paying as much attention to those around me as I thought.

"Besides," Renni said. "If anyone was to come looking for us tonight, they will probably be well trained themselves. Better that Tuta or me is there to greet them. And you need to sleep. It will be you who must do the thinking tomorrow. We are just there to protect you."

Nenwef still hadn't returned by the time we went to bed. After a quiet conversation with Istnofret, Renni slipped back outside. He signalled a message to Tuta on his way out and received a nod in return. I assumed they were planning for Tuta to relieve him.

Merti was subdued as we cleaned up the dishes and prepared for bed. She stood at the window, peering out into the dark. I went to stand beside her.

"He will be fine," she said quietly, as if reassuring herself as much as me. "He is a sensible man. We need to wait patiently and he will come home when he can."

"You are obviously well accustomed to being the wife of a guard," I said. "How long have you been married?"

"Almost ten years. It took some adjusting to, I must say. It is hard on a young woman when her husband so often comes home late from work and cannot tell her where he has been, or what he was doing, or who he was with. I understood when I married him that there would be secrets, especially since he had very recently been appointed to your personal squad. But when you are young and newly married and have spent all day waiting for your husband to come home, it is difficult to accept when he is late and can tell you only that he was working."

"I am sorry."

I didn't really know what else to say. I had rarely considered what impact my decisions, and the subsequent need for Intef to rearrange the schedules of his men, must have had on my guards, let alone their families.

Merti gave me a small smile.

"He was well paid for it. I didn't realise until after you were gone just how well paid your men were."

"They were Intef's men, not mine. And I never even knew what they were paid. Intef looked after all the details."

She shrugged a little, seemingly unwilling to argue with me and turned back to the window.

"I am sure he is well," I said, but my voice didn't sound convincing even to my own ears.

"He will be home by morning," she said.

I went to bed shortly after, leaving Merti to her lonely vigil by the window. But when I rose the next morning, Nenwef still hadn't returned. Merti had finally left her post by the window and sat on a cushion. Her face was pale and tight, and I wondered whether she had waited up all night. Istnofret sat nearby, while Renni and Tuta both prowled around the chamber. Behind me in the sleeping chamber, I heard Behenu beginning to rise from her blanket.

"We need to make a decision," Renni said as soon as I entered the chamber. "We must assume that Nenwef was caught. Do we continue with the plan? Or do we abandon it and make a new one?"

He and Tuta both looked to me.

"What would Intef do?" I asked.

"He would continue," Renni said. "It was the best plan we had, so unless we can come up with something better, I think we should go ahead."

"I think he would change the plan," Tuta said. "If Nenwef has been caught, Intef would not risk that he might have told them our plan."

"I thought we could trust him," I said to Renni.

"We can," he said, quickly. "Nenwef won't tell them anything unless he has to, and even then, he won't tell the full truth. We were taught to tell our captors enough to satisfy them, but to twist everything just enough that it doesn't quite reveal the plan."

"Will they torture him?" I asked.

A small sob caught my attention and I realised Merti was quietly crying.

"I am so sorry, Merti," I said. "I never would have let him go if I thought he would be caught."

She sniffed and wiped her eyes. "He knew the risk."

It was the same as what Istnofret had said after Sadeh was killed. She knew the risk, Istnofret had said, and she went willingly. I prayed to Isis that Nenwef would not lose his life because of me. I didn't think I could bear to know that another person had died out of loyalty to me.

Renni crouched down in front of Merti.

"I know this is difficult," he said, "But I think you should prepare to leave. Go to Babylon like Nenwef wanted. If he is alive, we will get him out of there. He will follow you if he can."

She looked at him for a long moment and I could see her indecision. She wanted to tell Renni that he was wrong, that Nenwef was fine and would be home soon enough, but she already believed he was dead. Eventually she got to her feet.

"I will pack a bag," she said and left the chamber.

My heart broke as I watched her go. Another life ruined because of me. If I hadn't come back to Memphis, Nenwef and Merti would have continued as they had. Renni put his hand on my shoulder.

"Don't fret," he said. "Merti is right. Nenwef knew the risk. I expect they have locked him up somewhere. Once we have dealt with Ay, you will release him and he can go after Merti."

"If you are so sure he is well, why did you tell her to leave?"

"Out of caution, and because I know it is what Intef would do."

"What would you do if you were not thinking about Intef?" I asked.

He gave a heavy sigh and took a long time to answer.

"To be honest, I don't know. Intef was my captain for a long time. I have never really thought about whether I would do things differently myself. I just do what he tells me to. Or rather, what he told me to. Do you still expect to turn around and find him standing there?"

"Not really," I said. "I know he is not coming back."

"With every decision I make, I expect to find him there, judging me for not thinking it through carefully enough."

My throat was suddenly choked and I couldn't respond.

"I cannot pretend to know how you feel," he said. "But I know how I would feel if it was Istnofret there."

"I wish…" My voice broke and I stopped to compose myself. "I just wish he didn't hate me. I think I could bear it a little easier if I didn't know that. He might live forever there and he is going to hate me for all that time."

"He does not hate you," Renni said. "He was angry, but he is a reasonable man. Sooner or later he will understand why you did what you did."

"But I will never know."

"No. I suppose you won't."

We were silent after that. I had no words left. How could I tell him how much it hurt? How much I regretted that one decision had cost me both my daughter and her father? I didn't even know whether I was doing the right thing anymore.

EIGHTEEN

My heart was heavy as I prepared to leave Merti's house. I bathed and put on my other gown, combed my hair and applied some kohl around my eyes. The gown was reasonably clean and I supposed I looked tidy enough. It was a far cry, though, from what I used to wear. The sheer linens and expensive jewels. The multitude of wigs and the careful makeup. It had been a long time since I had missed those things, but today I needed to feel regal and it was hard to do that dressed as I was.

I examined my hands: chipped and broken nails, peeling skin. Once upon a time, my ladies would rub lotions into my hands twice a day. My skin had been as soft and smooth as a baby's. I was still staring at my hands when Istnofret appeared in the doorway.

"Samun, they are waiting for you."

Did my face look as heavy as my heart felt? She looked me up and down and gave me a small smile.

"You look lovely, my lady."

The title might be jarring to my ears, but it seemed to roll smoothly off her tongue.

"I suppose I should get used to calling you that once again," she said.

"No, Ist. You can always call me Samun. No matter what happens today."

"Are you nervous?"

I inhaled. Held my breath. Let it out slowly. If I lied, would she be able to tell?

"Nervous, no. Petrified. Uneasy. But somehow at the same time, exhilarated. I have waited such a long time for this day and I can hardly believe it is here. I just hope…"

"What?"

"I hope I will make Intef proud today. That it will all be worth it."

She gave me a steady look. "I will support you, no matter the outcome. Renni too."

I reached for her hand and held it while I tried to figure out exactly what I needed to say.

"Thank you, Ist. For believing in me. For getting me out of the prison in Thebes. For travelling all the way across the world for me."

She had told me once that she believed I would take control of my throne. That she would be proud to serve me, whether I was Queen or Pharaoh. I hope she would never live to regret that statement.

Istnofret squeezed my hand and tears shone in her eyes. She started to say something but choked on a sob. Eventually she just shook her head. I released her hand and we went out to the chamber where the others waited. Behenu got to her feet with a groan and I suddenly remembered her injured leg.

"Behenu, we should have sent for a physician last night," I said.

"I will last another few hours," she said.

"Perhaps you should stay here today."

"No, I am coming with you. Once you have done what you need to, I will send a runner for a physician."

"You should send for the royal physician," I said.

"Maybe I will."

She gave me a small smile and I returned it, although I wasn't sure it looked convincing. Renni reached into his pack and pulled out the wooden box that contained the artefact we had given up so much to find.

"Are you ready?" he asked, his fingers on the clasp.

My heart pounded and I suddenly wasn't sure I was. I took in a shaky breath and nodded. He opened the box and held it out to me.

"Wait," Istnofret said. "Maybe you should not touch it until we get to the palace."

"We don't know what waits for us there," Renni said. "There might not be another opportunity for me to give it to her."

"But what if something goes wrong and there is no chance for her to use it?" she asked.

"Then you must take it from me," I said. "No matter what you have to do. No matter what I say. Promise me that if I cannot use the Eye today, you will take it back from me. I fear what it could make me do, especially if it thinks I will not use it. You know how it makes me crave power. I don't know what lengths it might go to in order to obtain the power it wants."

Renni and Istnofret both nodded. Tuta's eyes were round.

"Has anyone…" I gestured towards Tuta.

"I have told him," Renni said.

"All of it?" I asked.

"All of it. I doubt that he can fully comprehend it though. It is an unbelievable tale to anyone who was not there."

"I believe you," Tuta said. "But as you say, it is hard to

comprehend. I am still not sure that I understand where Intef is and exactly whether he is dead or alive."

"I don't think it matters," I said. "Either way, he is not coming back."

Nobody disagreed with me and for a few moments we all just looked at each other. Then I reached for the box in Renni's hands and took the Eye.

I hadn't touched it before. In fact the only time I had seen it was in that moment when Osiris allowed me to check that he wasn't tricking me with an empty box. It was smooth and almost weightless, made perhaps of a very light wood. It seemed to nestle into my palm. My fingers closed around it, almost without conscious intent. From the Eye came a very faint thrumming. Like a heartbeat. As if it was alive.

My own heart responded to its call, beating in time with it. I closed my eyes, trying to steady myself, but all I was aware of was the slight weight of the artefact in my hand. The sound of my heart beating in time with it. It wanted me to use it. It wanted me.

"Samun?"

From the exasperation in Istnofret's voice, it was clear she had been trying to get my attention for some time. Reluctantly, I opened my eyes. They all stared at me.

"Samun, are you well?" Istnofret asked.

My entire focus was on the Eye clasped in my fist. There was nothing left in me to make my mouth work. Eventually, when I still said nothing, Renni gestured towards the door.

"We should go," he said. "Nenwef may well need us."

The others said their farewells to Merti. I tried to farewell her with my eyes as I couldn't make myself speak. She gave me a serious nod and seemed to understand. Renni had secured passage on a boat which was sailing north to Rhakotis this afternoon. The captain knew of a ship that would be leaving for Sardis in a couple of days and had agreed to see Merti on board. If Nenwef was still alive and I freed him today, he would be able to get to Merti before the ship sailed.

As we left the house, I kept my fist closed around the Eye. I had a feeling I didn't need to fear losing it though. The Eye would not allow itself to be lost or to be taken from me. I was certain that if I were to trip and fall, the Eye would stay stuck to my skin even if I opened my hand. It would never leave me. Not until I had used it.

The walk to the palace was not overly long, but I was barely aware of it. With every step, the beat of my heart matched the thrumming of the Eye. My blood pulsed through my veins in response to it. I breathed in time with it. Eventually I realised I even walked in time with it. My entire body had synchronised itself to the Eye.

Somewhere, in some tiny corner of my brain that wasn't yet entirely consumed by the Eye, I wondered whether this was dangerous. Would I lose myself entirely to it? What would happen if I decided not to use it? No, that was not a possibility. The Eye would demand to be used. It would make me use it, and I would not resist. I wanted to experience its power. I had been queen once, but I had never experienced true power. This time I would.

I was aware of nothing around me until Renni spoke.

"Samun, are you ready?"

I hadn't even realised we had stopped walking. We were not far from the palace — in fact, I could see it at the end of the street ahead of us. How long had it been since I was here last? Two years perhaps, maybe a little more or a little less. The Eye pulsed, drawing my attention back to it.

"Samun?"

"I am ready," I snapped.

I was the only one who could wield the Eye. They couldn't possibly understand how it felt to hold such an artefact. I could feel the possibilities. Feel its power. My heart still beat in time with it.

"Samun?"

They had started to walk again and I never even noticed.

"Perhaps I should take the Eye until you need it." Renni held out his hand.

I wrapped my fingers more tightly around the precious artefact.

"You will not take it from me," I snarled.

Never again would I let power be ripped from my grasp.

Renni quickly held up his hands and took a step away from me.

"That was not my intention. I only thought to help you."

"Nobody will touch the Eye." I glared at each of them in turn. "Only I can wield it and only I will touch it."

Renni was the only one who met my eyes. The others all stared at the ground or the sky or anywhere but me.

"If we are going to do this today, we should go," Renni said.

"I am ready."

I clasped the Eye more firmly and strode towards the palace. Renni rushed to walk in front of me.

"Behind me," I said. "Nobody will walk in front of me this time. I will approach Ay myself."

"It is not the way things are done here," he said. "You know that. The queen should have one of her guards out in front of her."

"If you cannot follow my instruction, you can stay behind," I said. "I have no need for a guard who cannot obey orders."

He gave me a steady look and I saw the way he calmed

himself. Just as Intef used to do. It always irritated me that Intef wouldn't let himself express his emotions. It was no less irritating when Renni did it, but as long as he held his tongue and did as he was told, I supposed I didn't particularly care what he thought. It was not his place to think.

I kept walking and Renni fell in behind me with Istnofret, Behenu and Tuta. It was a sorry entourage for a queen and a memory tugged at my mind. Intef had always walked in front of me. My thoughts began to clear and I realised I had fallen under the Eye's spell again. The power it made me crave was not what I wanted for myself. Then the Eye thrummed and the thought slithered away. I held the power of the gods in the palm of my hand. What other mortal could say such a thing?

The palace loomed over us, much larger than I remembered. At the entrance, a pair of oversized wooden doors were flanked by a guard on either side. Was two men all the security Ay believed the palace needed? I didn't even need help for this. I could manage them myself. But as I approached, a curious thing happened. Instead of stepping forward to challenge us, both guards turned away to face out to the side. I hesitated, confused.

"Keep going," Renni whispered from behind me. "Nenwef said he would make arrangements. They are ensuring they do not see you enter."

As I walked up the shallow steps, the guards gave no sign that they had either seen or heard me. Someone behind me stumbled and scuffed a sandal against the step. Still the guards didn't react. I pushed open the doors. The wood was smooth and cool beneath my fingers, and they swung silently on well-oiled hinges.

An array of familiar impressions hit me. The smell of incense and lamp oil. Many-coloured murals covering every surface. The cool relief from the heat outside, which I hadn't even noticed.

Now I felt the sweat which trickled down my back and behind my knees. My gown was loose linen but even that felt too heavy in this heat. The Eye pulsed and once again I was drawn into its sphere. My breathing steadied to its pulse, my heart kept time to it.

"We need to keep moving," Renni said, drawing me from my reverie.

"Where is Nenwef?" Istnofret whispered.

"Nenwef will look after himself," Renni said. "Pharaoh will be in the audience hall since today is his monthly audience. That is all we need be concerned about."

We moved quickly along the hallways. I wasn't sure I would remember where the audience hall was after all this time and without Intef to lead me there, but my feet remembered the way even if my head didn't. People moved out of our way as we strode past. There were gasps and whispered comments, perhaps shock at my appearance or at my presence. I paid them no attention.

We rounded a corner and Renni, who had somehow gotten ahead of me, suddenly halted. I crashed into his back. He reached behind himself to steady me but didn't turn around. There was a long moment of silence before he spoke.

"Will you allow us to pass?"

"Is that her behind you?" a familiar voice replied.

Renni moved aside and I came face-to-face with Horemheb. He had been commander of the army when my brother was pharaoh. He had also been my brother's heir and had expected to marry me when my brother went to the West.

Horemheb looked me up and down. His lip curled slightly as if he saw something distasteful.

Behind me, Behenu made a small sound, almost a sob.

"I heard a rumour you had returned," he said. "I didn't believe it to be true."

"Why not?"

"I never thought you were that foolish. You barely got away with your life last time. You think he has forgiven you for making a fool of him?"

"I care nothing for what he thinks."

What did the opinions of worms like Ay or Horemheb matter when I possessed the power of the gods?

"You should remove yourself from my path," I said.

Horemheb seemed to hesitate. He looked from me to Renni and to Tuta, Istnofret and Behenu who stood behind me. He must have seen something that made him decide not to test me, for he stepped aside with a mocking bow. I didn't spare him another look as I swept past.

NINETEEN

As we turned towards the audience hall, I clutched the Eye tighter. Nothing could stop me now. I would remove Ay from the throne and take back my rightful place. Then I would rule as I had been born to. My only disappointment was that Intef wouldn't sit on the throne beside me. For a brief moment, my thoughts became more lucid and I remembered that I had not wanted to be queen again. But then the Eye pulsed and the desire for power rose within me, overwhelming everything else.

Before we reached the audience hall, Renni slowed to a stop. It was only then that I realised he had been walking in front of me. I was so accustomed to following one of my guards that I hadn't even noticed. Right now, though, the only thing I wanted was to get there quickly. I couldn't wait to see the look on Ay's face when he realised I was back.

"Keep going," I muttered.

"There are too many," Renni said.

I stepped around him and saw the guards. They lined the hall, two deep. It wasn't just one or two squads either. There were dozens of men.

"How many?" Istnofret asked quietly.

"Five squads," Renni said.

"I guess he thought we were bringing a larger force than we did." Tuta sounded almost amused.

I shot him a look and the smirk quickly disappeared from his face.

"I meant no disrespect, my lady."

I looked away, back to the waiting men. He would understand I was dissatisfied with him. There was no need for me to say anything.

"Halt!" came a voice from ahead of us.

"Metjen," Renni said. "It is good to see you."

"Why did you come back?" The man sounded almost disappointed. "I would have expected better of one of Intef's men."

"The queen wants to speak with Pharaoh."

"Is she still the queen? My understanding…"

"Metjen, don't be a fool. She will look favourably on those who aid her today."

Metjen shook his head.

"I am sorry, Renni, but she is not the queen any longer. Pharaoh has made that very clear."

"Who is queen then?" I asked.

Metjen looked surprised, although I wasn't sure whether it was because I had spoken or because I addressed my question to him.

"His Great Royal Wife, of course," he said. "Queen Tey."

For a moment I was confused. Tey had been in Crete with my sisters. Then I remembered this was not the same person. But it also wasn't who I had expected to be queen.

"Not the high priestess then?" I asked.

"Who?" His face showed his confusion.

I waved away the question. I had thought it would be Mutnodjmet who had taken my place. That's what my dream had shown me all those months ago. It would be either Sadeh or Mutnodjmet who sat on my throne. The dreams had never been wrong, but then I had never before possessed the power of the gods. If Mutnodjmet's day had not yet come, it never would now. The throne would be mine again.

"Will you let us pass, man?" Renni asked.

The Eye pulsed harder and I could hardly hear their conversation over it. It wanted my attention to itself. I squeezed the artefact, letting it know that I heard. The pulse subsided slightly as if the Eye was mollified.

"Not you," Metjen said. "Pharaoh's orders are that only she is to enter."

"I cannot send her in alone," Renni said. "She would be defenseless."

"It is her or none of you. I am sorry. If there was anything I could do, I would, but those are my orders and they came from Pharaoh himself. He has noticed me recently and I have the chance to impress him. I might be able to get a position in his personal squad and you know what kind of pay rise that means."

"And I suppose they all have the same orders?" Renni gestured to the other guards.

"They are all under my command." Metjen puffed out his chest. "Me. Can you believe it?"

"I have to say I find it hard to believe," Renni said.

Metjen's face reddened. "You could have been here yourself, you know. You never will be now. You are a traitor and everyone knows it."

Behind me, Tuta shifted slightly. Just enough to draw attention to himself. I supposed he was reminding Metjen that Renni wasn't here alone. Or maybe he reminded Renni.

"I have seven squads here under my command today,"
Metjen said.

"Five actually," Renni said. "Or were you too busy getting
yourself promoted to learn how to count?"

Metjen flushed and he pointed towards Renni.

"Arrest him," he cried. "Take him away. He is the traitor who
helped the queen when she tried to flee from Pharaoh's
custody."

Men stepped forward and took Renni by the arms. They
seemed to handle him more roughly than was necessary considering he made no effort to resist. I started to object, but the Eye
pulsed, reminding me I had no use for a mortal man. I closed my
mouth and watched them lead Renni down the hallway.

"Arrest him as well." Metjen nodded at Tuta.

"Hey, man," Tuta said. "I didn't do anything."

"You were acting suspiciously," Metjen said. "And associ-
ating with a known criminal."

Did he mean me or Renni?

Other men came to take Tuta away. He shook them off.

"I have done nothing," Tuta said. "Would you arrest an innocent man?"

"Take him away," Metjen said. "His whining offends my
ears."

No matter, I had the Eye. I didn't need men to protect me.

"As a matter of fact, take them all away," Metjen said. "They
are all known associates of a criminal."

"Wait," Istnofret said. "Let me stay. I am just a serving
woman. I attend to her."

Metjen pretended he didn't hear her and other men came to
lead her and Behenu away. Istnofret protested, but Behenu
murmured something to her and she stopped.

Soon only I was left. I glared at Metjen.

"Now will you let me pass?"

He nodded at one of his men.

"Advise Pharaoh that his *guest*-" his tone made a mockery of the word "-has arrived."

A guard slipped into the audience hall and I waited, lost in the pull of the Eye. It wanted me to use it. I could feel its desire, its longing to be used. The gods would not have given me such power if they didn't intend me to use it. All those years I had done what the advisors ordered. I had never understood true power before.

Perhaps I waited a long time. Perhaps it was only minutes. At some point Metjen gestured for me to enter the hall.

"Pharaoh will see you now," he said. "My orders are to see that you are kept under control so do not give me a reason to act on them."

I didn't deign to look at him as I entered the hall. I might have expected Ay would keep me waiting, but he had already dismissed whichever sycophant had been giving a report. The guard at the door didn't announce my titles or even my name.

I strolled down the aisle towards Pharaoh on his throne. I matched my pace to the pulse of the Eye, although it throbbed four times for every leisurely step I took.

The hall was full and around me I heard the whisper of fabric and the scuff of sandals as folk shifted in their places. Comments made in lowered voices were too soft for me to hear, but I didn't care. Let them say what they wanted. Last time they had seen me I was powerless. Now I held the power of the gods.

At last came the moment I had waited so long for: I stood in front of Pharaoh with the Eye of Horus in my hand. Ay looked older than I had expected. Weary, perhaps. Certainly fatter. The weight didn't sit well on him. He looked me up and down and seemed to sneer a little. Just as he had so many times when I had been Queen and he was merely an advisor.

"So," he said. "You return. You look quite the peasant woman in that garb."

"This country was built on the backs of peasants," I said.

"That does not mean that one of royal blood should dress like them."

"What would you have me do? You took away everything I owned. You left me with no resources to dress myself like a noble."

"Is this why you have returned? To ask that I fund your life-style. You, a slave and a known criminal."

I had almost forgotten I was supposed to be a slave. Many, maybe most, of the folk present here today, probably considered me to be such. The Eye pulsed, reminding me that today I would rule over them.

"I am not a slave just because you call me one," I said. "Just as you are not Pharaoh merely because you call yourself that."

He narrowed his eyes at me.

"That is exactly how it works. I am Pharaoh and you are a slave because I say you are."

"Sitting on a stolen throne does not make a man pharaoh. Nor does it make a queen."

I turned my attention to the woman who sat beside him. I was pleased to see that her fine linen dress wasn't one of mine, but the tall crown with the ureas at its front was, as was the pendant with an enormous chunk of lapis lazuli.

"Helping yourself to my belongings I see," I said to her.

I might have expected her to blush, but she only glared down at me with cold eyes.

"You would be wise to remember your place, slave," she said.

"Does it not bother you to know what kind of man you are married to?" I asked.

"I am queen because I am married to him."

"Not legitimately. I would rather be a slave than an illegitimate queen on a stolen throne."

"Fortunately for you that is exactly what you are."

We glowered at each other. The Eye pulsed. *Use me,* it seemed to say. *We can end this.* I was tempted. By the gods, I was so tempted. But I could only use it once. Use it too soon and I would lose my chance to deal with Ay, and everything I had endured would be for nothing.

"Why are you here?" Ay asked.

He slumped back in his throne and seemed to be making a show of finding our conversation exhausting. Or perhaps boring. That was only because he didn't yet know what I held in my hand.

"To restore the throne to the rightful bloodline. To punish you for your crimes."

There were other reasons, weren't there? I couldn't remember them now, but I had told Intef of my reasons for coming back. The Eye clouded my head, preventing me from remembering anything but what it wanted me to know. For a moment, I was alarmed. How could I control it if I could only remember what it wanted me to?

Ay took a long time to reply. I had surprised him. Exhilaration rushed through me and my momentary concern slipped away.

The Eye pulsed louder.

End this, it said.

"I am curious," Ay said. "How exactly do you propose to do such a thing? You are here alone. You have no guards, nobody to help you. How do you — a slave — propose to take the throne?"

The urge to taunt him welled within me, shocking in its ferocity. I didn't want to merely take the throne. I wanted him to know it was about to happen. I wanted him to fear it.

"Have you ever known true power?" I asked. "Ultimate power."

He frowned a little, but he wasn't sneering anymore. I had intrigued him.

"There exists an amulet. An artefact of the gods. Made from the eye of Horus himself. It has power that you cannot even begin to imagine."

Ay's face paled. It was clear he had indeed heard of the Eye and, more than that, he already feared it. This would be too easy.

"Think of what a person could do with that kind of power," I said. "One could do anything they wanted, could they not? They would be as powerful as the gods."

I raised my clenched fist. I couldn't hold back any longer. The Eye pulsed harder than ever before and I could barely string my words together. I wanted to focus on nothing but the Eye, but I had to remember my goal. Remove Ay from the throne.

"I possess the Eye. I have the power of the gods. And you will die."

The Eye pulsed, agreeing with me.

Ay gave me a bewildered look and shook his head.

"I do believe she has lost her mind," he said to the hall at large.

His voice was pitying. He shouldn't pity me. He should fear me.

"You must die!" I cried.

I squeezed my fingers around the Eye, waiting for it to act.

Ay pointed towards me and shouted.

"Guards, take her away. She is to be restrained for her own

safety. Alone. She is to have no opportunity to conspire with anyone to escape again."

Guards ran to grab my arms. I tried to shake them off. No, they couldn't take me away yet. Not before I saw Ay fall to the ground.

"Die!" I cried again.

My emotions bubbled over. I threw back my head and laughed.

But Ay continued to sit on his throne and look at me as if I was a rather bewildering bug beneath his sandal.

"Why are you not dying?" I felt as confused as he looked. I opened my fist and stared down at the Eye. "Why are you not working? What did I do wrong?"

Ay leaned forward a little, as if to see what I held. I closed my fingers around the Eye. Its power was not for the likes of him to see.

The Eye pulsed, reassuring me. It still wanted me to use it.

But I had tried and it didn't answer me.

They took me by my arms and led me away. They locked me in a chamber where there was nothing but a bed mat, a lamp and a pot in which to relieve myself. No window, no couches. Not even so much as a mural on the wall. I sank down onto the mat and examined the Eye. It still pulsed, still called to me. It wanted me to use it as badly as I did.

Exhaustion swept over me and suddenly keeping my eyes open was more than I could manage. I curled up on the mat, the Eye still clasped in my fist. I slept.

TWENTY

I t felt like time ceased to pass while I had nothing but a lamp to keep me company. Eventually the lamp's oil ran low and its flames began to flicker. I supposed that time really did pass after all.

It reminded me of something, this odd notion that maybe time had stopped, but I couldn't remember what. I had experienced a timeless place before. Perhaps it was something I had dreamed.

I dozed on and off. My dreams were jumbled and confusing, half-glimpsed fragments of things I didn't understand. Somebody whispered in my ear. *You should be careful of the jackal. He is a trickster.* I walked on a sandy shore in a grey world. I sank down into an ocean. Intef stood in front of a pair of tall black gates as they swung shut. The girl on the other side looked at him steadily and her face gave no hint of her thoughts. A falcon's eyes glittered. *The legend says the Eye has never been used with ill intent.*

The words rang in my ears when I woke. My fingers were

still tightly clasped around the artefact. I tried to let go but my fingers didn't move. My heart beat double time and for a moment I panicked, but then my fingers spasmed and twitched. Finally I was able to unclasp my fist. I stared at the amulet in my palm. Reddish-brown paint coated its surface, or maybe it was blood. It didn't look like anything special. Certainly nothing powerful.

The legend says the Eye has never been used with ill intent.

That was what Hemetre had told me, long before any of this started. Before I ever left Egypt. And yet I had tried to use the amulet to kill Ay. I couldn't explain why I had done it. It had not been my intention. I had never been able to see how our eventual confrontation might play out. After all, I had no idea how the Eye worked. I had expected to figure it out when the time came. But why had I tried to kill him? Had the Eye told me to do it? Or had that dark desire come from within me?

"What do you want from me?" I whispered. "If you have never been used for ill, why do you want me to kill him?"

The Eye pulsed more weakly now, as if it was as exhausted as I. It did not respond to my question and eventually I fell asleep again.

I woke to the creak of a door opening.

"Breakfast," the guard said as he set a tray down on the floor. He turned to leave.

"Wait."

My voice was croaky and I had to speak twice before it was loud enough for him to hear. He turned back to me.

"How long does he intend to keep me in here?"

"I couldn't say," he said. "It is not my place to question Pharaoh's intentions. Nor is it yours."

"Do you know nothing of what is to happen to me?"

His face was slightly more sympathetic as he shook his head.

"I have heard nothing. I must go now. I have other duties to attend to and I do not intend to be late because I dallied to talk to a prisoner."

I caught a glimpse of other men in the hallway as the door closed behind him. The lock clicked.

At first, I decided that I would eat nothing. Ay would release me rather than let me starve to death. But when my stomach felt like it would gnaw its way out of me, I gave in. The bread wasn't terribly fresh and the beer might have been stale, but it wet my throat and filled my belly nonetheless. With nothing else to do, I went back to sleep, the Eye still clutched in my fist.

Light from the hallway flooded the chamber as the door opened. It was a different guard who brought food this time. He set a tray on the floor, then crouched to check the oil in the lamp.

"Are you well, my lady?" he asked, very quietly.

I stared up at him blearily.

"I am well enough."

"You must not lose faith. All will be well."

Was he trying to pass on a surreptitious message? Was this some code that one of the others thought I would understand?

"Do I know you?"

I squinted against the light, trying to make out his features more clearly, but he snatched up the tray from my previous meal and stood.

"I am nobody," he said. "Just a guard."

Then he left and I was alone again. This time the tray contained bread with a thin slice of cheese and more beer. I ate methodically, hardly tasting any of it. When I had finished, I looked down at the Eye, still grasped in my right hand.

"What do you want from me?" I asked.

It pulsed, weakly now. I could use it to free myself, it seemed to suggest.

But Hemetre had said I could only use it once.

"I cannot," I said. "You know that."

It didn't respond. If I would not use it, it would not talk to me anymore, it seemed.

I suddenly felt very alone. Everyone left me eventually. My sisters. My parents and my brother. Sadeh. Intef. Now even the Eye.

My head felt clearer and now that my thoughts were my own again, I finally understood what I had done. I had tried to kill Ay. As much as I hated that odious worm, I had not come here with any conscious intent to kill him, but perhaps that was what I had secretly desired. Perhaps the Eye had amplified my desire, even if I had never expressed it to myself.

I looked down at the Eye resting on my palm. It was just a wooden amulet now. Sleeping perhaps. Dormant. I set it down on the mat. It pulsed weakly but then seemed to retreat into itself again. My only consolation was that I had faced Ay alone. I had dreamed once that I would face him alone or watch the Egyptian army be slaughtered by the Hittites. Everything else might have gone wrong, but at least I had saved my country from Suppiluli-umas's revenge.

It was a different guard again who next brought me food. Unlike the last one, he made no attempt to talk to me, just set down the tray, checked the oil in the lamp and left.

I was beginning to wonder just how long Ay intended to leave me in here, but the next time they brought me food, it was the kindly guard again, and this time Istnofret followed him into the chamber.

"Ist? What are you doing here?" I asked.

I tried to get to my feet but after lying down for so long, my head spun and I almost fell over. Istnofret rushed forward to steady me.

"Quiet," she whispered. "We don't have much time. Have they treated you well?"

"Well enough. Where are the others?"

"Still locked up. Setka here couldn't risk letting us all come to see you."

"So you are not here to rescue me?"

"I am afraid not. Setka will have to take me back to our chamber in a moment."

At the door, Setka looked out into the hallway.

"Hurry." His voice was terse. "You know we cannot afford to get caught."

"Setka offered to watch your door while the guards went for a quick drink," Istnofret said. "I wanted to see you. He said you were well, but I had to see for myself."

"Does Renni have a plan? How are we to get out of here?"

"We don't know. Setka is the only guard we have seen so far who is well inclined towards us. He and Renni used to have some shifts together before Renni joined your personal squad. All the others are treating Renni as a traitor. They have not forgotten that he was caught helping you sneak out of the palace."

"So what am I supposed to do?"

"Just wait. We will figure something out soon. There are usually two men stationed at your door and half a squad at ours. Setka is the only one we can trust."

"Are you all in one chamber?"

"Renni is next door, but as long as we don't make too much noise, the guards don't seem to care if we talk to him. Tuta is in the chamber on the other side of his."

At the door, Setka cleared his throat.

"Time to go," he said. "They will be back any moment."

Istnofret leaned in to give me a quick, fierce hug.

"Trust us," she said. "We will get you out of here."

Then she was gone. The door closed behind her and the lock clicked.

TWENTY-ONE

Weeks passed. Months. Istnofret didn't return and neither did Setka. I hoped that meant they hadn't been caught before he returned Istnofret to her chamber, but I had no way of knowing. I could hardly ask anyone.

I saw nobody other than the guards who brought food, refilled my lamp, and emptied my chamber pot. Every few days someone would bring a bucket of water to wash in and once I was given a clean gown.

My entire world was nothing but flickering lamp light and solitude. At first, I felt like I might go out of my mind. I became angry. I yelled and cried. At Intef, at Maia. Horus, Ay, Keeper of the Lake. The Eye. Osiris. Even my friends for not having rescued me yet.

As the weeks passed, my anger subsided. At some point I threw the Eye into the corner of the chamber. It hit the wall and clattered to the stone floor. Remorse filled me immediately. What if I had broken it? I was gifted the power of the gods and I tossed it away in a fit of pique. I left it where it fell, though, and didn't check whether it was broken. I couldn't afford to touch it. I wasn't sure I would be able to resist it again.

I waited for someone to rescue me as Istnofret had promised, but eventually I realised that nobody was coming for me. Perhaps they had no chance to escape their own chamber. Perhaps they had been separated or taken elsewhere. Perhaps they weren't even alive anymore. It seemed it would be up to me to rescue myself.

So I began to pay more attention to my guards. I listened at the door to figure out how many men were there. Istnofret had said there were two. Being inexperienced in any such covert activity, I had no idea whether the sounds I heard were only two men.

I had no way of estimating time other than by how quickly my lamp burned down. The guards checked the oil each time they came in but only refilled it every second visit. As this pattern was so consistent, I concluded that they brought me food at the same times every day. There were only four guards who ever entered my chamber, other than Setka who didn't return, and none of them seemed inclined to talk to me. They didn't even look at me. I tried several times to speak with each of them. One — the guard who had told me he didn't want to be late because he stopped to talk to me — acknowledged my words with a grunt. The others pretended they didn't hear me. So I would get no help from them.

I had no way of knowing whether it was day or night, but if there were only two guards at my door, I guessed it was unlikely that their numbers would be reduced overnight. It was the guards outside my friends' chambers who might be fewer at night if I could figure out when that was. The hallway outside my chamber was always lit — this far into the depths of the palace, the lamps would burn both day and night.

With nothing else to base my decision on, I decided that perhaps the guards let my lamp burn a little lower at night, which meant the period after they refilled the oil must be day. It was a tenuous connection, but it was all the information I had.

I waited another four meals to be sure the pattern was consistent. There seemed to be a fixed order in which guards came as well. As luck would have it, the smallest was the one who brought my evening meal on the day I intended to act. As soon as he left, I went to the door and waited with my ear against it. I listened for a while but heard nothing and couldn't tell how many guards there were. This was it. My escape attempt. There would only be one chance. If I failed, they would guard me even more securely and I would certainly remain imprisoned here until Ay decided to dispose of me.

I tore a thin strip of linen from my skirt and used it to shield my skin as I snatched up the Eye from where it still lay in the corner of the chamber. I had not worn my pouch the day we came to confront Ay so I had nothing in which to carry the amulet other than my hand. I could only hope that by not touching it directly, I might give myself some resistance to it.

I dipped my fingers in my beer and wiped them around the edges of my face to make it look as if I had been sweating profusely. My meal tonight was a barley gruel. It was cold by now and probably barely edible anyway. I splattered some of it on the front of my gown, then dropped the bowl to the floor. With the dinner tray positioned close by for ready access, I lay back on my bed mat. I groaned and moaned, growing increasingly loud until a guard knocked on the door.

"Hey," he called. "Keep it down in there."

"I am poisoned," I cried. "Fetch a physician."

I heard a conversation between the guards. They were

worried enough to not keep their voices down. I groaned even louder and made retching sounds.

"Please hurry," I called to them. "I am dying."

Movement from the hallway. The door opened and the smaller guard entered. I could see little of the hallway behind him and could only hope the other man had gone to find a physician.

He stood in the doorway, clearly unsure what to do. I moaned and clutched my belly.

"It was the gruel," I said between sobs. "Someone has poisoned me."

Still he didn't come any closer.

"The police chief will want to inspect it," I said. "He will-" I paused to groan and sob. "He will look favourably on you if you keep it for him."

He finally approached me. I let one arm fall down to the floor, resting it just beside the dinner tray.

The guard crouched to inspect the spilled gruel. I grabbed the tray and hit him in the face as hard as I could. He cried out as he toppled over.

I got to my feet and snatched up the keys from where he had dropped them. The hallway outside was empty. I locked the door, although my hands trembled and I dropped the keys twice. With the guard secured, I raced along the hallway.

There were three other chambers in that hall. Two were unlocked. The third wasn't. I knocked very softly.

"Ist?" I whispered. "Are you in there? Behenu? Renni? Tuta?"

"Who is it?" came a gruff voice from within.

I left without reply. At the end of the hallway were two branching halls. Down the left, the hallway was empty. On the right, a solitary guard stood at a door. Wherever my friends were, I doubted they were unguarded, and if there was only one guard, my guess that it was night was probably correct.

I kept my head down as I walked towards him, hoping he wouldn't recognise me, and tried not to look as if I was panting. After barely moving for months, it was an effort to even walk, let alone run.

"What do you want?" he asked as I approached.

"A message for you, sir," I said. "I work in the kitchen. There has been a suspected case of a prisoner being poisoned. I was sent to ask if anyone guarding prisoners has noticed anything unusual."

I could feel him staring at me. I kept my face averted, looking to the floor as was appropriate for a servant and a commoner.

"They ate a while ago," he said, finally. "Have not heard anything from them since then."

"Do you think you could check on them? Just to be sure they are well? I am supposed to find out whether anyone else has been poisoned."

He grunted and fingered the keys that hung from his neck.

"If they were sick, I would have heard something. Run along now. You can report back that all is well here."

"The prisoner who was poisoned died very quickly. I heard the guard is being questioned as to why he did not notice earlier."

"I suppose it would not hurt to check," he said. "Just to be sure. Then you can report that I was conscientious about the prisoners' welfare."

"I am sure that will be viewed very favourably."

He unlocked the door and swung it open.

"Looks-"

He stopped abruptly as I kicked him hard in the back of his knee. He dropped to the floor and Renni was on him in a moment. A swift punch to the face left the guard howling and his nose bloodied. Renni snatched the keys from his hand.

"Move," he said as he gestured for me to get out of his way.

I tumbled back out of the chamber and he locked the door behind us. I was frozen in place as he unlocked the door to the next chamber. The lamp light revealed Istnofret and Behenu standing together. Istnofret held the chamber pot — she had used that trick before and we knew it was effective — while Behenu clutched the lamp. They were both tensed and ready to launch their objects at us. Renni motioned for them to follow and they set down their items and hurried out after us without a word. Another chamber contained Tuta and he too stood ready. We took off down the hallway.

"You have a plan?" Renni asked me.

"That *was* my plan," I admitted. "I did not really think past getting out of that chamber."

In truth, I hadn't thought I would need to plan past that. I had assumed Renni would take it from there.

"Is there anyone in Memphis you trust?" he asked Tuta. "We need somewhere to lie low for a few days while we figure out what to do next."

"Plenty of men I would have trusted once," Tuta said. "Now I am not so sure. I have been gone for two years. I don't know enough about what has been happening here to know who to trust anymore."

"If you had to trust someone, who would it be?" Renni said. "Don't think too hard. Tell me what your gut says."

"Nehi maybe." Tuta shot me a look as if he thought I would know who he meant, but I shrugged at him. "He was captain of Pharaoh's personal squad."

I vaguely recognised the name. Tuta didn't mean the current

pharaoh, but my brother. I wasn't sure I had ever met Nehi, but Intef might have mentioned him.

We reached an intersection and Renni indicated with a nod which way we were to turn. But as we did, we encountered a man. Renni stopped abruptly and we all followed his example. I didn't miss the subtle flash of hand signals between Renni and Tuta, nor the way Tuta began to edge around behind the man. They were preparing for trouble.

"Renni!"

"Sabu," Renni said. "It is good to see you, man."

"What are you doing? I heard…"

His voice trailed off as he took a closer look at me. His face was familiar and it took me a few moments to recall where I had seen him. He had guarded my brother's door on one of my last visits to his chamber. He had let me in, even though he had orders not to.

"Sabu." Renni's voice was very quiet. "It would be best if you forget you saw us."

"I heard you had all been arrested. That my lady threatened Pharaoh."

"Just let us pass," Renni said. "We don't want any trouble."

"And yet Tuta here has got himself in position behind me ready to take me down. You don't trust me."

"We don't know who we can trust," Renni said. "And we cannot afford to take any chances."

"Sabu," I said. "I remember the time Intef took a whipping for you."

"I had hoped at one time that he might ask me to join your personal squad," Sabu said. "Being in Pharaoh's squad gave me a very high status, but Nehi's men were not regarded in the same way as those who served under Intef. But when Intef took that whipping for me, I knew it would never happen. If he had thought I was strong enough to bear it myself, he would not have offered and he would never want a weakling in his squad."

"That was not why he took your whipping," I said. "He felt an obligation to you. You would not have been whipped if you had not let us into my brother's chamber. He considered it his responsibility to take the punishment for you."

"He didn't think I was weak?"

The look on Sabu's face said this was something he had never considered.

"He spoke very favourably of you after that incident."

I wasn't sure that was the truth, but it was what Sabu would want to hear.

He gave me a small smile and stepped aside.

"Go," he said. "Quickly before someone else sees you. If anyone catches you, I never saw you."

"Thank you," I said. "I am most grateful to you once again."

He gave me a low bow, then we were jogging past him. I wondered whether I would ever see him again.

TWENTY-TWO

We saw nobody else as we hurried through the palace. Renni led us on a circuitous path, and as well as I thought I knew this place, I was thoroughly lost. Eventually he stopped.

"Wait here."

He slipped inside a chamber and the door swung shut behind him. Tuta positioned himself beside the door. He nodded down the hallway.

"Watch that way," he said. "I will watch the other way."

I wasn't sure who he meant so I looked in the direction he had indicated, although both Istnofret and Behenu were doing the same thing. The door opened and Renni waved us in.

The chamber was all in darkness although the moonlight through the open windows gave enough light to ensure I didn't trip over anything.

"Are we waiting in here until morning?" Istnofret whispered.

"We will go out the window," Renni said.

"Are we not safer in here?" she asked. "They will search the city, but they surely won't search the palace. They won't expect us to still be here."

"If they are sensible, they will have men searching every last chamber." Renni's tone was grim. "We don't want to be here when that happens. However, we need somewhere to go."

I leaned against the wall while I thought. I had never known many people outside of the palace, but there was one person we might be able to trust.

"Hemetre," I said.

"The priestess?" Istnofret asked. "The one who told you about the Eye?"

"She took a great risk in telling me as much as she did."

"That was a couple of years ago," Renni said. "Are you sure you can still trust her?"

"People change," Istnofret said, very quietly. "She might not be the person you knew."

"They don't change that much in just a couple of years," I said.

"Do you know where she lives?" Renni asked.

"No, but she will be at the temple for dawn worship. I need to find a way to speak privately with her."

Renni shot me a look. "You don't trust the high priestess?"

"I always felt that of the two priestesses, I could only trust one and I am certain that is Hemetre."

"Let's go then. It is quite a walk to the temple and you will need to be inside before the priestesses arrive if you don't want Mutnodjmet to see you."

"Wait," Behenu said. "What about Nenwef? We should find him."

Renni and Tuta looked at each other for a long moment. Hand signals flashed between them, but at length Renni shook his head.

"We cannot risk it. We don't know where he is being held, if indeed he is even still in the palace. If we intend to leave here tonight, it must be now before they find us."

Renni was right when he said it was a long walk, especially after spending months being confined to a chamber. Still, I was far more accustomed these days to walking on my own feet rather than sitting in a palanquin carried by slaves, and I could bear the walk. The Eye pulsed, reminding me of its presence.

You could have that again, it seemed to say. *If you had the courage to use me.*

I tried to pretend I didn't hear it and instead kept an image of Intef in my mind. Thinking about him seemed to help me resist the allure of the Eye. My stomach growled, reminding me I hadn't eaten. I should have had some of the gruel before I threw it on the floor.

We wove through the alleys between buildings, keeping to the shadows as much as possible. The moon was close to full tonight and there was plenty of light for anyone who might be searching the city for escaped prisoners. As we walked, I remembered that Behenu had been wounded the last time I saw her.

"Behenu, how is your leg?" I asked. "Did they treat it?"

She didn't reply for a moment and I repeated my question, thinking she hadn't heard.

"They did treat her." Istnofret's voice was full of barely concealed rage. "But not until her blood became infected. She was very sick and we thought she would go to the West before they finally brought in a physician."

"The royal physician?" The title was held by Yuf, when I was here last, and he had kept his position even though he had been unable to save my brother.

"I doubt it," Istnofret said. "He was little more than a common magician. All he did to start with was pray over her leg and place amulets on it. Eventually Behenu told him to go find some honey to put on the wound. He insisted he could heal her with prayer, but I made such a fuss that eventually he got the honey. She started to improve after that, but she was sick for a long time."

"It is much better now," Behenu said. "It scarred badly, though, and the scar is too tight. It is a bit uncomfortable when I walk too fast."

We had run through the palace and she had never even said she was in pain.

As we approached the temple, Renni stopped us in the shadow of a cottage.

"Tuta, you go and check it out," he whispered. "If it seems safe, wave Samun over to you and find her somewhere to hide inside."

"He is not permitted inside," I said. "The priestesses are very strict about not allowing men in the temple of Isis."

"Either he or I must check the area, so we don't have much choice," Renni said.

"I will go by myself," I said. "Tuta can check around the outside, make sure nobody is waiting behind the temple. If it seems safe, I will go inside and wait for a chance to speak with Hemetre."

"Definitely not," Renni said. "Intef would kill me if I allowed you to go inside without checking it first."

"Intef is not here to kill anyone," I said, rather shortly. "And he will never know."

Renni gave me a steady look.

"You understand the danger you are putting yourself in? If there is some threat in there, we won't hear you from out here. You will have no back up if something happens."

"I understand. I would rather risk that than Mutnodjmet's

wrath if she finds you in there."

"It is on your head then," he said with a heavy sigh.

"Maybe you should leave the Eye with us?" Istnofret suggested. "If something happens-"

"It stays with me," I said. "I am the only one who can use it anyway."

I just had to keep thinking of Intef. He would give me the strength to resist the Eye.

"But maybe-"

"No."

I waited, but it seemed nobody had any further objection.

"I guess I am going then," I said.

Istnofret caught my hand. "Be careful, Samun."

Tuta and I darted across the street and I waited out the front of the temple while he slipped around the back. I stood close beside one of the giant stone lions that flanked the entrance. Depending on which direction someone was looking from, I might be visible, but it gave me some small feeling of safety.

Tuta returned and gave me a nod.

"All quiet back there."

As I pushed on the wooden door, it occurred to me that perhaps the priestesses would leave it locked overnight. It opened easily though, without even a creak. I glanced back to see Tuta returning to where the others were hidden.

The temple was all in darkness. When I used to come here for dawn worship, the halls were always lit by torches which sat in brackets on the walls. Today the torches were cold and the halls dark and empty. I crept along them, one hand on the wall to feel my way.

I had never been here without the priestesses and it occurred to me that I didn't know what their routine was as they prepared for the worship ceremony. Who would arrive first? Who carried out which tasks? Which chambers would they enter? Where did they store the items they needed for the ceremony? I didn't even know where the goddess herself was put to bed for the night.

Before I reached the inner sanctum where the priestesses would worship, I slipped into a chamber. I had passed it every time I came for worship but had never paid it any attention. Here in the depths of the temple, there were no windows and the chamber was in utter darkness. I felt my way around. Shelves with rows of bowls. A pile of cloths. Tidy bundles of incense, a basket of silky petals. A low bench along one wall. Mutnodjmet would undoubtedly come in here before the ceremony. I had a feeling she wouldn't allow Hemetre to handle such precious items. There didn't seem to be anywhere to hide, or at least nowhere I could find in the dark.

I tried the next chamber. A large table in the middle, more shelves. My foot caught on something which toppled over with a clatter. I froze, barely breathing. Had anyone else arrived yet? But nobody came to check on the source of the noise and eventually my heart rate returned to normal.

I crouched and felt around on the floor. Bronze items, perhaps, long and thin. I ran my fingers over one but couldn't guess what it was. I bundled them back up and stood them against the wall. How many were there and how exactly had they been positioned? I was acutely aware of the minutes slipping by as I ran my fingers over the cool stones, trying to find any I might have missed. Eventually I gave up. I would have to trust that either I had found them all or that nobody would think it odd if one seemed to have fallen over.

I made my way around the rest of the chamber. Nowhere to hide in here. As I returned to the hallway, I spotted a flicker of lamp light back towards the temple entrance. I was almost out of time.

I slipped into the next chamber and felt my way around it. Another long shelf. A stack of what seemed to be wooden tubs. A large clay pot. A wooden chest. Footsteps came along the hallway and the lamp light grew stronger.

I eased up the lid of the chest and felt around inside it. It held a stack of neatly folded linen and plenty of spare room. I climbed in on top of the linen and eased the lid shut.

My heart pounded so loudly that I couldn't hear the footsteps anymore. I breathed slowly, willing my heart to slow down. It was only now, confined in such a small space, that I became aware of my own odour. The stench of sweat, unwashed linen and gruel was fierce and I tried to breathe through my mouth so I wouldn't notice it as much.

I squeezed the Eye, seeking the comfort of knowing I possessed the power of the gods. As soon as I thought about it, the Eye started pulsing.

Use me, it seemed to say. *I could take you away from this.*

I quickly fixed an image of Intef in my mind again. I would not waste my one use of the Eye.

Through a crack between the panels of the chest, the lamp light grew stronger. Someone entered the chamber. The lamp was set on a shelf. Something moved, slid along its shelf or perhaps the floor. Someone passed right in front of the chest. I held my breath and hoped whoever it was couldn't hear the pounding of my heart or smell my stench.

The person started humming. It was so faint I could hardly hear the tune, but it seemed to be the song we sang to Isis. I eased a little closer to the chest wall, trying to put my ear against it. Then abruptly the chest lid opened.

Hemetre stared down at me, lamp light bright behind her. Her eyes widened and she sucked in a breath. The lid dropped back down again. She resumed her humming, although it sounded a little shaky now.

"Knock once against the side of the chest if you can hear me," she said, very quietly.

I knocked gently. The noise seemed much louder than I had anticipated.

"Are you here to speak with me?"

I knocked again.

"Will it be a problem if Mutnodjmet finds out?"

I knocked.

"Does anyone else know you are here?"

Another knock. Whether she meant my friends or perhaps someone in the temple, I wasn't sure.

"Are you in trouble?"

I knocked.

"And you think there is something I can do to help you?"

I hesitated. I wasn't sure that anyone could help. She repeated her question, perhaps assuming I hadn't heard. Not knowing what else to do, I knocked.

Her footsteps retreated as she checked the hallway. She returned quickly.

"Mutnodjmet has arrived. You will need to stay here until after the ceremony. She won't have reason to come in here so you are safe enough as long as you are quiet. I will return when I can."

Then she was gone, taking the lamp with her. She called out a greeting and Mutnodjmet replied, although her voice was too low for me to make out her words.

I waited until they seemed to have left before I wriggled around to try to get myself into a more comfortable position. I knew how long the morning worship took and no doubt it would seem even longer trapped as I was in the chest.

TWENTY-THREE

I must have fallen asleep at some point and I woke with a start. Lamp light flickered through the cracks of the chest. Hemetre hummed. As she passed by, she whispered to me.

"Be quiet. She has not left yet."

I lay on my side with my legs tucked up. A cramp spasmed my calf muscle. I longed to stretch out my limbs. Just as it got to the point where I thought I couldn't bear to be in here for another minute, the lid lifted and Hemetre peered down at me. She held out a hand to help me out.

My legs were numb and at first all I could do was sit up. Even that was a welcome relief though. I shielded my eyes against the lamplight, which seemed unbearably bright. My hand which clutched the Eye spasmed.

"Slowly," she said. "You have been in there for hours. It will take time for your blood to move again."

"Are we alone?" I murmured.

"Yes. You are fortunate that Mutnodjmet has been called to a meeting at the palace. She would be here for some time yet otherwise."

"At the palace? Do you know why?"

"She said only that Pharaoh's chief advisors had asked for her."

"They will warn her that I might come here."

She gave me a steady look. "I wondered if that might be the case."

"Do you intend to tell her?"

"I suppose that depends on why you are here."

"I need your help."

"Come. Let's get you out of there and we can talk."

Getting to my feet was painful, with my legs spasming and my feet numb. Even once I was standing, I had to wait in the chest for another few minutes until I trusted my legs to hold me while I climbed out.

At the door, Hemetre checked the hallway, then indicated for me to follow. We walked as quickly as I could manage. The chamber she took me to was bare other than for a rug on the floor and an overturned chest on which rested a miniature statue of Isis, no taller than the length of my thumb.

"I use this chamber to pray," Hemetre said. "If anyone notices me in here, they are unlikely to interrupt. Wait here and I will get you something to drink."

She took the lamp and closed the door behind her, leaving me once again in the dark. The absence of light was a welcome relief. Hemetre returned quickly with two mugs of melon juice and a thick slice of bread.

"I guessed you might not have eaten for some time," she said.

"Thank you."

Hemetre didn't speak again until I had finished eating.

"Tell me what you think I can do to help you."

I took another sip of melon juice. It was sweet and tangy and I still found myself surprised at the taste. When I left Egypt, I had thought I would never taste melon juice again.

"I found the Eye of Horus," I said.

Hemetre appraised me for a long moment, as if trying to determine whether I told the truth.

"I thought that if anyone could find it, it would be you," she said eventually. "The Daughters of Isis have tried to keep track of it over the generations, but we lost its trail about twenty years ago."

I gave her a short accounting of our journey. My conversation with Maia in Behdet, which led us to Indou where we found Abha and Dakini, only to realise that it was Bhumi who Maia had sent me to find. I had arrived too late to see anything other than her grave. Travelling to Babylon where we met Shala and her archivist husband, Belasi. Finding Antinous's account of how he intended to fulfil his promise to his friend Djediufankh to hide the Eye away where no man would ever find it again. Searching the island of Crete and how we accidentally crossed into the underworld. How our shadows became unattached and we had to leave Intef behind as a companion to Keeper of the Lake. I drank the rest of my melon juice while I talked and my throat was still dry when I had finished.

"I will get you some more juice," Hemetre said.

She rose and left without any comment on my story.

I was a little stunned at her hasty departure. Did that mean she didn't believe me? Was she sending a message to Mutnod-jmet to come back to the temple? Had I said the wrong thing and made her think I was delusional, or worse, cursed?

When Hemetre returned, she handed me the mug, then settled herself on the rug again. I longed to ask whether she believed me, but I figured I had said enough. Let Hemetre speak now. If she didn't believe me, she would say it soon enough and I would know I was wasting my time. I had no idea who else we might go to, but we would come up with a new plan. We always did.

"Maia obviously had information she had not shared with the rest of us," Hemetre said. "Why would she tell you and not us?"

"I don't know her motives. I only know that if she had not sent me to Indou, we never would have found the Eye."

Hemetre studied me as if carefully considering her next remark.

"I assume you intend to use it to take back the throne," she said at last. "Why have you not done that already?"

I hadn't expected her to ask this. My cheeks heated as I remembered how I had tried to use the Eye.

"You yourself said it can only be used once," I said. "And I have not yet figured out either what to use it for or how to activate it."

"So what do you need from me? I have told you all I know about the Eye. If you seek more information, it seems it is Maia you should speak with. She is still in Behdet as far as I know."

"We need somewhere to hide for a few days. Time to plan. Perhaps a chance to speak with a priest who might know more about the Eye and how it works."

"Just you alone?"

"And my friends. There are five of us."

And Nenwef who was still imprisoned and Woser who might be waiting for us somewhere in the city.

"It would be too dangerous for you to stay here at the temple," she said. "I could perhaps hide one person but not so many."

"Is there a place you can suggest? We know how to be quiet and we can look after ourselves. We just need somewhere to stay."

"If you are willing to be separated, there are other Daughters who would give you and your companions shelter for a day or two. I know of nobody who could take you all though."

I had only just found my friends again. We couldn't afford to be separated again already.

"We need to make plans. We must stay together."

Hemetre sighed, sounding troubled in a way that surprised me until her next words.

"I suppose you will have to stay at my house. I have a son, though. Can you promise me he will not be in any danger?"

A son. I had not expected that. Hemetre had always seemed somewhat mysterious to me. After all, she was a member of the elusive Daughters of Isis who were apparently sworn to protect the bloodline of the rightful queens. I had never pictured her as having a family or even a home. If I had thought of her at all, I would have only imagined her here at the temple.

I looked Hemetre in the eyes and swallowed hard as I considered her request. As soon as Pharaoh knew we were gone — and I had to assume he already knew — he could devote his army to looking for us. He could seal off the city and ensure that nobody left until he found us. He had the resources of an entire country to put into his search. If he wanted me badly enough, he would find me.

"I cannot promise such a thing," I said, at last. "What I can promise is that we will do all we can to protect him. If we are found, we will keep him safe if we are able to. That is the best I can promise."

Hemetre looked at me for a long moment and finally she nodded.

"I suppose that will have to be enough then. I am sworn to protect the rightful queen and it is my duty to help you if I can."

TWENTY-FOUR

H emetre led me to the temple's back entrance.

"Wait here. I will go find your friends."

Behind the temple was a pretty garden area. In all the years I had come here for dawn worship, I never knew about this garden. There were neatly arranged beds of flowers. Daisies, poppies and jasmine in full bloom. Chrysanthemums not yet in bud. A small pond with blue lotus and a ring of papyrus. Other plants that I suspected might be medicinal in nature. During my purification ceremony, Mutnodjmet had drugged me with wine that I suspected had been laced with poppy or blue lotus. Now I knew where her supplies came from.

The garden was orderly, its paths swept clear of leaves and the flowers all neatly trimmed. I stood on the edge of the pond and gazed down into the water. This place was like a balm on my soul. It reminded me of my pleasure garden, not the one here in Memphis but my beloved one in Akhetaten. With the brown ducks and the wooden bench that never had a single splinter. I used to sit on that bench and feel like I was the only imperfect thing in the garden.

My thoughts were interrupted by the swish of sandals behind me on the path. My heart began to pound, but it was only Tuta.

"Come," he said. "The others are just around the side."

Hemetre led us to her home which was only a short walk from the temple. I was surprised to discover how small her cottage was, just a single chamber. It was tidy enough although a pair of small sandals kicked under a chair and some wooden playthings discarded on the floor were testament to a child's inhabitance. In the corner of the chamber two rolled bed mats sat neatly against the wall. I had expected three since she had mentioned a son.

"Do you have no husband?" I asked.

Hemetre's face was tight.

"No."

She offered no explanation and I didn't know what else to say. Had he died? Run off and left her?

"Is your son at school?" Istnofret asked.

"Yes, he will be home later." At the mention of her son, Hemetre's face lost some of its tightness. "His name is Ptahhotep and he is seven."

"I remember when my brother was seven," I said, eager to make amends for upsetting her. "He was very annoying at that age."

"I suppose if Ptahhotep had a sister, she would say the same," Hemetre said.

I was suddenly at a loss for what else to say. We had talked before, of course, but it was usually about Isis. Mutnodjmet had often asked questions about my life — how I spent my days, what my ladies or my chambers were like — and Hemetre would listen, but she never offered any comment or asked questions of her own. In fact, the time Hemetre visited me at the palace to discuss the Eye was one of the few times I had actually had a conversation with her. It was strange to see her in such a domestic setting.

Hemetre seemed as uncomfortable as I as she began retrieving various items from shelves to prepare a meal. Behenu quickly offered her help. Not knowing what else to do with myself, I wandered back to the doorway where Istnofret stood looking out.

"Do you ever wonder if your life might have been like this had things been different?" she asked. "A little house, a garden. Peace."

"You can still have those things. You and Renni. We are almost at the end of this."

She sighed heavily and for a while, I thought she wasn't going to respond.

"I am not so sure of that," she said, at last. "The closer we get to the end, the further away it feels."

"You can go back to Crete." I didn't want to be the one who took her dreams away. "The little house by the sea."

Istnofret sighed again and this time she didn't answer. I stood beside her for a while longer, feeling increasingly awkward. Hemetre and Behenu chatted amicably as they prepared our meal. Renni and Tuta huddled together speaking in low voices. I would be intruding if I tried to join either pair so I went outside.

How long had we been locked up in the palace? I guessed *shemu* had passed, and perhaps most of *akhet* as well. The morning air was too cool for *shemu* and too warm for *peret* so perhaps the end of the inundation approached. That meant cooler days were on the way. I was a little sorry about that, for I had missed the hot, dry days and the breeze sweeping in from the deserts.

Behenu came to call me back inside and I took a deep breath

to steady myself. I must remember my purpose. I did this to save Egypt, to atone for my own failures. To restore my father's dynasty. I couldn't let him down.

Back inside, the others already sat in a circle on a mat with the food in the middle. I set the Eye down on a shelf, thankful to finally be able to put it aside for a while, and joined them. Hemetre and Behenu had prepared slices of grainy bread, some soft cheese, a salad of cucumber, lettuce and the tiny, sweet onions I loved. It was a simple meal but after weeks of nothing but bread and beer, and so many months of eating foreign foods while we travelled, it was reassuringly familiar.

"Tuta and I will go look for Woser," Renni said. "If he is in the city, he will be keeping an eye on Nenwef's home as we were supposed to meet there."

"Ay might have men watching the house," Istnofret said.

"We have to assume he does," he replied. "Intef always said to plan for the worst."

"Please be careful," she said, with a frown.

"You know I will, Ist." Renni took her hand and squeezed it gently. "And you know you don't need to say it."

He and Tuta left soon after. We women cleaned up after our meal, although Hemetre gave me more than one odd look. I supposed that since she had only ever known me as queen, it must seem odd to see me carrying dishes. Once we had finished, Hemetre took a basket from a shelf.

"I should go to the market," she said. "If I am to be feeding you all for a couple of days."

"We can pay you," I said.

"I could go with you," Behenu said. "Carry your basket for you."

Hemetre hesitated. "Is there any possibility you might be recognised?"

"I was just a slave here," Behenu said. "Nobody remembers the face of a slave."

"But people have seen you," Istnofret said. "The day we entered the palace and the men who guarded our chamber. I don't think you should risk it."

Behenu looked to me, obviously hoping for my support, but I shook my head.

"I agree with Istnofret. It is too risky."

I felt like less of an intrusion on Hemetre's home once she left. Behenu took up a broom.

"We may as well do her cleaning for her while she is out," she said and began sweeping.

Istnofret found a cloth and wiped down the shelves. I stood there awkwardly, wanting to help and not seem useless, but unsure of what else might need doing.

"Samun, perhaps you could see if the garden needs weeding or if there are any vegetables ready to be picked," Istnofret said, obviously guessing my dilemma.

This, at least, was a task I was familiar with. I had dug and planted a garden when we lived in Babylon, in those days when we waited for a reply from Hemetre. Of course, I had almost forgotten. I had sent her copies of the two Egyptian scrolls we had found, in the hope that she might know someone who could translate them for us. We waited in Babylon for some months afterwards, but then I found Antinous's scroll, in which he talked of taking the Eye to Crete. We had left Babylon before any reply from Hemetre could reach us.

By the time Hemetre returned from the market with an overflowing basket, I had almost finished weeding her little vegetable garden. It was badly in need of attention and I supposed it must be difficult for Hemetre to find the time to do everything herself. I still felt like I had little understanding of how the common people lived, but surely a woman with a son but no husband struggled to do everything herself. When I had been a princess, and then a queen, I never thought about things like sweeping or dusting or weeding. There were servants who did all those things and I had regularly found myself inconvenienced by their presence as they bustled around my chambers.

"I sent you a letter." I suddenly felt awkward about asking. "From Babylon, months ago."

"Oh?" Hemetre peered out of the window and hardly seemed to be listening. "I never received it."

"It contained two scrolls written in ancient Egyptian. I hoped you would be able to find someone who could translate them."

"I would have tried if it had reached me."

I supposed they must have fallen victim to shipwreck, as so many ships did. Something tugged at my memory. Falling down through deep water. I had drowned. Or had that been a dream?

Istnofret went to stand beside Hemetre at the window. "Is something wrong?"

"I thought someone might have followed me," Hemetre said. "Perhaps you should stay away from the windows. Just in case."

I cast my gaze around the chamber. My heart suddenly beat far too fast. There wasn't anywhere to hide here. Not even a back door from which to flee. Hemetre's home had only one entrance and a single window.

"We should keep calm," Istnofret said, clearly sensing my panic. "If they have found us, we must comply with whatever they want. Renni and Tuta will come for us."

Behenu looked as unconcerned as Istnofret. How could they both be so calm? Fatigue rushed over me and I yawned. We had been up all night after all. From its place on the shelf, the Eye thrummed. *Use me. Escape capture.* My servants could stay up

and keep guard. I needed my sleep. It was, after all, more important that I was rested than they.

"Lay out a bed mat for me."

I directed my words to the chamber at large, not particularly
caring which servant did it.

Istnofret and Behenu froze. Hemetre just looked bewildered.

"Samun-" Istnofret started.

I glowered at her.

"My title, if you please. Servants should not be so familiar
with their mistress."

"You are tired," she said. "You know the Eye influences you
more easily when you are tired."

I yawned again, trying to ignore her words. Why did she
prattle instead of carrying out my order?

"I will do it." Behenu started to get up, but Istnofret quickly
stopped her with a hand on her arm.

"No," she said. "We must not pander to her or she will have
no reason to fight it off."

"I don't understand," Hemetre said. "What is happening?"

"She gets like this when she is fatigued," Istnofret said. "The
Eye corrupts her. It reminds her of what it was like when she
was queen and she starts thinking we are her servants again. She
can fight it if she tries hard enough."

She turned back to me.

"Samun, remember you promised you would listen if I said
you must. I hold you to that promise."

I yawned again, barely able to keep my eyes open.

"Will you hurry up? Or must I do everything myself."

"I am afraid that if you want a bed mat, you will have to do it
yourself," Istnofret said.

I glared at her.

"You are an impertinent servant."

"And you are not a queen, no matter how much the Eye might be making you think you are right now."

Anger welled up within me. A servant should never speak like that.

My feet found their own way over to the shelf where the Eye lay. I took it up and it nestled into my palm.

"Samun." Istnofret's voice was wary now. "What are you doing?"

She was afraid. I could feel it washing off her. So she should be. I would punish her for her impertinence. She would never dare speak to me in such a way again.

"Great goddess," Hemetre said.

A rush of pleasure ran through me. Finally, a servant who knew her place. But then I realised she prayed, and not to me.

"Mother Isis, watch over your daughter. Protect her and remind her of who she is. Let her not act hastily, lest she regret what cannot be undone."

Her words grated. How irritating to hear her praying to someone else. She should be on her knees before me. But as Hemetre continued to pray, the words began to worm into my brain.

You are not a goddess, something deep inside me whispered, a part of me that had not yet allowed itself to fall under the sway of the Eye. *You are not even a queen.*

I took a deep breath, trying to ignore both the voice inside of me and Hemetre's increasingly annoying prayer.

"Samun," Istnofret said. "Samun, are you listening?"

I huffed my annoyance, but as much as I tried to ignore it, the voice inside of me continued.

Friend. She is a friend. Not a servant.

"Listen to me with your heart, Samun," Istnofret said. "Remember what we have given to get this far. Remember that

Intef gave up his mortal life so that you could bring the Eye to Memphis."

Hemetre continued praying, her voice even and steady.

The mention of Intef sent a ripple through my mind. This had happened before. The Eye twisting my thoughts, making me think I was a queen again, or even a goddess.

"Remember this happens when you get too tired," Behenu said. "We have been up all night."

Her words made me yawn again and suddenly I was so tired it was all I could do to keep standing. A random memory from one of my dreams flashed into my mind. Intef standing in front of a set of tall black gates as they swung shut. The Gates of Anubis. The haze began to fade from my mind and I shook my head to try to clear it.

"Are you yourself again?" Istnofret asked.

"Yes, but I need to rest."

"Let me lay out a bed mat for you," Behenu said, but I put out my hand to stop her.

"I should do it myself. I am not strong right now. If you do something for me, it might be enough to trigger the Eye again."

I went to the corner where the bed rolls were and fumbled to unroll one. I was asleep almost as soon as I lay down.

TWENTY-FIVE

I woke to Istnofret shaking my shoulder.

"Samun," she whispered. "Wake up but be quiet."

My head was fuzzy and for a few moments I couldn't even figure out where I was. Eventually I remembered. We were at Hemetre's home. Renni and Tuta had gone to look for Woser. Hemetre's son was at school. Ay probably had guards searching the city for us.

"Someone is hiding behind the house across the street."

I sat up too quickly and my head spun. "Are you sure?"

"Hemetre thought earlier that someone followed her home."

"I never quite saw him so I was not certain." Hemetre's pace was pale, but she looked composed enough. "Every time I looked back, I caught only a glimpse of someone, but he was always gone before I could see him. I have been watching from the window, though, and there is definitely someone out there."

"Is it a guard? One of Ay's men?"

"We don't know," Istnofret said.

"How long was I asleep?"

"Less than an hour I suppose. I was sorry to wake you, but we weren't sure until now."

"I saw him move between the houses," Behenu said. "I stood to the side of the window so he couldn't see me."

"Only one man?" I asked. "Surely Renni and Tuta will be back soon. They will easily deal with one man."

"We have only seen one, but we don't know whether he has passed on a message already," Istnofret said. "There could have been two of them earlier."

"They would have come for us by now if that was the case," I said. "Ay would not wait."

Hemetre stood at the window in full view of anyone who looked.

"What are you doing?" I asked. "He will see you."

"It is my house," she said. "Anyone who knows that would expect to see me here. Besides, if he is trying to be surreptitious, he will not approach as long as I am watching."

Someone rapped quietly on the door. We all jumped.

"Dear Isis, protect us," Hemetre said. "Spread your wings over us. Spread your wings over Ptahhotep and keep him safe if I am not able to."

"We will stand out of sight behind the door," Istnofret whispered. "Whoever it is already knows Hemetre is at home, but maybe they don't yet know about us."

Hemetre waited while Istnofret, Behenu and I huddled behind the door, then she unlocked it and cracked it open.

"Can I help you?"

"I am looking for my lady," came a low, male voice. It was vaguely familiar.

"I am sure I do not know who you mean," Hemetre said. "It is just my son and I who live here."

"I know you are not alone in there."

"I—"

"Please, it is urgent," he said. "I cannot be seen here."

I had no idea who the speaker was, but he didn't sound like he was one of Ay's men.

"Let him in," I said to Hemetre.

She stiffened although she didn't acknowledge my words. The man had heard me though.

"My lady," he said, his voice still low. "It is Woser."

"Woser!"

I stepped out and as soon as Woser saw me, he came in and shut the door behind him. His face was lined and weary.

"You must keep out of sight," he said. "There are men searching for you."

"Did Renni and Tuta find you?" I asked.

"I have not seen them."

"Then how did you know we were here?"

"Just a hunch. I could not think of anyone else in Memphis who you might view as an ally. I have been checking here for you every day or two for the last three months."

"If Woser has thought of Hemetre, he is probably not the only one," Istnofret said with a frown. "We should be ready to leave as soon as Renni and Tuta come back."

"Where are they?" Woser asked. "Is Nenwef with them?"

"They went to find you. Nenwef was captured before we were imprisoned. We have not seen him since. We don't even know whether he is still…"

My voice trailed away. I couldn't bear to think that Nenwef might have lost his life because he tried to help me.

"Where is Merti?" Woser asked. "I have been keeping an eye on their home but have seen no sign of her either."

"She went to Babylon. We have friends there. If Nenwef… If Nenwef is able to, he will find her there."

"I see." Woser frowned. "I notice you have not mentioned Intef."

I exhaled sharply. My heart hurt at the mere mention of him.

"No," I said at last. "I have not."

He gave me a steady look.

"I see," he said again.

"Another day," I said. "I cannot today."

He gave me a brief nod, then looked towards Hemetre.

"Your son should be home from school by now, should he not?"

She glanced out the window, checking the location of the sun. "He must have been delayed. I am sure he will be back soon."

"Maybe I should go meet him," Woser said. "I know the route he takes home."

"You have been following my son?" Hemetre's voice was sharp and she looked at Woser uneasily now.

"Standard surveillance tactics," Woser said with an apologetic smile. "Learn all you can about the subject. And besides, you think I will be the only one to wonder whether my lady came to you? I did not dare try to get a message to her inside the palace. Was not sure who I could trust anymore. But I thought she might be able to get a message out and I could not think of many people she might try to contact. I remember the day you visited her at the palace."

"If you have been watching me so carefully, how did you miss them all arriving here this morning?" Hemetre asked. "You obviously did not see Renni and Tuta leave either."

"I was following Mutnodjmet this morning. Heard she had been summoned to the palace and wondered if it might be something to do with this lot escaping."

"You knew we escaped?" I asked.

"The whole city is talking about it. The palace is trying to downplay it, but everyone knows exactly who it was. A lot of people saw you enter the palace that day, but nobody saw you come back out. There was no sign that you had reunited with Ay, so the obvious answer was that you were a prisoner. So when word gets out that prisoners have escaped, it is not a hard thing to guess who it might be, especially not with men like Renni and Tuta accompanying you. The only thing that surprised me is how long it took you."

"We were separated," I said, almost absently.

Was there a way I might yet use the situation to my advantage? As if it knew the direction of my thoughts, the Eye pulsed.

Behenu had positioned herself beside the window where she could look out without being seen.

"Here come Renni and Tuta," she said.

The door opened.

"Woser." Renni slapped him on the back. "We have been looking for you."

"So I hear. What news?"

"The city is in uproar," Renni said. "The fact that prisoners escaped from the palace overnight is common knowledge. We heard a lot of speculation and the general consensus is that Samun has returned to take back the throne."

"There are also rumours about who escaped with her," Tuta added. "Theories range from Intef to some of the Medjay to a whole squad of magicians."

"Magicians?" I couldn't keep the scepticism from my tone.

"You escaped from somewhere that should have been pretty much impossible to get out of. The guards were all killed and not a person saw you leave. Must be magicians according to most folk."

"The guards are not dead," Istnofret said, indignantly. "We killed nobody."

"We are not sure whether it is true," Renni said. "It could be a false tale spread by the palace to make us seem dangerous. The more fearful folk are, the more likely they are to report it if they see us. Or they might have been executed for allowing us to escape."

"My son really should be home by now," Hemetre said with a worried glance out of the window. "It is not like him to be so late. I think I should go look for him."

"I will go," Woser said. "Better that you stay here in case he comes home. He will be concerned about finding his home full of strangers and you not here."

"I will come with you," Renni said. "Tuta, you stay here."

Hemetre watched them leave from the window. She clasped her hands tightly and even from the other side of the chamber, I could feel her rising anxiety.

"I am sure Ptahhotep is fine," Istnofret said. "You know what boys that age are like. They have no focus. He is probably off playing with friends and has not even considered that you might be worried."

"He never does things like that," Hemetre said. "It is just the two of us, so he tries to be the man of the house. He comes straight home from school to make sure that I am well. He has never come home late before."

"Renni will find him," Istnofret said. "In the meantime, I think one of us should keep an eye on what is happening outside. Just in case. It will only take one person to recall seeing us this morning for folk to start putting the pieces together."

We took turns to keep watch from beside the window where we were out of sight to anyone spying on the house. I was the last to take my turn as the sun sank behind the surrounding buildings. Hemetre's face was increasingly tight and she had given up any pretence of occupying herself with chores. She paced up and down the length of the small cottage.

"It is taking too long," she said, abruptly stopping her pacing. "They should have found him by now. I will go out and find him myself."

"Stay here," Istnofret said. "He will want to see your face when he returns. Renni and Woser will find him. You don't need to worry."

"What is taking them so long then? They have been gone for hours."

Istnofret looked to me and Behenu, clearly hoping one of us would answer Hemetre's question. I shrugged at her. I had no answer to give. In truth, by now I was convinced that something must have happened to Ptahhotep. If he had simply stopped somewhere to play with friends, Renni and Woser would have found him long before now. I couldn't say that in front of Hemetre though.

"You know what Renni would say," Behenu said. "A good soldier waits patiently and does not wonder about what he cannot see."

"Worry, not wonder," Istnofret said. "He would say we should not worry about what we cannot see."

"I know you are trying to make me feel better," Hemetre said. "But you don't understand how out of character this is for Ptahhotep."

I spotted a figure that seemed to be keeping to the shadows beside the houses across the street. A second figure followed not far behind. I waited as they came closer, but at last I was sure.

"Here they come," I said.

"Oh thank the goddess." Hemetre already had the door open as they reached the house. "Where is he?"

Renni and Woser came in, quickly closing the door behind

them. Renni nodded towards the window and Woser came to take my place there. He gave me a small smile. He looked tired. Or worried. I wasn't sure which. But Ptahhotep wasn't with them so it was clear something was wrong.

"He was picked up by a couple of Pharaoh's guards." Renni spoke very gently as if he thought Hemetre might fall apart at the news. "Shortly after he arrived at school this morning."

Hemetre swayed a little and he quickly grabbed her arm.

"Sit down," he said. "Disturbing news can do all sorts of funny things to your body. Better that you are sitting."

Hemetre crumpled onto the floor and buried her face in her hands. I thought she was crying, but she simply sat like that for a few moments.

"Tell me everything you know," she said at last.

"There is really nothing else. Two armed guards arrived at his school and said he had been summoned by Pharaoh. The teacher let them take him, of course."

"Did they give their names?" I asked. "Was it anyone you know?"

"They said only that they were from the palace. The teacher didn't recognise their faces. We spoke to all the boys in his class and nobody else knew them either. That is why we were gone so long."

"But why take my son? He is only seven years old. What do they think he can do for them?"

"More likely it is what they think you might do with enough motivation," Renni said. "I doubt they intend to hurt him. He is a hostage. I am sure there will be a message soon."

"I don't think we will have to wait much longer," Woser said from the window. "Someone is coming."

"Back against the wall," Renni said to the rest of us as he

offered Hemetre his hand and helped her to her feet. "And stay quiet."

Istnofret, Behenu and I once again stood against the wall behind the door. Renni waited on the other side of the doorway, his dagger ready in his hand.

Someone knocked. Renni nodded at Hemetre to answer. She cracked the door open just the tiniest bit to peer out.

"Are you the priestess Hemetre?" a gruff voice asked.

"Yes. What do you want?"

I was surprised at how unflustered Hemetre sounded, considering only moments ago she had all but collapsed on the floor.

"I have a message for you. Can I come in?"

"I would really prefer you did not."

"It is a rather personal matter. I am sure you would want to hear it in private."

"I am sure you can understand my point of view," Hemetre said coolly. "You are a stranger to me and yet you ask me to let you into my home? I am here alone and have no wish to start rumours of dalliances with strange men."

"Of course," he said. "I bring a message from the palace. Your son is being held there. If you wish to see him released, you will go to the palace. Ask for Ahmose and tell him everything you know about the escaped prisoners."

"Escaped prisoners? I am sure I know nothing."

"Then I am afraid your son is in for a rather long stay at the palace. You don't need to fear for him. He is being treated as an honoured guest. For now."

Sandals crunched on the packed dirt path as he walked away. Hemetre closed the door firmly and leaned against it, as if hoping it would keep her on her feet.

"I cannot do this," she said in a whisper. "I am sorry, but I cannot trade my son's freedom for yours, regardless of my vow."

"We will get him out of there," Renni said. "Do not be afraid for him. We just need a couple of days to figure out a plan and put it in motion. I will personally retrieve your son for you before we leave."

"What exactly do you intend to do though? I know little of your plans. How can I weigh up whether my son's freedom is more important than your task?"

They all looked to me for an answer. Thoughts of my daughter swirled through my mind. I had given her up for the sake of my task and it had broken my heart. How could I ask another mother to give up her child in service of my quest? Hemetre spoke again before I could find a response.

"I am sure you mean well," she said. "And as a Daughter of Isis, I am sworn to work towards your aims. But my son is all I have. Give me reason to believe that you can get him back."

"I will give you three reasons," I said at last. I pointed to each of the men in turn as I said their names. "Renni. Tuta. Woser. They are from Intef's squad. The best of the best. As long as your son is alive, they will get him back for you."

"Give us twenty-four hours," Renni said. "That is all we need. Time to make a plan and then I will go get your son. I was second in command of the queen's personal squad. I trained with the Medjay. I *will* get your son back."

Tuta and Woser murmured their support. Hemetre looked at them for a long moment before she finally nodded.

"Twenty-four hours," she said. "As a Daughter of Isis, I owe the rightful queen that much. But then you will go get Ptah-hotep, regardless of whether you have your plan in place or not."

TWENTY-SIX

None of us spoke much that evening. Behenu and Istnofret helped Hemetre prepare dinner while I sat with my back against the wall and tried to keep out of everyone's way. I didn't want to attract any attention in case Hemetre looked at me and remembered it was my fault that her son had been taken.

We ate quietly, then went to sleep. But when we woke in the morning, Hemetre was gone.

"How could she have gotten out of the cottage without you noticing?" Istnofret gave Renni, Tuta and Woser each a fierce glare.

"I was sleeping," Renni said. "Whoever was on guard should have seen her."

"Uh, I don't think we had anyone on guard," Tuta admitted.

"I never even thought of it," Woser said.

"I was exhausted and just went to sleep." Renni gave Istnofret an embarrassed shrug. "There are enough of us here that I guess I assumed someone else would take care of it."

"Intef would be ashamed," Istnofret said.

"I know. I feel bad enough without you rubbing it in."

"It is not Renni's fault," I said. "We all went to sleep without thinking about who would keep watch."

Istnofret included me in her scowl.

"Renni should be more responsible," she said. "Intef trained him better than that."

"Ist-" Renni said but stopped when she threw her hands up in the air. "Let's just try to figure out where Hemetre might have gone and what we are going to do about it."

"She must have gone to the palace," I said. "As the messenger last night said to."

Istnofret sighed and nodded. At least she wasn't glaring anymore. "She went for her son. We cannot blame her really. Any mother would do the same."

"I think we can trust her." Behenu's voice was soft and when we all turned to look at her, she took a step back as if she was afraid to disagree with us.

"Then where is she?" I asked. "If we could trust her, she would not have left without telling us where she was going. We made a mistake in coming here."

"Did not we say just yesterday that Intef would say not to worry about what we cannot see?" Behenu said. "If she wanted us to know what she was doing, she would have told us. We just need to wait."

"I wish I believed that, Behenu," Istnofret said. "Truly I do, but I don't think we can afford to wait. We need to assume she has gone to the palace."

"I agree," I said. "We should leave straight away in case they come looking for us. In fact, we should have left already instead of standing around arguing about it."

Another thing that Intef would not have allowed. He would have had us out the door long before the rest of us even noticed

Hemetre's absence. My heart ached, but I steeled myself. Intef had made his choice.

"Get your things together then and let's go," Renni said. "We will find a safe place and figure out our next move from there."

It took us only a minute or two to be ready to leave. I wrapped some linen around my hand to keep the Eye from touching my skin. We had hardly anything else, having left almost everything at Nenwef's home when we first went to confront Ay. My stomach grumbled, reminding me that we didn't even have any supplies of our own.

"Maybe we should take some food," Istnofret said, as if she had heard my thoughts, or perhaps my stomach.

"No," Behenu said. "Life is hard enough for most folk without us taking what she has worked for."

"Would you say that even knowing she has probably betrayed us?" I asked.

Behenu gave a small shrug. "We know nothing for certain just yet. I will think the best of her until it is proven otherwise."

I puzzled over Behenu's comments as we left Hemetre's house. Perhaps having been a slave, Behenu was acutely aware of what it was like to be judged without anyone really knowing her. But then wasn't I in the same position? How many people were like Merti and had an opinion about me or about my father without ever having so much as met us?

The sun was well on its way up into the sky, the remnants of sunrise fading to blue. A thought struck me, startling me enough that I stopped walking.

"What is it?" Renni scanned our surroundings, clearly thinking I had spied some threat.

"I think I know where Hemetre is," I said. "She has probably gone for the dawn worship."

"Oh," Istnofret said. "I feel terrible."

Behenu gave me a small smile, obviously pleased that I had found grounds to trust Hemetre.

"She has every reason to go straight to the palace," Woser said.

"We have to assume the worst until we know otherwise," Renni said. "We cannot afford to continue thinking she is a friend without being certain."

The more I thought about it, the surer I became. Hemetre wouldn't miss the dawn worship. Her devotion to Isis would require her presence and, if nothing else, she wouldn't want to explain her absence to Mutnodjmet. How could she tell the head priestess what had happened to Ptahhotep without giving the reason for him being taken? She would keep up the appearance of normalcy, even if she secretly wondered whether she should give us up in order to get her son back.

"I think we should go to the temple and wait for the dawn worship to finish," I said.

"If Ay has Ptahhotep, it is because he already knows that you have made contact with Hemetre," Tuta said. "They might be watching the temple."

"Perhaps he merely thinks I might contact her," I said.

"A preemptive strike?" Renni frowned. "I think you give the man too much credit."

"Either way, if we wait near the temple, we will know soon enough. And would it not be better to know for sure? If Hemetre is not there, the only other place she would have gone is the palace. She would not miss the dawn worship for anything less."

"How certain of her are you?" Renni asked. "Can we trust her?"

"Yes," I said. "We were foolish to think otherwise."

"Fine," he said. "We will wait to see if she is at the temple. I think Samun should wait somewhere else though. Even if

Hemetre has not given us up, the palace may well be watching her."

I agreed and we set off. Some distance before the temple, Renni turned down a narrow alley behind a bakery.

"You all wait here. I will go watch the temple."

"Not alone you won't," Istnofret said. "Take Tuta with you."

"I would rather he stayed here," Renni said. "What if someone finds you?"

"What if someone finds you?" she countered.

"I can look after myself."

"And the four of us together will be safe enough. It is broad daylight and even if you take Tuta, we still have Woser."

"I am not worried about people with nefarious intentions. I am worried the palace guards will find you."

"How many men would they need to take all four of us? Woser has been through the same training as you. If we are found, he will fight and we will scream and carry on. You will hear us from the temple."

Renni hesitated, shooting looks between Istnofret, Tuta and Woser.

"You need at least two people to watch the temple," Tuta said. "Hemetre might leave from the front to make it seem that nothing has changed, or she might slip out the back to avoid being seen. You cannot watch both at once."

"You should both go," Woser said. "I will stay with the women."

Renni gave a heavy sigh as if they were being completely unreasonable.

"Fine then," he said. "Stay out of sight as best you can, though. Stand against the wall and keep your heads down. Don't draw any attention to yourselves."

"Go," Istnofret said. "Woser can tell us these things just as well as you can. The dawn worship might be finished by now and you will miss her if you don't hurry."

Renni reached for her hand. She resisted for a moment and I expected her to bat him away, but then she relented. The two men left.

We did as Renni had said. We stood in a line with the wall against our backs and our faces averted so that anyone peering down the alley from the street wouldn't identify us on first sight. We were silent for a while, but soon enough my feet started to hurt. The stone wall was cool against my back, leaving me a little too chilled. It was Istnofret who eventually broke our silence.

"Brr," she said. "It is far colder here than it is out there."

Nobody answered and she lapsed into silence again.

"Ist," I ventured at last. "Is everything all right between you and Renni?"

She took a long time to answer and I began to feel awkward about having asked. After all, whatever was going on between the two of them was none of my business.

"He is tired of living like this," she said at last. "He says we should walk away. Go back to Crete. Make our own lives. He wants his own house and a job."

My cheeks heated at the realisation that I was the source of the tension between them.

"You can go if you want to," I said. "None of you are obliged to stay with me. I have told you before."

Istnofret shook her head firmly. "As I keep telling Renni, we will see this through to the end. It is just that he is starting to think the end will never come."

"My goal has not changed," I said, a little defensively. "I always said I wanted to find the Eye and bring it back to Egypt so I could make things right again. This will be over any day now and then you and Renni will be free."

"That is what I keep telling him," she said.

I felt the sting of her words. It hurt to know they were so keen to go off to make a new life of their own.

"I long to go home," Behenu said into the awkward silence that lay between Istnofret and I. "But I am not sure that I actually will when the time comes."

"Why not?" Istnofret asked.

Her voice was gentler than the casual tone she had used with me and I again felt the sting of her judgement.

"Because here I am free. I can be whoever I want to be. There... there are expectations on me."

"What kind of expectations?" I asked, but Behenu only shook her head and didn't answer.

She always clammed up when she got too close to telling us about her home. What was it she was trying so hard not to reveal?

TWENTY-SEVEN

F ootsteps at the entrance to the alley made us all jump and
my heart began to race.

"It is only Tuta," Woser said, needlessly for we could all
see him.

"We found Hemetre," Tuta said without preamble when he
reached us. "She slipped out the back door and I was able to
speak with her very briefly. She fears for her son, but I don't
think she has betrayed us. She is going home and Renni will tail
her to make sure she is safe. We will take the long way around
and meet them there."

Tuta led us on a circuitous path which seemed to involve
trekking halfway around the city before we turned back towards
Hemetre's home. If nothing else, the long walk gave me time to
think although I had more questions than answers. Why had I
been so quick to believe that Hemetre had betrayed us? What
was it that Behenu didn't want us to know about her life in
Syria? Why was Istnofret so determined to see this quest through
to its end, even though she obviously feared it might cost her

Renni? My mind whirled and the longer I thought, the more questions I came up with.

"Wait here," Tuta said eventually. "Hemetre's house is just two streets over. I will go and make sure all is well. As far as I can tell, we were not followed, but keep your eyes and ears open."

"What if Ay's men are there?" Istnofret asked. "If they didn't follow us, it might be because they were following Hemetre."

Tuta was already gone before she finished speaking. She looked to Woser, but he only shrugged. Of course, he knew no more about what was happening at Hemetre's home than we did.

Tuta was only gone for a few minutes before he reappeared and waved for us to follow. We hurried the rest of the way and I was thankful to finally have walls between us and anyone who might be spying. I set the Eye back on a shelf, relieved also to no longer have to hold it. It made no effort to talk to me. Perhaps it was dormant again.

Hemetre was preparing a meal and seemed to be making an unnecessary amount of noise.

"Can I help you with that?" Behenu asked her.

"Oh no, you all just relax," Hemetre said. "It is not like I opened up my home to you without question. My son was not abducted to try to persuade me to betray you. It is not like I helped you plot against Pharaoh." She shot me a fierce look. "And yet the moment I am out of sight you all believed I had betrayed you."

"I did not," Behenu said, very softly.

Hemetre just shook her head and returned to her banging and clattering.

"I am sorry," I said. "It was not that we actually thought you would betray us. We didn't know what to think when we woke up and you were gone."

"How many years did we worship together, Ankhesenamun?" she asked, without turning around. "All those years of dawn worship and yet the first thought that came to your mind when I was gone at dawn was that I had betrayed you? Even though I have told you time and again that I am a Daughter of Isis? You know I am sworn to protect the queen."

The dawn worship should have been my first thought. It was where Hemetre was every morning. Why had I thought that today would be any different? *Because you were in her house and her son was taken,* a little voice inside of me whispered. *It was perfectly reasonable to assume she would go straight to Pharaoh to give you up in exchange for her son.*

But no matter how hard I tried to convince myself, I knew I had been wrong.

Hemetre and I were both silent as we broke our fast. The others talked, perhaps a little too cheerily as if to make up for our lack of trust. It was only when we had all pushed our bowls aside that Hemetre finally spoke again.

"I suppose you have a plan then."

They all looked to me. I looked to Renni. It would have been Intef who came up with our plans once and I still expected that Renni would take his place. It really wasn't fair of me. Renni wasn't Intef and I doubted he had any desire to pretend to be. Renni just looked back at me. It seemed even he waited for me to come up with a plan.

"We need to figure out how we will remove Ay," I said. "If I am to use the Eye, we need to make sure it doesn't think it is being used for ill or it won't cooperate."

"It chooses whether or not to obey you?" Hemetre gave me a calculating look and I suddenly feared I had said too much.

"The Eye does not obey anyone," I said quickly. Could the Eye hear her? "That is not how it works. But it has a very strong desire to be used, especially, I think, when it is in the hands of someone who the gods have deemed worthy of wielding it."

"How do you know it wants to be used?" she asked.

"It tells me," I said. "It talks to me. Sometimes constantly. At other times it seems to go to sleep or perhaps it just isn't interested in what I am doing because it knows I have no intention of using it at that time."

"We know little about the Eye but this is such as I have not heard before," she said. "I always pictured it as an object. But you make it sound like it is alive."

"I suppose it is, in a way," I said. "It is supposed to be Horus's own eye after all, not that it looks like any such thing."

"May I see it?" she asked.

I hesitated and tried not to look at the shelf where the Eye lay. It felt wrong to show it off as if it was a prize.

"Never mind," she said quickly. "I feel like that may have been inappropriate. So how do you intend to use it?"

"I don't really know. My aim has always been to remove Ay from the throne. But when I confronted him…"

My voice trailed off as my cheeks heated. It still embarrassed me to remember that I had tried to use the amulet to kill Ay. But if Hemetre was going to aid us, she deserved to know the truth.

"I told him to die, but he did not, of course. I had forgotten you said that the Eye cannot be used for ill intent."

"Have you learned anything else about it?"

"Not really. It wants to be used, but I think it only wants to be used in a certain way. Or for a certain aim. It seems to only think about power. I think it is sleeping now, though. I don't know whether it will continue to speak to me if it doesn't get the power it wants soon."

"Hemetre, do you know anything else about the Eye that you haven't told us?" Istnofret asked.

Hemetre considered her question for a moment but eventually shook her head.

"I told Ankhesenamun everything I knew the day I visited her at the palace. It is little enough, but it took the Daughters years to learn even that much. I would love to know where Maia's information came from. It is clear she found a source she didn't share with the rest of us."

We stared at each other in silence for a long moment. It was Renni who finally spoke.

"We still need a plan," he said. "The day is getting away from us. If we are going after Ptahhotep, we need to figure out how to do it."

"I think the bigger issue is how you are going to deal with Ay," Hemetre said. "I am sure they are treating Ptahhotep well. He will be fine there for another day or two. Do what you need to do first but Ankhesenamun, if you want my help, you must promise me that as soon as you have done it, the first thing you will do is release my son."

"I promise."

"Then what is your plan?" she asked.

"I think I need to figure out how to use the Eye," I said, slowly. The pieces of the puzzle were starting to fall into place. "It can only be used once and not for ill. So I need a way to remove Ay from the throne without the artefact thinking I am trying to harm him."

"So you cannot kill him," Woser said. "You cannot drive him mad or make him sick."

"I wonder if you could make him fall asleep?" Istnofret suggested. "The gods know we could all do with more sleep. You could be doing a really good thing for him."

Would I have to specify how long I wanted him to sleep for? And how long should that be? A few days? Months? Forever?

"Could you make him voluntarily give up the throne?" Tuta asked. "Could the Eye make him say that he does not want to be pharaoh anymore?"

"Has he named an heir?" I asked.

"Nakhtmin," Hemetre said. "His grandson. His mother, Iuy, is a priestess of Min."

"Do you know her?" I asked.

"Barely. We have spoken once or twice at festivals. I know who she is and I have no doubt she knows who I am, but that is about it."

"What is Nakhtmin like?"

My thoughts were tripping all over each other. What if I could remove Ay and put his heir on the throne? I had never had a clear plan of what I would do with the throne. I wasn't the same woman as the one who used to be queen. I would no longer be satisfied with spending my days sitting around my chamber and watching my ladies do needlework. Outings to the market or the temple or my pleasure garden. But what if I didn't need to be queen again? What if I could put a good man on the throne and then walk away?

"I know little of him other than his name," Hemetre said. "He is rarely seen in public."

"Is he a good person, do you think?"

I wasn't sure I knew anymore how good should be defined. Was I good? Was Intef? We both had blood on our hands.

"I really don't know," Hemetre said. "I saw him in the street once. He was surrounded by guards. I glimpsed dark hair and a white *shendyt*, but that was as much as I saw."

That could describe almost any man in Egypt. I couldn't count on him being the kind of person I hoped for, but if he had already been named as heir, he was probably my best option for a stable transition of power.

"Do you really think you could use the Eye in that way?" Renni asked. "To force Ay to step down and give Nakhtmin the throne?"

"It doesn't seem to break the rules," I said. "It is not an ill use."

"You could argue it would be ill for Ay," Woser said.

I shot him a look and he raised his hands in submission.

"I didn't say that was my opinion, but we don't know how your amulet thinks, if that is what it does. I am merely saying that perhaps it will view the situation from Ay's perspective as well."

"I don't know what I could do that would be positive for both Ay and for Egypt," I said. "I don't think those two things are reconcilable."

I waited but nobody offered any other suggestion.

"Is this the only plan we have? I use the Eye to make him give up the throne and pass it to Nakhtmin?"

"And if that doesn't work, you make him go to sleep," Istnofret said.

"So how do we get into the palace?" I asked. "We cannot merely stroll in the front door again. They will arrest us on sight. I need to make sure I can confront Ay, not just be locked away again."

"Can we get a message to him?" Tuta suggested. "Do we know someone who has access to him?"

"We know plenty of people with access," Renni said. "It is more a matter of who can we trust to pass the message to Ay rather than straight to their captain. If we try to send a message through the wrong person, guards will be waiting for us at the front door."

"Could we use Mutnodjmet?" Hemetre spoke slowly as if still considering the possibility herself.

They all looked to me.

"You are the only one other than Hemetre who knows her," Renni said.

"I don't know her well," I said. "In fact, I barely know her."

"But you worshipped with her for so long," Istnofret said. "Surely you know her. I remember you talking about your conversations."

"We never talked about her though. She asked lots of questions about me but gave little information about herself."

I had wondered at the time whether I could really trust Mutnodjmet. It always seemed a little odd that she wanted to know every detail about my life. I had wondered what she did with that information.

"After my purification ceremony, she said she would send a message to Ay to tell him that I should not try to produce an heir yet. That I should wait. That the one was not yet ready."

"The one?" Istnofret asked.

"During the ceremony, Isis said that the one was not ready. I thought it might be about my attempts to produce an heir."

"Who is the one?" she asked.

"I was never sure. At the time I thought it might be whoever I was supposed to marry. The man who would produce the heir with me."

"Maybe she meant Intef," Istnofret said. "After all, he was in love with you for years. Maybe she meant you needed to wait until he was ready. Perhaps he was the man she intended to father the heir."

"Maybe the one was Samun," Behenu said.

"Me?" I asked.

"That makes even more sense," Istnofret said. "Perhaps you

could not produce the heir until something specific had occurred. Until you were ready."

"Yet even now, I still have not managed to do it," I said, rather bitterly.

And without Intef, I couldn't imagine I ever would. Once I had thought I would do my duty, no matter who the man was. Now I couldn't imagine doing such a thing with anyone else.

TWENTY-EIGHT

We decided to wait until morning since the day was more than half passed by the time we had finalised our plan to try to send a message through Mutnodjmet. We spent a long time talking about what Hemetre should say to make it sound like she was merely a messenger with no real knowledge of our intentions.

I slept restlessly that night and was awake long before Hemetre rose. The plan was for her to speak with Mutnodjmet after the dawn ceremony. I itched at the delay although I knew Mutnodjmet wouldn't be interested in anything else until after her worship. I might not be sure we could trust her, but there was no doubt in my mind as to her devoutness to Isis.

We had decided to wait at Hemetre's home for as long as possible in case Ay had men watching the temple. The less time I spent where anyone might recognise me, the better. I paced around the chamber, unable to sit still. Today was the day. The end of my long quest. I tried not to think of all the ways our plan might go wrong. By the end of the day, I would have succeeded or I would likely be imprisoned again. Perhaps Ay would execute me this time to ensure I caused him no further problems. This might well be my last chance to complete my task.

Behenu prepared breakfast for us, but I couldn't eat. The sun crept up above the horizon before Renni decided it was time to leave. We walked at a sedate pace so as not to draw attention to ourselves. When we reached the temple, Tuta stayed out the front to keep an eye on things there. Woser waited around the side in case Tuta needed to get an urgent message to us but couldn't leave his post. The rest of us went to the garden at the back. There wasn't anywhere to hide so we sat beneath a tamarisk tree. I felt horribly conspicuous but there was nobody else around and it seemed unlikely that anyone would have reason to be wandering in the temple garden, especially at such an early hour. It was mid-morning before Hemetre came out.

"She will consider sending a message," she said. "But she wants to speak with Ankhesenamun first."

"What did you tell her?" Renni asked.

"Only what we agreed. That Ankhesenamun wishes to speak with Pharaoh. That she regrets the circumstances in which she last left and wishes to make amends."

"Do you think she believed you?" I asked.

"I have no way of knowing. Mutnodjmet keeps her thoughts to herself. All I can say is that she is eager to speak with you."

"I am coming too," Renni said.

Hemetre shook her head.

"I am sure you know the rules as well as I do."

No men permitted inside. It brought an ache to my heart to remember my first visit to the temple when Intef had wanted to come in with me. Mutnodjmet didn't allow him then and I knew she wouldn't allow Renni now.

"Stay here," I said to him. "I am safe enough in the temple."

Isis will protect me, I had said to Intef that first time. I was no longer sure whether that was true. She hadn't protected me from the loss of both of my babes or of Intef. Why would I think she would protect me now?

"I will go with you," Istnofret said. "It would not be inappropriate for you to have an attendant and if things go badly, perhaps I might be able to help."

I looked to Hemetre. "Do you think Mutnodjmet would allow that?"

"She did not explicitly say it, but I think she expects you to come alone."

"Then I will go alone," I said.

Besides, it wasn't like Mutnodjmet had guards in the temple. There would be other priestesses, but no men. I was probably safer within the temple walls than I was out here.

"Do you have any advice for me?" I asked Hemetre as we went inside. After all, she had known Mutnodjmet for much longer than I had.

Hemetre paused in the doorway and gave a heavy sigh.

"In truth, I don't know what you should expect. Mutnodjmet is not a Daughter of Isis and I don't know whether she even knows about us or our pledge to support the queen. She plays a very long game and I have never been able to figure her out. There is something she wants, something she has been working towards for many years. Agreeing to send this message for you could well be another step in that."

I could guess Mutnodjmet's goal. My dream years ago had shown me that either Sadeh or Mutnodjmet would sit on my throne. Sadeh went to the West before she ever had the chance. Mutnodjmet's time had not yet come. Perhaps today's events would push her closer towards it.

Hemetre led me along a hallway before stopping at a closed door.

"She said she would be in here. May the goddess spread her wings of protection over you."

I entered the chamber to find Mutnodjmet standing with her back to me. She faced a statue of Isis whose wing-shadowed arms were wrapped around a child. Isis's face was serene and knowing.

"Horus," Mutnodjmet said as I hesitated in the doorway. "Her son. Ever his mother. Ever his protector."

"As all mothers are."

She turned to face me at last and looked me up and down. My appearance must surely be vastly different from when she last saw me, but she made no comment and her face didn't even register any surprise.

"So, Daughter," she said. "You have come home."

Did she mean home to Egypt? Or home to Isis?

"I came as soon as I could."

"Yes, your quest. The Eye of Horus."

Had Hemetre told her more than we had agreed or had Mutnodjmet gleaned that information from elsewhere? When I didn't respond, she continued as if she hadn't expected a reply anyway.

"I assume you were successful. You would not have returned otherwise. Not now. Not today."

"What is to happen today?"

"Pharaoh will announce his new heir."

"I heard his grandson was his heir. Nakhtmin."

"Nakhtmin departed for the West a few days ago."

I was surely unsuccessful at keeping the surprise from my face.

"Does Hemetre know?"

All I could think was that Hemetre should have told us. This was information we could have used when we made our plan.

"It has been kept very quiet. None other than a few of Pharaoh's most senior advisors know."

"And that includes you."

"It does." She arched her eyebrows at me. "I told you once that Pharaoh seeks advice from me."

"You did, but I did not realise you were quite so intimate with him."

She merely looked steadily at me.

"What do you want?" I asked.

"I believe it is you who wants something from me."

"But you want something in exchange for helping us."

"I want what I always have, Daughter," she said. "The throne."

I was taken aback at her baldness. I had suspected that was her aim but had never expected to hear her say it.

"The throne passes through my father's bloodline," I said. "You are not entitled to it."

"It was me he was supposed to marry, you realise." Her tone was conversational as if we returned to a conversation already had many times. "Before he met your mother."

I could make no reply, could only stare at her.

"It was all arranged. His parents and mine had agreed. I would marry him and through me he would be pharaoh. Then he saw Nefertiti for the first time, and once he had seen her, he would have no one else."

I looked carefully at her, noticing for the first time how the curve of her chin and the arch of her brows echoed my dim memories of my mother's face.

"You are her sister?" I asked. "My mother's sister?"

"So she never mentioned me. She would not, of course. Not after she had stolen both my husband and my throne."

My mother wouldn't have done such a thing. Would she? I had been young when she died and we were never close. My beautiful mother. The perfect queen. Impeccable. Emotionless. Had she ever loved my father or did she marry him for his throne?

"I watched you girls grow up," she said, and the way her mouth twisted made her look almost wistful for a moment. "You never saw me, of course. My sister made a lot of mistakes, but the one thing she got right was you girls. She instilled in you an unshakeable confidence. She made sure you never doubted for a moment that you were meant to be princesses. That you were better than everyone else. It was her way of protecting you. In case I ever tried to assert my prior right to her throne."

If Mutnodjmet was the oldest sister, she undoubtedly had the strongest claim to the throne at the time my mother married. And yet somehow my mother had been the one to become queen and the throne became merely something that might have been hers but never was.

"I am sorry we did not know about you," I said, a little stiffly. "We would have liked to have known our mother's sister."

I had longed for guidance and wisdom in those dark days after my father died. If I had known my mother had a sister, I would have summoned her to the palace to be with me. How might events have transpired had I a strong woman at my side to counsel me?

"Why did you not come after she went to the West? You might have convinced my father to marry you then. You might have been queen after all."

She gave a heavy sigh and shook her head a little. "Your

father would not even receive my messengers. I never spoke with him again after he chose your mother over me."

And when she went to the West, he had married my oldest sister in order to retain his claim on the throne. I had never questioned that decision. The right to the throne ran through our blood, but Mutnodjmet had probably been equally eligible to be queen as Merytaten at that time.

"So what are you going to do?" I asked. "Even if Ay was to take you as a second wife, I doubt his queen can be persuaded to give up her position and he likely won't be persuaded to remove her."

"You are not thinking clearly, Daughter," she said. "I have no wish to take the throne beside Ay. I don't want a man who is already pharaoh and set in his ways. It is his new heir who interests me."

Finally, I started to understand her game.

"And you think you know who that will be."

"There are rumours, of course. Some suggest it might be Wennefer or Maya. They have been his chief advisors since the day he became Pharaoh."

"Sons of donkeys," I muttered.

"There are whispers that it might be the captain of his personal squad. He is a young man and well favoured by Pharaoh."

"And who do you think it will be?"

"If I had to guess?" She shrugged. "Horemheb."

"May his sandals be forever lined with donkey dung."

She gave me a steady look.

"He may well be your next pharaoh. And if he is, I intend to be his queen."

"Is he not already married? Armenia?"

"Amenia, I believe, and she went to the West a couple of years ago. Not long after you left Memphis, as a matter of fact."

"And you think I can make sure he marries you?"

"If you want my help, that is my price."

"It is a steep price for merely passing on a message."

"It is your decision, of course, Daughter." She turned her back on me and returned to her contemplation of Isis. "I will give you one hour to decide. If we are not in alliance by then, you can expect no help from me. Not today and not ever."

TWENTY-NINE

"She wants what?" Istnofret asked.

I had returned to the garden at the back of the temple and relayed my conversation with Mutnodjmet.

"She is your mother's sister." Behenu's voice was a little wistful. "It must be wonderful to know you have a living relative here in Egypt when all these years you thought there were none left."

"It explains why she has always called me Daughter. I thought it was because she was the high priestess and that she probably called all women the same thing."

"She has never called me that," Hemetre said. "And I have never heard her use the term with anyone else."

"So what do we do now?" Tuta asked.

"She wants the throne," Istnofret said. "Are you willing to give it to her?"

"I don't want it."

But I had at one time. There was a time when my aim was to find the Eye and use it to take back my rightful place on the throne. Back then my whole identity was so interwoven with being queen and princess and Great Royal Wife that I didn't know who I was if I wasn't those things. After the loss of both of my babes and of Intef, I wasn't sure who I was anymore. The only thing I knew was that I wasn't the person I used to be.

Once again, my purification ceremony came to mind. *The one is not yet ready.* Perhaps Behenu had been right when she suggested I was the one. But what was it that Isis thought I wasn't ready for at that time? And was I ready now? Did Isis already know of the journey that was ahead of me, even back then? Perhaps she never intended for me to keep the throne. Maybe she intended for me to be, like herself, a guardian of my country, but not the one who ruled?

"The Eye wants you to have the throne," Istnofret said. "Will it allow you to use it if it realises you don't intend to be queen again?"

We had left the Eye at Hemetre's home, carefully hidden away under a chest in case anyone searched the place while we were gone. I could only hope it couldn't hear us from this distance.

"Maybe I could pretend the throne *is* what I want. Not let myself think about anything else until I have done what I need to. Then Mutnodjmet can have the throne and I can… I don't know. Do something else."

I had never really thought about what I would do afterwards. Intef had talked about a house and a garden, but I had never been able to see that for myself. Without Intef, my future seemed empty. Interminable. Unbearable. What would I do with myself if I was not a queen and not a wife or mother or friend? What would I do if I was alone?

"Do you really think you can fool it?" Renni asked. "An arte-fact of the gods?"

"I don't think I have a choice. However it happens, Ay needs to be removed. He is not worthy to be pharaoh."

It was not just the fear and hatred he sowed. I had other, more personal, reasons to want him off the throne. He had raped me repeatedly in an attempt to get me with child after he had forced me to marry him. I still believed he was responsible for the arrow that had killed my brother, even if he hadn't shot it himself. He was responsible for Zannanza's murder, which had left Egypt and Hattusa on the brink of war. He had raped Sadeh too and he was responsible for her death, even if he was not the one who had run the knife across her throat. That had been Intef, to give Sadeh a fast death.

"But how will you convince the Eye?" Istnofret asked. "Surely you would have to constantly think about wanting the throne and power. You know how easily it corrupts your thoughts. It could make you really want such power and you would not even realise that the desire was not your own."

"Then you will have to remind me," I said. "As you have done every other time that has happened."

"What if I cannot get through to you? What if thinking about wanting the throne, even if you are only pretending, puts you even deeper under its influence? What if you won't listen to me?"

"You must make me listen. Thinking about Intef always seems to bring me back to myself. Talk to me about him."

She gave a heavy sigh.

"Ist, please. I cannot do this alone."

"I will try. That is all I can promise. It will be up to you whether you listen or not."

I supposed that was all I could ask. Dear Isis, let me hear her when I need to. I went back inside the temple. Mutnodjmet still stood in the same place, silently contemplating the statue of Isis.

"I agree," I said.

"To what exactly?"

"If you pass a message to Ay and help me remove him, I will do everything in my power to ensure that you are the next queen."

"Not good enough."

"But that is what you wanted."

"I want to *be* the queen, not just receive vague assurances of you doing *everything in your power*."

"I can hardly promise such a thing. It may not be up to me."

"If you handle Ay correctly, it will be."

"I suppose you know something about that."

She turned to look at me finally. Her gaze was cool and assessing.

"He likes power. Above all else. Power in himself, yes, but also power in other people. Confront with him an artefact like that you supposedly have and he will want to see it used. His desire to see such power might even outweigh his desire for power for himself."

"Surely not. He would not give up the throne simply to see the Eye used."

"I am merely telling you my impression of him," she said with a shrug that seemed to indicate she cared little whether I believed her or not.

"So what am I supposed to do?"

"That, Daughter, is your problem. If you will excuse me, I will freshen up before I leave for the palace. When shall I tell Pharaoh to expect you?"

"I will be there at dusk."

She gave me a brisk nod and swept out of the chamber. I stood there alone for a while longer, thinking about our conversation. What kind of queen would Mutnodjmet make? Would she be a tempering force if Horemheb needed it? Or would she encourage him as Ay's queen seemed to? Was this even my concern? My aim had been to remove Ay and it seemed I had a way to do that. As my mother's sister, Mutnodjmet was probably almost as entitled to be queen as I myself was. Perhaps that would have to be good enough.

Once I removed Ay, it would be time to entrust Egypt to the hands of the gods. And I would have to make a new life for myself. Without Intef. Without my friends. Without my sisters. I would be all alone.

THIRTY

I barely noticed the walk back to Hemetre's home. My mind whirled with all the things I had waited years to say to Ay. I supposed he probably had things he had been waiting to say to me too. I could hardly begin to fathom what I would need to do tonight. Would I really be able to use the Eye to make him give up the throne? Could I bear to put Horemheb in his place? It was only when we reached Hemetre's home and sat in a circle on the mat that I remembered to tell the others about Nakhtmin.

"I am not sure we can act tonight in that case," Renni said. "Ay needs to announce his new heir before we do anything."

"The heir won't be legitimate otherwise," Tuta said.

Woser swiftly agreed. "If you push him from the throne too early, it might create a power vacuum. Someone will seize the throne before dawn, but it might not be the man you want on it."

"I am not sure there is any man I particularly want on the throne." I pushed away memories of Intef. Of all the men I knew, he was the finest. He would be a strong and compassionate pharaoh, a far cry from the man we were about to confront.

"If you are going to do this, better that you choose the man yourself," Istnofret said. "You can only use the Eye once, so it will be too bad if the next pharaoh is even worse."

"Mutnodjmet thought he would choose Horemheb," I said.

He had been my brother's heir and after Tutankhamun went to the West, Horemheb should have been a certainty to be the next pharaoh. I had never quite figured out how Ay managed to steal the throne away from him and perhaps it no longer mattered. Horemheb would finally have his chance.

"He would be a sound choice," Renni said. "I cannot say I like the man any more than you do, but he is an experienced commander."

"Intef did not think much of him," I said. "He thought too many of Horemheb's men deserted."

"One deserter is too many," Renni said. "Every general loses a few men in that way."

I didn't want to argue with him, but Intef had given me the impression that Horemheb lost more than just a few. Renni surely knew this. I glanced at Behenu to find her staring intently down at her hands in her lap. I hesitated, wondering whether to ask, but Istnofret must have noticed my gaze.

"Behenu?" Her voice was very gentle. "How do you feel about this? I know that Horemheb was not kind to you."

Behenu's chin seemed to wobble a little before she could control it.

"He was my master and I was his slave," she said, eventually. "I suppose he treated me as well as any master treats his slave. He is not a kind man, no, but someone must sit on the throne and he is experienced if nothing else."

"So it is to be Horemheb?" Tuta asked.

I looked around the group. "Does anyone have a better idea?"

"I think that the closer we can stay to what Ay already intends, the more likely we are to be successful," Hemetre said. "We know very little about the power of such an artefact as you possess. We assume it has great power. Far more power than any mortal should wield. The closer we stay to intended events, the less of its power you will need. Perhaps you will better be able to control it that way."

"I am not sure that anyone can control the Eye," I said.

In the place we had hidden it, the Eye woke. It began to pulse, very faintly.

Use me, it whispered.

Soon, I promised. From now on, I could only let myself think what I wanted the Eye to hear and I must try not to lose myself in the process. *Soon you will make me queen again.*

As dusk approached, we left Hemetre's home. She had nothing in the way of fine garments or jewellery so I wore my usual clothes. A sturdy gown and sandals. A small pouch for the Eye, borrowed from Hemetre. A length of linen wrapped around my hand in preparation for when I retrieved the Eye from its pouch. My hair was neatly brushed and fell to just below my shoulders. Istnofret had made up my face with kohl and a little rouge borrowed from Hemetre. I had no jewellery other than the spell bottle and the acacia seed pod from the Syrian healer, both of which hung on cords around my neck.

Mutnodjmet met us at the palace entrance.

"He has agreed," she said.

"Safe passage?" I asked.

"For you and your companions."

"Can I trust him?"

She gave me a steady look.

"That I suppose you will find out. He awaits you in the audience hall. Before you go, you should know that he formally named Horemheb as his heir just a few minutes ago."

Once again I found myself walking the familiar hallways of the palace, only this time I didn't know what I was. First I had been a queen, then a slave and a prisoner. Then I suppose some might have called me a trespasser, an intruder. Now I was what? A guest? The Eye thrummed and I remembered that I could only think what it wanted to hear. So I might not be a queen right now, but very soon I would be once again.

I felt strangely calm as we approached the audience hall. My hands weren't shaking. My heart wasn't racing. We paused at the far end of the hall so I could retrieve the Eye from my pouch. I held it in my left hand, which was bound with the linen. When the time came to use it, I would take it in my right hand where it could sit against my bare palm. I still wasn't sure how to activate it, but we thought that contact with my bare skin might heighten my awareness to it. Perhaps that was all I would need to do. Perhaps the Eye would respond when the moment was right.

"Are you ready, Samun?" Istnofret asked me quietly.

I nodded.

"You don't have to do this," she said. "We could leave now. We have plenty of gems left. We could be on the next boat heading back to Rhakotis. We could go somewhere far away."

"He is my responsibility," I said. "If I had been stronger, he would not have been able to steal the throne. He would not have been in a position to order Zannanza's murder. He would not have been able to rule with fear and threats and intimidation. I allowed him to take the throne and now I must remove him from it."

She squeezed my hand. Her fingers were cold and they trembled a little. For the first time, I realised they must all be afraid.

Of what might happen here tonight and perhaps of what I might become if I succeeded.

"You must remember your promise," I said to her.

I couldn't say more without thinking about what I didn't want the Eye to hear.

"I will try," she said. "But it will be up to you to listen."

THIRTY-ONE

A guard pushed open the wooden doors as we approached the audience hall. They opened smoothly without even the slightest creak. I had almost expected the hall might be filled with Ay's supporters, come to witness him put a recalcitrant slave firmly back in her place. But it was almost empty.

At the far end was the dais, on which stood two thrones. For a moment I feared my brother's throne would be there, but I knew of course that it wasn't. I had sent it with him to his tomb. I had seen Ay's throne before, a gaudy thing of gold and inlaid lapis lazuli. It was a costly item but not made by someone with an eye for beauty. Beside Ay's throne stood his queen's. His queen, however, was nowhere to be seen.

Ay stared at me from his throne. I could barely make out his eyes from this distance, but I could feel his hostility.

"Ankhesenamun!" the guard at the door announced.

I waited for a moment, somehow still expecting he would add my titles, but he said nothing further. I gave him a hard look as I passed. He stared straight ahead and didn't acknowledge me.

As I walked towards the dais, I still felt calm. After all these years, this was the moment of my showdown with my most hated enemy and I was ready. Echoes from a dream slipped through my mind. Glittering falcon eyes. Sinking down into deep water. *Be careful of the jackal.* The black gates closing in front of Intef.

In my hand, the Eye pulsed. *Use me.*

I pushed thoughts of Intef from my mind.

Soon, I whispered to the Eye. *Very soon you will make me queen again.*

My friends followed behind me. Behenu whispered to someone, her voice too low for me to make out the words.

I stopped in front of the dais and studied the man I had come to depose. His cheeks were flabby pouches hanging off his face. His meaty arms rested on the arms of the throne, swollen fingers dangling from his hands. He wore the white *shendyt* that was usual for our menfolk and his round belly sagged over the waistband. Golden sandals on his feet and a large pectoral collar of blue faience. At least a dozen golden rings squeezed his fat fingers. I tried not to stare at the gems, acutely aware of how valuable they were. He wore enough jewels to feed the entire city.

Ay shifted in his seat and cleared his throat. When I finally met his eyes, I instantly remembered how he used to make me feel. Insecure, uncertain, suitable only to be kept hidden away in my chambers where I couldn't embarrass anyone.

Use me, the Eye whispered.

I straightened my shoulders and held my head high. *You will make me queen again.*

"That throne you are sitting on belongs to me."

It wasn't what I had meant to say, but the words were out of my mouth before I realised.

His eyes widened and his mouth dropped open just a little.

"I had thought you might be remorseful," he said. "Apologetic even. Grateful for my mercy."

"Mercy? You kept us locked up for months."

"I could have had you killed."

"So why didn't you?"

Because he wants me, the Eye whispered. But no, he didn't know about the amulet. He had more personal reasons for wanting me kept hidden away.

"Why?" Ay raised his hairless eyebrows and affected amusement.

But for the first time I could see through his act. He was afraid of me. Had that always been the case?

"Yes, why?" I prodded.

"I have no need to explain myself to the likes of you. You are a slave, and a bad one at that. Not worth the hassle of keeping you."

"You didn't keep me. You sent me to the slave mines."

"And it was most inconvenient that you escaped. You had help, though, didn't you? Your *friends* from the palace. But I see one of them is missing. Your captain. What was his name again?"

"You know his name."

I forced my jaw to unclench. He toyed me with me. He had tried to steal Intef away, to convince my captain to join his personal squad. He had met privately with Intef. He knew his name.

"Setau, perhaps?" His voice was mocking.

A flash of anger pulsed through me. Intef's father, Setau, had died because Ay's men tracked us down in Thebes.

"You murdered Setau," I said.

"I do believe I heard he died lying on the ground outside his own home. Rather pathetic really, but I wasn't even in Thebes at the time. You can hardly blame me."

I tried to rein in my temper. He was goading me. Perhaps hoping I would lose control and give him an excuse to arrest me.

He doesn't need an excuse, the Eye whispered. *Use me while you still can. You will be queen again.*

"And where is your captain?"

"Intef." My voice was flat.

"Of course. Setau's son."

I took a deep breath. I would not lose control in front of him. That was exactly what he wanted.

Use me. You know what you want to do.

I did know exactly what I wanted to do to this worm. I wanted to rip him from his throne. I wanted to crush his skull beneath my sandals. I wanted to-

Use me.

My fingers tightened around the Eye. For a moment, I almost forgot it couldn't be used for ill. In my mind's eye, I saw myself reach for Ay and tear him from his seat. Toss his broken body on the floor. Watch his head bounce against the stone until it dripped with blood.

My breath caught and for a moment I thought I had done those things. The image had been so vivid.

Use me.

"Gone to the West, I presume?" Ay said, when I didn't respond.

I almost panted with the effort to restrain myself. It was all I could do to breathe. I had to focus. Remember my aim. I was here to become queen again. To remove him from the throne.

"Shame, really. He was exceptionally dedicated. Except, of course, for when he came to tell me all your secrets."

In. Out. Focus on breathing. That wasn't what had happened.

Use me.

Or was it? Why was I always so ready to believe Intef's version of the event? Was it possible he really had betrayed me? Almost without thinking, I transferred the Eye to my right hand. Where it could rest against the bare skin of my palm.

Another image popped into my mind. Myself sitting on Ay's throne. I wore an elegant white linen gown, my crown with the sun disk rising between two horns on my head. People prostrated themselves before me. Ay prostrated himself.

Use me.

Yes. I had the power to make this happen. This worm who sat on the throne didn't deserve it. He had no respect for the institution of the pharaoh. He wasn't even of my father's bloodline. He was an illegitimate pharaoh sitting on a stolen throne. I opened my hand and held up the Eye, resting on my palm. Ay's gaze was immediately drawn to it and he learned forward a little to better see what I held.

"You," I said to Ay, barely aware of what I did. "You will give up the throne and walk away."

His eyes widened and he started to laugh but abruptly, he stopped. His eyes bulged and he gagged a little as if choking. Then he stood and came down the steps of the dais to stand in front of me.

"I forfeit the throne," he said.

His eyes looked like they would pop out of his head and his face turned an alarming shade of red.

"Leave," I said to him. "Walk out of the palace and keep going. Leave Memphis and never return."

He stood in front of me for a few moments too long. I started to fear that he wouldn't comply. Perhaps the Eye wasn't strong enough to make a man do something he was so opposed to. But then he stepped around me and walked to the door at the far end of the hall. The guard opened the door, shooting me a confused look. Ay passed through the doorway and was gone.

"Is that it?" Istnofret asked, her voice low. "Is it over?"

"It was too easy," Behenu said. "Something is wrong."

I didn't acknowledge their comments, only walked up the steps of the dais and settled myself on my throne. Why had I intended to be merely queen when I could be pharaoh? I straightened my skirt over my knees and leaned back. The throne was still warm from its previous occupant. Bile rose in my throat and I tucked my hands into my lap rather than rest them on the arms that Ay's flesh had touched.

"Tomorrow, I want this throne disposed of. It is to be replaced with a new throne. A new throne for a new pharaoh."

They stood in front of the dais with a variety of expressions on their faces. Istnofret looked horrified, Behenu resigned. Both Renni and Tuta's faces were carefully schooled to blankness, much the way Intef used to. Woser opened and closed his mouth. Hemetre looked confused.

"Should you not be prostrating yourselves?" I asked. "I am, after all, your pharaoh."

Behenu was the first to lower herself to the floor. The others soon followed although I didn't miss the way Renni grabbed Istnofret's hand to pull her down.

"Not now, Ist," he muttered.

I left them lying on the floor for some time while I looked around the chamber. It was too dreary for my taste. A pharaoh should be surrounded by beauty and elegance. Like I used to be.

"This chamber needs linen hangings for the walls. Some colourful rugs or mats. Perhaps a few side tables with trays of food. And there should always be a jug of fresh melon juice."

Nobody moved.

"You there," I called to the guard at the end of the hall.

He raised his hand to his chest as if asking *who me*?

"Send for runners. At least a dozen."

He hesitated, but I glared at him until eventually he slipped out into the hallway.

I waited a little longer while the servants at my feet lay on their bellies. It was rather boring, though, to just sit and wait. At length, I yawned.

"You may rise."

They got to their feet slowly, giving me cautious looks.

"Samun-" Istnofret started.

She stopped when I leaned forward and glared at her.

"Uh, my lady," she said instead.

I eased back into my throne a little. At least now she showed respect, even if it was insufficient.

A dozen runners filed into the hall. They were young boys, not quite into their teens but old enough to obey orders. They all wore white *shendyts* and their feet were bare. Most had the shaved heads of men, although one or two still wore the sidelock of youth. They hesitated when they saw me on the throne, looking amongst themselves, before one finally lowered himself to his belly. I stared pointedly at the others and they quickly followed. I left them to lie there for a while before bidding them rise.

"Send servants to prepare my chambers."

I hoped that between the lot of them they had enough wit to decide who would do what. I really didn't have the patience for servants who needed personalised instructions. Not today. I had far too much to do.

"I require fresh melon juice to be available at all times. Have the jugs replaced every hour. And make sure there is food laid out whenever I return to my chambers. I require new clothes, so send to me somebody who can instruct the weavers and tailors.

Have Pharaoh's private chapel prepared so that I may worship Isis at dawn. If there is no statue of Isis here, fetch the largest one from the temple."

Various runners left to convey my instructions.

"Send me the captain of Pharaoh's personal squad and the slave master. Send also the viziers of Upper and Lower Egypt, and the treasurer. And send me Pharaoh's chief advisors."

Two runners still stood in front of me, waiting for instructions.

"I want a cat," I said. "Find me an orange kitten."

My heart ached. That would remind me too much of Mau. I didn't need anything that would make me feel weak.

"No, find a grey one."

Another runner left. Just one boy remained. He looked at me steadily. What task could I give him?

"Find every messenger you can. Send word throughout the Two Lands. Egypt has a new pharaoh."

THIRTY-TWO

Once all the runners were gone, there remained six other people in the chamber. I ignored the guard at the door. He had not bothered to announce my titles when I arrived. He deserved nothing from me.

"You have been loyal," I said to the five who cowered in front of me. "You have travelled a long way with me, most of you. You will be rewarded for your faithfulness."

"If it pleases my lady." Renni's voice was suitably respectful. "We do not need any reward other than to be permitted to remain at your side."

The others nodded in agreement. I stared down at them, allowing them to wait a little longer for my reply.

"Fine, you may do so. You, Renni, and you, Tuta and Woser, will join my personal squad. You will be the guards who stand closest to me at all times. I hold you personally accountable for my safety."

"Thank you for honouring us in this way, my lady," Renni said.

They quickly took their places behind me, although I didn't

miss the look that passed between Renni and Istnofret. The women waited in front of me, their heads bowed in supplication.

"You will attend me," I said. "As you did before. You will be my companions. You will call for runners."

"I can look after your wardrobe and your makeup, my lady." Istnofret's voice was pleasingly meek. "If you will allow it."

I considered her request. She had looked after my wigs and accessories before, back when I had three serving women. Then when Charis went to the West, Istnofret had also managed my wardrobe.

"I suppose that will be fine, as long as it does not take too much of your time. When I want someone to sit with me, you will be available."

"Of course, my lady. Anything you require."

Behenu glanced up at me, just for a moment, but it was enough for me to see the fear on her face.

"Why are you afraid?" I asked her.

She quickly bowed her head.

"I am merely awaiting your instructions, my lady. You have not yet assigned me a task."

"What other task do you wish than to be my companion?"

"I could be your spy."

"A spy?"

I had not expected to be surprised at her request. The others had been predictable, but this was unexpected.

"What makes you think you would be a good spy? You do not exactly blend in with the people here."

Indeed, with her skin several shades darker than an Egyptian, Behenu was obviously a foreigner.

"I was a slave before. I know how to go unnoticed. People don't see me. They say things in front of me that they would never say in front of you. I could watch and listen and report back to you."

I needed someone like that. Someone loyal who I could trust to tell me exactly what the servants said. Then I could punish the traitors and the unfaithful. I would have only those who were loyal to me near me.

"A spy is useless if everybody knows they are a spy," I said.

"Then as far as anyone else knows, I am merely your serving woman," Behenu said. "You should—" She caught herself. "Perhaps you might give me some instructions from time to time so that other people hear them. I could fetch things for you, summon runners, direct the servants. It might be helpful if I am seen to be doing things at your bidding and then people will not suspect I am a spy."

And those things would give her more reason to be in places where she might hear things that were useful to me.

"Fine. You will be my secret spy."

The door at the far end of the hall opened.

"Usermontu, Vizier of Lower Egypt," the guard announced. "Arriving in response to... um... your summons."

"Renni," I said in a low voice. "If the guard cannot address me with the correct titles, he is to be relieved of his duties and replaced with a man who puts more value on attention to detail."

"My lady." Renni hurried away to speak to him.

I examined Usermontu as he approached. I had listened to him many times during my brother's audiences. He was of average height for a man and walked with a slight limp. His face was rounded, although his body wasn't overly fat, and he wore an elaborate wig of braids which came down to below his shoulders. He hesitated when he reached the dais. Tuta cleared his throat rather loudly and Usermontu dropped down onto his belly.

I left him there for a long time as punishment for all the boring reports I had endured from him when my brother was pharaoh. The man lay perfectly still, without twitching so much as a finger.

"You may rise," I said, when I grew bored with watching him lie so still.

He scrambled to his feet awkwardly. He had bad knees, it seemed. Usermontu bowed low from the waist and waited for me to speak.

"You will report every first day of the week," I said. "Your report will be brief, concise and interesting."

His face registered surprise and he opened his mouth. I raised my finger to stop him.

"I have no patience for tedious speeches. I am uninterested in flattery. I want factual reports and I do not want to be bored listening to them."

"Uh, of course," he said.

"Leave now."

"Uh, you do not want me to provide a report while I am here?"

I held his gaze for a moment, letting him think I considered his request.

"Is today the first day of the week?" I asked.

"It is not."

"Was there something about my instruction that was unclear to you?"

"No, no, of course not."

"Then why are you still standing there?"

He bowed and left without another word. He walked much faster than when he had entered.

"Wennefer and Maya," the guard called. "Chief advisors to the previous pharaoh."

He was, at least, a quick learner. Perhaps I might forgive his earlier errors.

The two advisors ambled towards the dais. They made no effort to seem like they were hurrying and irritation flared within me. This was their first appearance before me and already they showed me disrespect. I had intended to allow them to keep their positions. After all, they had advised the previous three pharaohs and had much knowledge that would have been valuable to me. Knowledge, however, was less important than obedience.

They stopped in front of the dais and stared up at me. Neither man prostrated himself, nor even bowed from the waist. Wennefer towered over Maya whose hunched back made him seem shorter than he really was. They both wore white *shendyts* and decorated themselves with far too many jewels.

"Are those jewels your own or did you steal them?"

I fixed my gaze on a particular ring on Wennefer's hand. It had belonged to my father. Wennefer followed my gaze down to his hand. Maya just blinked at me.

"Where is Pharaoh?" Wennefer asked.

His tone was belligerent and I bristled.

"Gone."

"If he has been harmed, your life is forfeit. I am sure you are well aware of that."

"He is uninjured. He simply chose to leave."

"And I suppose he gave you the throne, did he?" Wennefer's tone was sarcastic now.

"She *is* of the bloodline," Maya ventured timidly. "If it is true that Pharaoh has abdicated, she probably has the most legitimate-"

"You surely don't support such an abomination? A woman on the throne?"

"It would not be the first time a woman has ruled."

"And many decent men swore last time that it would be the last," Wennefer said. "She gave up her position as queen. She has no right to the throne, either as queen or as *this*."

"I never gave up the throne," I said. "It was stolen from me."

"Where has Pharaoh gone?" Wennefer asked.

I shrugged. "As long as he has left Memphis, I don't particularly care. I have more important things to worry about."

"So you think you are going to run the country?" he asked with a sneer.

"I called you here to see whether you might be of use to me," I said. "It seems you are not. You are relieved of your duties."

"Relieved?" Wennefer gave an astonished laugh. "You have more nerve than most men I know. If Pharaoh is indisposed, it falls to us as his chief advisors to manage affairs until he returns."

"This is the last time I am going to tell you. Pharaoh has stepped aside and you no longer have positions in this government. Leave."

They didn't move. I raised my hand and twitched my fingers at the men behind me. Renni and Tuta stepped forward, their daggers already in their hands. Woser came to stand at my left hand.

"Time to go, gentlemen." Renni's tone was amicable. "You will wait in the hallway until we have guards available to escort you from the palace."

"You cannot be serious," Wennefer said.

"My lady has spoken," Renni said. "I am sure you heard her as well as I did, unless you are hard of hearing?"

"My hearing is perfectly fine."

"Then go wait in the hallway and someone will attend to you in due course."

Maya already headed back to the door.

"Maya!" Wennefer said sharply. "You cannot intend to comply with this nonsense."

"I don't particularly care for being stabbed through the heart today," Maya called over his shoulder. "I would rather live to see tomorrow. You may do as you please."

"But this is an abomination," Wennefer said.

Renni and Tuta took him by the arms. He briefly resisted, then allowed them to lead him out of the hall. Renni returned alone. Presumably Tuta was keeping watch over the advisors.

"Nehi," the guard at the door announced. "Captain of, um, Pharaoh's, um, the royal personal squad."

It had been more than a hundred years since a woman had last held the title of Pharaoh. It would take time for people to adjust. At least the fellow was trying.

As Nehi approached the dais, I saw echoes of Intef in the way he moved. He was alert, looking all around the hall, but without seeming anxious. His back was straight and his hands loose. I supposed he was being careful to look unthreatening. He would know that no matter how good his training, he would have no chance of overcoming my men on his own. When he reached the dais, he didn't hesitate before dropping down onto his belly. Since he was so compliant, I left him there for only a moment.

"You may rise," I said. "Your name is Nehi?"

"That is correct, your majesty."

So, he didn't know whether to consider me his queen or his pharaoh and was careful to ensure he offered no offence either way. This was a smart man.

"I have a place for you in my personal squad," I said. "But I warn you, I have no patience for disloyalty or scheming."

Nehi gave a low bow.

"I am honoured that you would consider me, majesty. How may I serve you?"

"Go assemble the men you consider worthy of joining my personal squad. Renni will meet with them in one hour. Both they and you should be prepared to justify why they should be selected."

He bowed again and left without another word.

"Where is the Vizier of Upper Egypt?" I asked.

"He would need to travel from Thebes, I expect, my lady," Woser said. "Even if a messenger left immediately, the vizier will not be here for several days yet."

"Then he shall learn that when I summon him, I expect him to arrive promptly." A wave of weariness rushed over me and suddenly I could barely keep my eyes open. "I will go to my chambers now."

As I rose, Istnofret swooped in to straighten my skirt. Renni steadied me as I made my way down the steps. As I crossed the chamber, he walked in front of me, in the place where Intef always used to. My resolve momentarily wavered. What was I doing? I had not come here with any intention of claiming the throne for myself. Then the Eye pulsed and the thought slid away.

Woser followed closely behind me and my ladies were behind him. It was just as it had always been. Guards ahead and behind me. My ladies trailing me. I was Pharaoh and things were right again.

THIRTY-THREE

As I walked through the palace, I realised things weren't exactly as they had been before. Once people would have quietly stepped aside to let me pass. Servants and slaves would have stood with their backs to the wall and their gazes on the floor. They would not have whispered amongst themselves or smirked or shared knowing looks. I pretended not to see them. They were not worthy of my attention.

At a branching hallway, Renni hesitated.

"Which chambers do you wish to use, my lady?" he asked. "Your previous chambers or those of pharaoh?"

Which chambers had the runner I sent made arrangements for? Pharaoh's chambers likely had the stench of Ay all over them. His belongings would need to be cleared out and the chambers thoroughly cleaned before I could bear to step foot in them.

"My old chambers," I said.

"I will go and see that they are unoccupied," Istnofret said and rushed on ahead of us.

I walked at a sedate pace, my gaze fixed on the back of

Renni's head, just as I had always watched Intef. My heart hurt suddenly and for a moment I was tempted to walk away. Leave all this behind. What did I want with power and authority? I had achieved my aim of removing Ay from the throne. Let his heir deal with whatever else needed to be done. It did not have to be me who stayed.

I was on the verge of opening my mouth to tell Renni I had changed my mind when the Eye pulsed. It was weaker now, as if tired. If it spoke to me, I couldn't make out any words. It was more of a feeling, a desire for power. For influence. To control the course of things. My resolve firmed. I had only done part of what I had intended. I had yet to deal with the ongoing conflict with the Hittites. I could root out Ay's supporters and remove them. I could restore my father's works, replace his face and his name in all those places where it had been chiselled away since his death. I could make Egypt the same as it had been when my father was pharaoh.

When we reached my chambers, I waited in the hall while Renni checked inside. A flurry of servants already made their way in and out of the chambers, carrying cleaning equipment and bundles of linens. Dusting, sweeping, hanging fresh curtains.

My chambers bore little resemblance to what they had been before. Someone had tried to remove all trace of me, just as they had done to my father all those years ago. The furniture had been replaced. The wall hangings were new. Even those that had been stitched by my ladies were gone. I felt a pang of regret at that. They had worked so hard on those wall hangings.

I made my way over to the little sitting chamber. Someone had torn out the vine that used to grow across the mud brick wall in the courtyard. I stood at the window for a long time, looking at the bare wall. Surely they could have left the vine.

In my sleeping chamber, the bed had been replaced. The chests where my clothes used to be stored were new and when I opened the lid of one, it was empty. The shelf that held my wigs was bare. The dresser with my makeup and jewellery was gone too. Unexpected tears sprang to my eyes. Could they not have left something? Anything?

I noticed Behenu bend to retrieve something small from the corner of the chamber. She studied it for a moment, then offered it to me.

"I think it is one of your rings," she said. "Someone must have dropped it and it rolled into the corner here."

I took the ring from her. A band of gold inlaid with a circle of lapis lazuli all around its diameter. It wasn't particularly elaborate and I had worn it infrequently, but it was indeed something that had belonged to me. I slipped it onto my finger. At least one thing from my former life had survived here. Istnofret disturbed my mournful contemplation as she bustled in with fresh linens for the bed.

"Are you tired, my lady? Perhaps you would like to lie down?"

I was about to say that I had far too much to do to lie around, but another wave of exhaustion swept over me and my head suddenly spun with fatigue.

"I am rather tired," I said. "Perhaps a short rest. Wake me up if I fall asleep."

She made the bed up neatly with a linen sheet and a cushion. While she was occupied, I tucked the Eye back into the pouch at my waist. I climbed into the bed and Istnofret draped a light blanket over me, then left without another word. I was asleep before she even made it out of the chamber.

I dreamed I rummaged through a pack. I searched for something and I grew increasingly frustrated at not finding it. Then my fingers closed around a papyrus scroll. I slowly withdrew it from the pack. It was a little squashed and the seal had crumbled at the edges although it was still intact. Nobody had read this letter since the seal was set on it. I ran my finger under the edge, breaking the seal, and unrolled the scroll.

Then the dream shifted and this time when I withdrew the scroll from the pack, I didn't open it. Instead I crushed it in my fist and tossed it to the floor.

THIRTY-FOUR

I woke to Istnofret shaking my shoulder.

"My lady," she whispered. "You asked me not to let you sleep for too long."

My mind was foggy and I couldn't remember why I had wanted her to wake me or even why she used my old title. Nobody called me that anymore. Then it all came rushing back. I sat up a little too quickly and my head spun.

"The master of the slaves came to speak with you and I told him to come back tomorrow," Istnofret said. "The head cook came to ask about your dietary requirements, but I managed that. The servants have finished cleaning out in the main chamber. They will return later to do in here. It needs to be properly aired out and have a good dusting."

She cast a critical gaze around as if the chamber itself was to blame for getting dusty.

"Also Horemheb sent a messenger to ask for an audience with you."

"I see."

Horemheb, ever the heir, never quite the pharaoh.

"I assume he hopes I will honour Ay's decision to name him as heir."

"Will you?" Istnofret's tone was frank. "You did say you didn't want the throne for yourself."

"I never said any such thing." I gave her a scornful look. "If you are to be my serving woman, you really must pay better attention to what I say."

"Where is the Eye?" she asked.

"Somewhere safe. Why do you want to know?"

"I think we should put it away. Somewhere you cannot get to it, like we did before."

"You will not touch it. It belongs to me. Anyone who I even so much as suspect of trying to steal the Eye will pay dearly for it."

She took a couple of steps back away from me.

"You misunderstand me," she said. "You asked me to help you to remember that the Eye twists your thoughts. It makes you crave power."

"What power would I want that I do not already have? As Pharaoh, I have the power of life or death over every living creature in Egypt. As holder of the Eye, I have the power of the gods. What more is there to want?"

"You don't want those things. You, the real you. It is the Eye corrupting your thoughts. You need to remember that you don't have to do what it wants you to."

"I am really quite disappointed in you, Istnofret. I have never heard you speak such utter nonsense before. Perhaps you should learn to think before you speak again."

"Of course, my lady." Her tone was suitably meek and she bowed her head so that I no longer looked into her face. I wondered whether she did so because she knew her eyes would be filled with defiance. "I do apologise."

Istnofret returned to the main chamber and I lay back down again. My gaze landed on the image of Hathor over my bed and for the first time I wondered how the gods became gods. Were they born that way or were they originally mortal? The stories we told of them said they had always been gods and yet Pharaoh was a mortal man until he became a god. Did that mean that a mortal woman could become a goddess? Like my dreams, my thoughts were tangled and only confused me even more. I finally dragged myself from my bed.

When I went out to the main chamber, my eye was immediately drawn to a grey kitten. He sprawled on the floor in a patch of sunlight. I looked at him for a long moment and my heart ached remembering an orange cat who used to enjoy sunny spots. The kitten opened his eyes and looked straight at me. He yawned and poked out his tiny pink tongue. Warmth flooded me and I started to smile but caught myself just in time.

"Remove the kitten," I said. "I do not want to see it again."

There seemed to be a never-ending list of decisions to be made over the next few days. My servants wanted to know which gown I wished to wear in the morning and how I would like my face made up. They asked about what I wanted to eat and when I would like to bathe. There was a constant stream of new items procured for my chambers and apparently I had to inspect every one of them. I personally approved every wall hanging, every floor mat, every cushion. Every new gown and pair of sandals and necklace.

"Can you do nothing yourselves?" I asked at last, exasperated with the constant barrage of questions.

"We don't wish to have any item here that you don't like, my lady," Istnofret answered, her gaze demurely downcast. "What is pleasing to my eye may not be pleasing to you and I only want for you to be surrounded by beautiful things."

I sighed and flung myself down onto a day bed. I stared up at the image of Osiris on the ceiling. Memories swirled in my mind. Memories I didn't want to remember. Ay grunting as he moved on top of me. His hand pressing my throat to the bed. I quickly got up.

"Have the image of Osiris painted over," I said. "Immediately."

I sat on a couch and looked around the chamber. My gaze fell on a patch of wall that was still bare. A piece of linen used to hang there, stitched by Sadeh in the early days. I quickly averted my eyes.

I went to the little sitting chamber where a couch was positioned so that I could sit and look out at the courtyard. A new vine had been planted against the base of the wall but it had not yet grown anything more than a few shoots. Still this spot in the sun was pleasant and the wall itself did not trigger memories I no longer cared to remember.

Tell me about your sisters.

His voice was as clear as if he was in the chamber with me. Intef and I had sat here together and I had talked about my sisters. He held me as I cried, then he kissed me. I hadn't realised at the time that I loved him. My cheeks felt wet and it was only when I wiped them that I realised I was crying. What was I doing? Why was I still here? Intef and I had planned to have a little house with a vegetable garden. I could still have that, even if I had to live there alone. From my pouch, the Eye pulsed and thoughts of the life Intef and I had intended to share slipped from my mind.

"Prepare Pharaoh's chambers," I said to Istnofret. "I will not sleep in here again."

As servants began packing up my gowns and jewels, Behenu came to stand in front of me.

"My lady, Hemetre has sent a messenger," she said. "He waits in the hallway if you would care to hear his message."

"Fine. What does Hemetre want?"

Behenu ushered in the messenger. He was a boy of around eleven years and looked much the same as any of the runners who waited around the palace for the opportunity to make themselves useful. There were always at least five or six waiting in the hallway outside my chambers.

"What is your message?" I asked.

"The priestess Hemetre wishes to remind your majesty that you promised to release her son, Ptahhotep, as soon as you were in a position to do so."

I waited, but it seemed he had said all he intended to.

"Is there anything else?" I asked.

"No, majesty. That is the whole message."

"You may leave then."

"But..." He looked towards Istnofret, obviously seeking some intervention from her.

"My lady," she said. "Do you not wish to send him back with your reply?"

"I have no reply to make."

Istnofret opened her mouth but clearly thought the better of it. She showed the runner to the door and no doubt arranged for the boy to receive a trinket for his service.

"My lady, you did make Hemetre a promise," she said when she returned. "She is frantic with worry about her son."

"I am sure he is being well cared for. She has no need to be worried."

"Do you not intend to release him?"

I lay back on a day couch with a yawn and closed my eyes. I had slept restlessly last night, plagued with dreams I couldn't quite recall now.

"Not just yet. Hemetre may prove to be a useful ally at some point and her son could be valuable in ensuring her compliance."

Istnofret didn't respond although I could feel her staring at me, even with my eyes closed.

"What?" I asked.

"Hemetre is your friend. She helped us, even after her son was taken. You promised you would release him as soon as you were able to."

"Then tell her I have not yet been able to do such a thing if you feel she needs a reply."

"She wants a reply from you, not from me."

"Send it in my name then. I hardly care. She is just a priestess."

"A moment ago you said she might be a useful ally."

I opened my eyes just enough to squint at her.

"Are you questioning me?"

"No, I am just..." Her voice trailed away and she gave a heavy sigh. "Samun, may I speak frankly?"

Something in the way she said my name made my heart hurt, but I steeled myself. I had no need for sentimentality.

"You should take care to address me using my correct titles."

I closed my eyes again.

She stood there for a few more moments before I heard her walk away.

THIRTY-FIVE

To Suppululiumas, King of Hattusa

Words cannot express my regret at the death of your son. I write to assure you that my offer to you was genuine and I had no part in Zannanza's death. I desired to align my country to yours. I wanted your son to be my husband. However he was a pawn, used to steal my throne from me.

The man responsible for your son's death has been removed from the throne and banished from Memphis. He will never again set foot in this city. I hope this gives you some small amount of satisfaction. I have ordered that should he ever return, he is to be tried for his crime and if found guilty, he is to be executed. Perhaps this will assuage your anger.

My people should not be held responsible for the actions of one man. I send with this letter compensation for the loss of your son. One hundred rolls of fine linen. One hundred shabti to serve you in the afterlife. One hundred woven baskets made by the best of our artisans. One hundred beads carved from precious stones.

I trust that our two countries will continue to be allies.

Ankhesenamun

Pharaoh. Lady of the Two Lands. Great of Praises. Lady of Grace.

THIRTY-SIX

I had been feeling unsettled ever since I had taken my rightful place as Pharaoh. In the evenings, once there was nobody left to hear reports from, I roamed the hallways, unable to sit still. When I turned my head, I sometimes caught the image of a woman. She faded from my view too quickly and I could never quite make out who she was.

My appetite was poor and my mood irritable. I had trouble falling asleep and when I did, my sleep was plagued with dreams of a sandy shore and waves that made no noise. Someone walked beside me but I could never see who it was. I sank down into deep water. Falcon eyes glittered.

I woke in the middle of the night, startled into wakefulness by a sound that was gone before I could hear it. In the corner the room, faintly lit by the moonlight, stood a woman. But as occurred every time I saw her, she quickly disappeared from my sight. I pulled the linen sheet up over my head and didn't let myself look again in case she had returned.

"You could go to the temple," Istnofret suggested one

evening. "For the dawn worship like you used to. I am sure Mutnodjmet would welcome you back."

She didn't mention Hemetre whose messages I continued to ignore. Still, her suggestion of worship seemed like a good idea. I had found peace in worshipping Isis before. Perhaps that was what I needed.

"Send runners to prepare the private chapel here at the palace. I will worship at dawn tomorrow."

When Istnofret came to wake me early the next morning, I already regretted having said I would go. I had slept little as usual, plagued with dreams of sandy shores and deep water, and was really too tired to bother getting out of bed so early. But I rose and allowed the servants to dress me. The best seamstresses in Memphis had put together an elaborate new wardrobe for me. The gowns were much fussier than I was accustomed to with many ribbons and ties and layers. Today Istnofret had selected a gown of pale green linen, which fell to my ankles in stiff pleats. Its long sleeves dangled past my wrists, leaving me uncertain as to what I was supposed to do with them.

An assortment of wigs had been procured for me, but when Istnofret tried to set one on my head there was too much of my own hair for it to sit neatly.

"We will have to shave your head," she said. "Behenu, send a runner to fetch warm water and a razor."

As I waited for the shaving implements to be brought, I studied myself in a hand mirror. My hair came down to my shoulders now, thick and glossy. I ran my fingers through it and was sharply reminded of the day I met the three women from Indou and how envious I had felt at the knowledge that the hair they wore was their own.

"No wigs," I said. "I will wear my own hair."

Istnofret shrugged and didn't comment. So instead of

having my head shaved, I sat on the stool for another hour while they arranged my hair in rows of tiny plaits threaded through with silver and green beads. From the corner of my eye, the half-seen woman watched. When I turned to look at her, she was gone. I had never seen her when I lived here previously.

The sun had almost risen by the time they were satisfied with my appearance. A half squad led by Tuta escorted me to the private chapel where everything I would need was laid out on a long table. There was an array of musical instruments, obviously selected by someone who was unaware of whether I knew how to play any of them. A lyre. A flute. Two tambourines and a sistrum. A pair of clappers, which I reached for. They were shaped like human hands, much like the ones I had used at the temple of Isis, but these were somewhat larger and they didn't fit my hands as neatly. Still it was the only instrument I had ever played, although I could probably manage the sistrum or a tambourine if I must.

Also laid out were an assortment of offerings for me to present to Isis — dried fish, a jar of wine, a loaf of bread, a mound of dates. There was a bowl of water sprinkled with lotus petals and a pile of soft cloths for washing the goddess. Another bowl was filled to the brim with loose lotus petals. And there was the goddess herself. For a moment I thought they had brought the statue from the temple, but as I studied her more closely, I noticed subtle differences. This Isis looked a little less serene and a little more knowing. The wings shading her outstretched arms had different markings. Her wig was slightly longer.

As I stared into Isis's eyes, my heart already rejected this image of her that wasn't the statue I was so familiar with. Looking at her didn't fill me with the peace and serenity I was accustomed to. Instead I was irritated that she didn't look the way she should.

Nevertheless, I took up the clappers and positioned myself in front of the statue. I began to sing the song we always sang in the dawn worship. The one that was composed in an ancient version of our tongue. Over time I had come to understand most of it, even if I had never been able to translate it word by word. My voice was thin and thready, unused to singing alone and without the accompaniment of Hemetre's lyre.

It had been a long time since I had worshipped in this way and I couldn't remember the whole song. I began skipping the parts I had forgotten and I jumbled several passages. Frustration grew at my inability to remember a song that used to be as familiar to me as breathing. Eventually I came to the end, although the song had been much shorter than it should have. I tossed the clappers down on the table and took a deep breath, trying to calm my swelling irritation. Worship was supposed to make me feel peaceful.

I took the bowl of water and a cloth over to the goddess. Bathing Isis would help to relax me. Mutnodjmet always performed this task herself and I had envied her for it. As high priestess, the most sacred tasks were reserved for her alone. But it was no more interesting than washing a stone block. I finished far too quickly and was left with the dissatisfied feeling that the goddess judged me for having failed to do the job as thoroughly as Mutnodjmet would have.

It was Hemetre's fault. Without her here to keep up a tune on the lyre, I had rushed instead of letting myself move calmly and slowly. I set the bowl and the towel aside and fed the goddess. This too should have been a sacred act, but I felt ridiculous waving pieces of dried fish and dates beneath the statue's nose.

I inspected the table wondering whether I had missed any

steps and spotted the bowl of petals. What was I supposed to do with those? Sprinkle them over the goddess? Over the floor? Uncertain, I did both. The bowl was still mostly full so I dumped handfuls of petals on the floor at Isis's feet. The servants would clean it up and I felt slightly better at having an empty bowl.

With those things done, there seemed to be no reason to linger in the chapel. As I turned to leave, the now-familiar image of a half-glimpsed woman faded away.

THIRTY-SEVEN

I stnofret had acted oddly since the day I told her she had disappointed me. She was meticulously careful to address me with my titles and she never said anything that was overly familiar. The distance between us felt strange, but I ignored it. After all, I was Lady of the Two Lands again. Pharaoh even. I had more important things to concern myself with than an obstinate servant. She was surely smart enough to know that if she wanted to retain her position, she could not afford to step out of place again. So I let the distance between us fester and said nothing.

As I walked through the palace one day with Renni in his usual place in front of me, I spotted a familiar doorway.

"Renni," I said. "I want to visit my pleasure garden."

"It has not been very well maintained since you left," he said. "The gardeners are restoring it, but it will take them some time yet to put it back in order. Perhaps you would like to wait until it looks more like how you remember?"

"I want to see it now."

"As you wish."

He led me out into the garden and I immediately understood why he had thought I should wait. Weeds threaded the flower beds which used to contain orderly rows of poppies and chrysanthemums. The shrubs were either overgrown or dead. Dirt and encroaching weeds spread across the paths. A thick layer of green slime covered the empty pond, the papyrus which used to grow around its edges gone. Tears came to my eyes as I looked around the garden, but I quickly blinked them away. Had they thought so little of me that nobody bothered to maintain this place once I was gone?

Renni disappeared behind the overgrown shrubbery, leaving me to walk the disorderly paths alone. At length I reached the place where I had planted the *kathal* tree. It had been a gift from the ladies of Indou and I had often sat here beneath its boughs. Back then, the area beneath it had been kept tidy, but now it was just as much of an overgrown mess as the rest of the garden. The tree's branches were heavy with yellow blossoms. Had anyone had eaten its fruit last year or had they had fallen to the ground, as unwanted as a former queen?

I looked at the *kathal* tree for some time. This garden used to be a place of peace for me. A place to centre myself. Now all I could see was the disorganisation around me. Whatever beauty had been here once was long gone. Perhaps it would be restored when the gardeners finished their work. Nevertheless, this tree had symbolised something for me once. Friendship. Alliances. I inhaled deeply and focused on the tree, trying to block out the mess around me and the quiet sounds of the gardeners going about their work.

Something dropped onto the ground with a heavy thud and someone groaned. A servant tripping over something perhaps. How was I supposed to focus with all this noise?

"Renni," I said. "Get everyone out of here."

"They are working hard to restore the garden, my lady," he said. "Would you not rather that they complete their work as soon as possible?"

"Now."

There were quiet conversations just out of my earshot and soon I had the garden to myself. I sat cross-legged on the path and faced the *kathal* tree, focusing my attention on it. It suddenly seemed important that I felt the connection to it that I used to have. That it meant something to me instead of being just another tree in an untidy garden.

A breeze rustled my hair and an ant crawled over my foot. I brushed it away and focussed again on the *kathal*. A bird squawked and some kind of flying insect buzzed around near my ear.

"Why is it still so noisy in here?" I asked.

"My lady, they have all gone. There is nobody here but you and I."

"I can hear birds and bugs and the wind."

There was a long pause before Renni replied.

"I am afraid I cannot do anything about them. I have no way of communicating your wishes to the birds and the bugs and the wind."

"Well, find a way then," I snapped. "How am I supposed to concentrate with all this noise?"

Another long pause.

"How exactly do you wish me to communicate with the bugs and the birds, my lady?" he asked. "Or the wind? If you can tell me what I must do, I will do it gladly."

"I don't know. Is it not your job to figure that out?"

I tried again to focus, but the wind blew, harder now, and the *kathal's* branches creaked. Blossoms drifted to the ground. I sighed and rose to my feet. It was pointless. Nobody could concentrate with so much noise and disorganisation. I would not return here again until it had been restored and was once more a place of beauty and symmetry.

As I turned to leave, my gaze landed on my shadow, moving in perfect unison with me.

"Hello, Shadow."

I had promised to talk to it, to remember that it could think and feel. I couldn't remember the last time I had paid it any attention.

"Do you feel as disturbed by all this chaos as I do?"

I waited, but of course there was no reply. I raised my hand, wriggled my fingers, and my shadow mimicked my movements.

"Can you still hear me?"

There was no reply and my shadow didn't even so much as twitch a finger unless I did it first. I felt morose all of a sudden. Everyone I had thought I had a connection with had abandoned me. Intef, my shadow, Istnofret. Even Behenu now kept her distance and had reported nothing useful to me in her capacity as secret spy. Renni, Tuta and Woser were meticulously polite and restrained. Hemetre sent messengers every third day, but the words they conveyed were never anything other than yet another reminder about her son. Even Isis was distant. Once I had felt a connection with the goddess. Now she felt impossibly far away.

A thought occurred to me which was so startling that for a few moments I forgot to breathe. My lungs started to ache and I inhaled a noisy gulp of air. If even Isis distanced herself, did that mean that I was now a goddess too? After all, Pharaoh was a living god.

Was this why I had felt so distant from those around me? Why I seemed so sensitive to noise and disruption and lack of beauty? No wonder I had found it so difficult to worship. It was I who was meant to be worshipped.

"Renni, I want a worship ceremony."

"Of course, my lady. Do you wish to go to your private chapel now?"

"No, I intend to be worshipped. Build a temple for me. One large enough that everyone in the palace can worship me at the same time. I will see nobody until this is done."

I left the garden with Renni trailing behind me instead of walking in front as he should have. I supposed it didn't matter if he neglected this duty. After all, I was a goddess. What need did I have for a mortal to walk ahead of me?

THIRTY-EIGHT

Work on my chapel began the very next day. Every morning I toured the site and finally I found a purpose again. The building rose quickly, for Renni had brought in as many workers as could fit into the site at one time. I found little to correct at first, given my lack of knowledge of construction. It wasn't until they plastered the walls and began painting that I could provide them with feedback. Art, after all, was something I had been well schooled in as a girl. My father had been a tremendous lover of art.

The images they made were of me, of course. In one, I stood beside a towering papyrus plant. In another, I held a bunch of lotus flowers as I stared serenely out at the viewer. I stood in front of a rising sun, a pleasing tribute to my father and his god, although perhaps unintentional. In each image I wore a crown just like Isis's with a sun disk emerging from between a pair of horns. Lady of the Two Lands proclaimed the hieroglyphs down the length of one wall. Great of Praises. Mistress of Upper and Lower Egypt. I pointed out images where my body was not quite symmetrical or my face was not pleasing enough. Several times I had them replaster a whole wall in order to start a painting again.

"They see me as merely a queen," I complained to Renni one day. "Look at the pictures. They are all a queen."

"The images are feminine, my lady, yes," he said, very carefully. "I thought that was what you wanted? To be shown as a goddess. Have I misunderstood?"

"I am not merely queen but pharaoh as well. They should depict me as such. I want future generations to be in no doubt that I ruled in every way."

"Of course, my lady. I will speak with the artists."

When I toured the chapel site the following day, a new image had been sketched out on an empty stretch of wall. In it I held the crook and the flail, the traditional symbols of pharaoh. My queenly crown had been replaced with the double crown of Upper and Lower Egypt and my chin bore pharaoh's false beard. I nodded my approval.

When I returned the day after that, several of the existing paintings had been modified. They were slight adjustments, perhaps nothing that anyone would notice unless they were very familiar with the original images. My face took on a sterner expression. My figure became more androgynous. Where my hands had been empty, I now held a crook and flail, and wherever my name was written, it was now surrounded by a cartouche to symbolise my importance.

As the day neared when my new chapel would be ready, I pondered exactly who would worship me there. I wanted a proper ceremony and that included music and singing. So I needed a trained priestess. The answer was obvious: it had to be Mutnodjmet and Hemetre, but two worshippers felt insufficient. They would need to train other women.

This temple was smaller than I wanted, but Renni had

convinced me its size was necessary for the sake of completing the building quickly. There was adequate space for only six worshippers, but I would build another, larger temple with room for a dozen. No, fifty. Better yet, a hundred. I would create the biggest temple ever built. Bigger even than Hatshepsut's. I had never seen her temple for myself, but I had heard people talk of it. They said it had been designed to last for millions of years. I would have a temple better than Pharaoh Hatshepsut.

In the meantime, this small temple was almost complete. I sent runners to advise Mutnodjmet and Hemetre that they would come the following morning to worship me.

For the rest of the afternoon, I sat on my throne in pharaoh's audience hall. A new throne rested on the dais now, one which was better suited to my size and more carefully carved to fit my body. It was elegantly wrought of thin sheets of gold inlaid with carnelian, ruby and lapis lazuli. I sat here every afternoon. No longer did Pharaoh hold audience only once a month. I was here every day for my officials to make their reports.

Many people came to my audiences, but their reports were surprisingly trivial. Perhaps I had misremembered what my brother's audiences used to be like. I had thought he made more important decisions. The things presented to me seemed minor and petty. A dispute about who owned a particular cow. An argument about the boundary between a farmer's land and his neighbour's. A priest from the House of Life who was accused of stealing the amulets that were supposed to be inserted between the bandages of the dead. Nothing about defence or trade. No strategy or politics. Just minor disputes that could surely be handled by someone other than Pharaoh.

Before I left the audience hall that afternoon, the runner returned with a response from the priestesses.

"The high priestess sends her regrets that neither she nor her assistant are available to attend you tomorrow."

The boy trembled a little under my fierce glare.

"Why not?"

"They did not say, majesty."

"Renni," I snapped.

He stepped out from behind me.

"My lady?"

"Go to the temple and tell the priestesses that a squad will be sent before dawn to collect them. They should ensure they are ready."

He bowed and quickly left.

The boy still stood in front of me. His hands shook and he shoved them behind his back when he realised I had noticed.

"Why are you still here?" I asked.

He fled.

When Renni returned, his face was troubled.

"Tell me," I said.

"My lady, they say they cannot worship you because they worship Isis every dawn. If they were to attend you, there would be nobody to worship Isis at the dawn ceremony."

"That is not my concern."

"You still wish me to take a squad to collect them tomorrow?"

"They are to be here in time for the dawn ceremony. Tomorrow and every day after. If they will not come willingly, tie them up and carry them."

THIRTY-NINE

W ell before dawn the next morning, I waited in my chapel, darting impatient glances out at the lightening sky.

"Where are they?"

I shifted restlessly on my throne. Nobody was here to respond. Renni waited at the chapel entrance, accompanied by a full squad, but like Isis, I had decreed that only women would be permitted inside. Woser led the men who went to retrieve my worshippers.

With nothing else to do, I smoothed my gown down over my thighs. I had selected my attire today rather than entrusting it to Istnofret. A mortal woman would surely not expect to make such a decision anyway. For my first appearance as a goddess, I had chosen a linen sheath made of an almost sheer and brilliant blue fabric. It fit close to my body and ended at my ankles with an elaborate band of lotus flowers stitched all the way around the hem. The top of the gown consisted of little more than thin straps which reached down to my navel, leaving my breasts exposed. I wore a wide pectoral collar patterned with a mosaic of precious gems, and on my head I bore a crown in the shape of a throne, which was modelled on that of Isis herself. It was newly made, fashioned during the construction of my chapel, and it pleased me greatly that it was ready in time for my first worship ceremony.

The sky was already streaked with the brilliant colours of dawn before Mutnodjmet and Hemetre arrived. They stood in front of me with sour faces.

"You are late," I said.

Neither gave me the courtesy of a response.

"Do you have no reply for me?"

"You did not ask a question," Mutnodjmet said. "It seemed no reply was needed."

I glared down at them for a few more moments. Neither prostrated themselves before me as they should have. I thought about ordering them to do so, but it was clear they were in recalcitrant moods and if they refused, I would have to either let them get away with it or allow guards into the chapel to force them. Neither was the way I wanted my first worship ceremony to commence.

"You may begin," I said finally.

I leaned back against the throne and made myself as comfortable as I could in my tight gown. For the first time, I would be worshipped in the way I deserved.

With a final sullen glare towards me, they chose instruments from the assortment laid out for them. I had expected they would select their usual instruments but Hemetre took up a tambourine and Mutnodjmet a rattle.

"You have not lit any incense," I pointed out as they poised themselves to begin playing. "Nor have you scattered lotus petals on the floor."

Mutnodjmet inhaled sharply and for a moment I expected

her to argue. It seemed that being escorted to my chapel under armed guard had not shown her how serious I was. She lit some incense, although not without several withering glares in my direction, then took a handful of petals and tossed them to the floor. As she did, the leopard skin draped around her shoulders shifted, revealing the markings on her throat and arms. She moved to pull the skin back up.

"Stop," I said.

Mutnodjmet froze.

"Take off the leopard skin."

"It signifies my rank as high priestess."

"I want to see the marks on your skin."

With another glare at me, she lowered the skin to her waist. The designs were finely done, starting at her throat and spidering across her shoulders and down her arms. I had never seen them clearly before and I took my time in examining them. I recognised many of the images - the *ankh* for life, the lotus and the scarab beetle which both symbolised rebirth, a *was* sceptre for the power of the gods. A throne of Isis covered the entirety of one upper arm.

"You may proceed," I said when I had finished.

Mutnodjmet pulled the skin over her shoulders and with one final glare at me, began to shake her rattle and sing. Her voice was sure, even without the accompaniment of Hemetre's lyre. It was not the song I had expected, the one we always sang to Isis. That song spoke of the glory of the gods, of eternal life, the peace of a good life lived beneath the gaze of the gods. This song was unfamiliar to me. From what I could make out, it seemed to be about war and death.

"Stop," I said.

They both froze.

"Why are you singing that? Sing the usual song."

Mutnodjmet's fist clenched around the rattle as if she expected to use it to defend herself.

"That song is for the worship of Isis," she said. "It would not be appropriate in a setting such as this."

"You are here to worship me. You should do it correctly."

"You are not Isis. You are not even a goddess."

"I am Pharaoh and if I say I am a goddess, it is so and you will worship me appropriately. Now sing the song."

She shook her head, her face resolute.

"I will not sing that song. Not here and not to you."

I looked at Hemetre.

"You then," I said. "You will lead the worship and sing."

She glared at me with even more fury than Mutnodjmet had.

"Why should I? You promised to release my son and you didn't. Now you want me to worship you as a goddess. What have you done to deserve such worship?"

I rose to my feet, almost speechless with fury.

"You will worship me because I demand it," I shouted at them.

"I will not worship a false goddess," Mutnodjmet said. "I sing because you order it, but I will not worship you."

I looked at Hemetre.

"Worship me and I will release your son."

She looked back at me for a long moment.

"I don't believe you," she said eventually. "You have given me no reason to trust you."

"Renni!" I called.

One way or another, I would be worshipped this morning. Even if it meant a man must step foot inside my temple.

"My lady?"

"Locate Hemetre's son. He is to be executed at noon."

"No!" Hemetre cried. "Please, my son is innocent. Leave him out of this."

"His life is in your hands," I said. "Renni, send a runner to make arrangements."

Renni left swiftly, although not before I saw the indecision on his face. He at least had the sense not to question me in front of the priestesses, although I had no doubt I would hear of it once they were gone.

A long look passed between Hemetre and Mutnodjmet. Eventually Hemetre turned back to me and bowed her head.

"I will worship you if you spare my son's life."

"Then do so," I said. "And I will decide whether your worship is adequate enough to change my mind."

"I need your assurance first."

Was she brave or just exceptionally foolish? Perhaps she did not take my threat as seriously as she pretended.

"Renni!" I called. "Remove one of the boy's fingers and bring it here for his mother to see."

Hemetre whimpered and I gave her a cold stare.

"For every minute you delay, another of Ptahhotep's fingers will be removed. Once we run out of fingers, we will take his eyes."

"Please, no," she said. "Please don't maim him. I will worship you."

She returned the tambourine to the table, took up the lyre, and began to play. Her voice was weaker than Mutnodjmet's, something I had never noticed when they sang together. She didn't have the same control over her breath and her voice wavered a little on the highest notes.

Mutnodjmet stood with her hands at her side, making it clear that she didn't intend to participate.

"Must I remove one of your fingers also?" I raised my voice to be heard over Hemetre's song.

Mutnodjmet glowered at me for a moment longer, then lifted her rattle and joined her voice with Hemetre's.

I relaxed back into my throne. This was much better. Together their voices made a pleasing harmony and Mutnodjmet's rattle provided a proficient accompaniment to Hemetre's lyre.

The song ended and I started to lean forward, expecting that the worship was over, but Hemetre began another. This one was about birth and rebirth, the pleasure of a beautiful scent in one's nostrils and silky petals beneath one's sandals. I settled back again and closed my eyes.

It was indeed pleasant. The spicy scent of the incense. The priestess's skillful strains. My heartbeat began to slow and my earlier irritation faded. I lost myself in the sound and aroma of my worship.

When the music finally faded, I kept my eyes closed for another few moments. I was queen no longer. I was not even a mere pharaoh. I was a goddess and I would be worshipped like this every day for the rest of my life. It was a beautiful thought.

When I finally opened my eyes, the priestesses stood before me with their instruments lowered. I glanced towards the table of offerings and Hemetre moved quickly. She presented various items to me, waving them beneath my nose as if I was a statue. My stomach growled, having not yet eaten today, but as a goddess, I could absorb the offerings through their scent. I had no need to eat them. At length both priestesses bowed, although Mutnodjmet's was rather cursory.

"The worship is concluded," Hemetre said.

"You may leave."

"My son?" she asked quickly. "You will release him now?"

"Renni, have them returned to the temple." To the priestesses

I said, "You will return for tomorrow's ceremony. See that you appear before me in a more willing frame of mind."

Renni came to usher the priestesses away.

"My lady, please," Hemetre said. "Will you release Ptahhotep now?"

I waved my hand towards Renni and he took Hemetre by the arm. I couldn't hear what he said to her, but she shot me a glare as he led her from the room.

"You promised," she called as she disappeared from my sight.

I leaned back on my throne, seeking to regain the peace I had felt while being worshipped. It was gone, though. Shattered into pieces by Hemetre's ungracious clamour. At the edge of my vision, a woman faded from sight.

FORTY

R enni came to me as I sat on my throne a few hours later, wishing the day would pass faster. I wanted it to be tomorrow morning already so that I might be worshipped again. Perhaps I should have a dusk ceremony as well. I could be worshipped twice a day and the wait would not be so long.

"My lady, may I speak with you?"

"Go ahead."

"Do you wish me to return the boy to his mother?"

"Hemetre's son, I assume you mean."

"Ptahhotep. You did tell her this morning that you would release him."

"She was not very compliant today. I think I need to see that she can be more obedient first."

"I am not sure she will worship you again if you don't release her son. She spoke to me on the way back to the temple. She was not happy about the possibility that you might not keep your word."

"I care little about whether she is happy or not provided she does as I say. And as long as her son is in custody, I think her obedience can be assured."

"My lady, Hemetre does not believe her son is still alive. She thinks this is the reason you have not released him."

"I assume you set her straight."

"I tried, but she won't believe me until she sees him with her own eyes."

"Do you question my decision?"

"Of course not, my lady, but—"

"It sounds like you are questioning me. You know I have little patience for such things."

"I just think this would go easier for you if you release him as you said you would."

"Did you send his finger to his mother?"

He hesitated for a long moment.

"Renni."

"I did not remove his finger, my lady."

"I ordered you to. Why did you disobey?"

He opened and closed his mouth, seemingly undecided how to respond. At last he said, "I didn't think you meant it. That you said it simply to assure Hemetre's compliance. I did not think you actually wanted me to cut off one of his fingers."

"I do not make empty threats. Now go. Have the finger sent to his mother."

"You would disfigure a boy in order to threaten his mother?" Renni asked.

I gave him a cold glare.

"I will not warn you again."

Renni turned to leave and I felt a small surge of victory. He, at least, would obey me. But he stopped and turned back to face me.

"I am sorry, my lady. Truly I am. But I cannot do as you ask."

"I am not asking. I am commanding."

"I don't know how we came to be here," he said. "But this is not you. This desire for power, to be worshipped, to be obeyed. You are not a goddess. You are merely a mortal woman and if you don't remember who you are soon, I fear you will do something you will regret for the rest of your life."

"Get out of my sight," I snarled.

He left without another word. I rose and paced around the audience hall. Tuta followed a few paces behind me, although my other guards kept their positions around the dais. My mind whirled and my stomach felt unsettled. If Renni would say such things to me privately, what did he say when I wasn't there? I couldn't allow such a situation to continue. I would have to make an example of him.

"Have Renni arrested," I said to Tuta. "He is to be imprisoned for seven days. I will consider his fate after that."

"My lady." Tuta's voice was tentative. "Renni is loyal to you, but his men are loyal to him. I am not sure how the rest of the squad will react if I arrest their captain."

"You are Renni's second. The job of captain falls to you and it will be up to you to ensure their loyalty."

"Their loyalty is to Renni, my lady. Not to me."

"Then make them loyal to you," I said with a snarl. "Now go and do your job."

Tuta bowed and left, having signalled to one of the men to take his place behind me. I continued to pace around the chamber. Gone was my sense of peace after being worshipped. Now I felt frustrated. Angry. Vengeful.

"I will go to my pleasure garden now."

The guard behind me — I had never bothered to learn his name — gestured to the rest of the squad and they formed up around me. As we marched along the hallways, folk stared at me more than usual. The whispers were louder. Several people boldly met my eyes instead of averting their gaze as they should have.

"Why are they looking at me?" I asked as we stopped in front of the door that led to my pleasure garden.

None of my guards replied.

"Answer me."

"My lady." It was the guard who had taken Tuta's place. "There have been… rumours circulating through the palace."

"What kind of rumours?"

He cleared his throat.

"That, well, that you have lost your mind."

"I am a goddess." My tone was haughty. "I do not need to conform to the expectations of mortals. I do as I please."

"They fear that you will become like Sekhmet, my lady," he said.

The Lioness. Lady of Pestilence, Lady of Plague. She came close to destroying humanity once. Her rage made men tremble. I had long admired her. Being compared to Sekhmet did not displease me.

"Perhaps I will," I said. "If they give me reason to."

I glanced pointedly towards the door and he stepped forward to open it. I strolled in. Gone were the days when I wasn't allowed to enter any area without Intef or his men checking it first. Now I walked where I wanted to and nobody even tried to stop me.

The garden was tidier than it had been when I was here last. Flower beds had been weeded, shrubs pruned. The paths had been cleaned of duck excrement. A soft breeze whispered through the trees around me and their branches bowed as I passed. See, even the trees acknowledged me. Peace returned as I walked, but it was shattered with Istnofret's arrival.

"My lady?"

Her voice was tentative, which immediately fuelled my irritation.

"What is it?"

"I heard that Renni has been arrested."

"What of it?"

"My lady, you know he is loyal to you. He travelled all the way across the known world to aid your quest. He followed you into the underworld. Yet now you arrest him?"

"He disobeyed an order."

"Can you not show mercy to one who has been as loyal as he?"

I whirled around to glare at her.

"Mercy? There is no mercy for anyone who disobeys."

She shrank away from me.

"What has happened to you?" she whispered. "I never thought to see you like this. The Eye controls you so strongly that you have no interest in anything but power."

"Be careful, Istnofret, or you will not live long enough to see much else."

"And now you threaten *me*?" She drew herself up and glared at me. "I, who have been your loyal servant since the day I was sent to you? Your friend for the last several years. Like Renni, I gave up everything to follow you across the world. My friends, my position, my livelihood, gods damn it. And this is how you repay me? By threatening me? Arresting the man I love? You swore you would listen if I told you it was happening again, but you have broken your promise."

"I will be treated with the respect I am entitled to," I shouted at her.

"What respect?" she shouted back. "You are no better than Ay. You rule with fear and intimidation. You demand that folk abide by your whim at the threat of their lives. I thought that if we helped you, you would make things better, but you have become a tyrant."

"Get out of my sight," I snarled. "If I see you again, I will have you executed on the spot."

She sniffed at me.

"Gladly."

Then she was gone and I was left to walk my garden alone.

FORTY-ONE

When I returned to my chamber, several crates had been brought in and stacked neatly against the wall.

"Why are those here?" I asked.

"I found your jewellery, my lady," Behenu said. "Or what is left of it anyway. I think some of the best pieces are gone, but there is still a lot there, including the ones Istnofret took gems from."

I lifted the lid from one of the crates and peered in. My jewellery had been tossed in with no care given to either tidiness or preservation. On the top lay a silver bracelet which I immediately recognised. It had once contained half a dozen blue sapphires, some of which I had given to the courier who transported me from Sardis to Smyrna. Did I still have the gems that matched any of these pieces?

In my sleeping chamber, my travelling pack lay on the shelf where it had rested ever since we returned to the palace. I had not brought it here myself. It had simply appeared one day and I had cared little enough to bother finding out who had retrieved it from Hemetre's home. I had not expected to need anything inside it, but for some reason I had been reluctant to have it disposed of.

I rummaged inside, searching for the little pouch that contained my gems. It wasn't there. I took the pack over to the window so I could see inside better and rummaged through again. Anger welled in me. Someone had stolen my pouch.

Just as I was about to toss the pack to the floor, my fingers found a scroll. I pulled it out, careless in my haste. It was somewhat crumpled but the seal was still intact, even though the edges had crumbled away. It was my own seal from when I had been queen.

My heart thudded double time. It was the letter to my sisters. The sole letter Behenu had saved from Setau's house. I stared down at it for a long time. I had never been sure I wanted to know which letter she saved. It might be something trite, something that would show how foolish and immature I had been back then. It might simply contain something I had no wish to remember.

I had no need to relive old memories. I started to crumple the papyrus but stopped as a memory teased at the edges of my mind. I had seen this, in a dream. The decision I made now about whether or not to read this letter would be important. If the dream had showed me the consequences of my decision, I didn't remember. I had nothing to guide me, other than the knowledge that this moment would be pivotal.

FORTY-TWO

My Dear Sisters

I am afraid. Ay grows more insouciant by the day. I have long known that he has little respect for me, but until now I believed that he respected my bloodline, and my father, if nothing else. Now I wonder if there is anything at all he respects. I fear that being my father's daughter is no longer enough.

Intef assures me you are well hidden and I can only trust that this is true. I fear daily that I will enter a chamber and you will be there, having been found and brought back to the palace. If they find you, the advisors will not need me. They only need one of our father's daughters for his bloodline to continue and I know they would prefer it was not me.

I often look back at what has happened and wonder how we got here. I have so many regrets. All the things I should have said, the things I should have done. The ways in which I could have encouraged our brother to be stronger or how I could have fought back against the advisors. How might things be different now had I been a stronger queen?

If I ever have an opportunity for real power, I will be stronger. I will be wiser. I will remember that we live by the grace of the gods. I will model myself after Isis and remember her dedication to her brother-husband, her love for her son and for her people. I will remember her sense of duty and her compassion. I will never be like Ay. I will never forget my humanity.

I pray to Isis, my dear sisters, that you are safe and well. I pray you have made a life for yourselves and that you do not regret that I sent you away. If the gods ever allow us to be reunited in this life, I will wrap my arms around you and never let you forget how much I love you. And if we do not meet again until the afterlife, I will do the same then.

I love you and I hope you remember me fondly.

Your loving sister
  Ankhesenamun

FORTY-THREE

Tears blurred my vision and I could barely make out the letter's final lines. I didn't even remember writing it, and yet this, out of all the letters I wrote to my sisters, was the one Behenu had chosen at random to save. This letter in which I swore I would never be like Ay. That I would never forget my humanity.

What had I become? Istnofret called me a tyrant and I supposed that wasn't far from the truth. I had imprisoned Renni. I had threatened to have Istnofret executed. I had tormented Hemetre by keeping her son from her and demanded that Renni cut off one of the boy's fingers. I had not made a single enquiry as to where Nenwef was being held.

A flash of anger spiked through me. I was a goddess. I had no need for the pathetic musings of a woman who no longer existed. Why was I letting human emotions such as regret and sadness fill me like this? I doubted Sekhmet ever felt any such thing, even as she destroyed the earth. Even as she slaughtered her people and drank a river of blood.

I read the letter again, searching for some hint that I had not truly been so pathetic as I sounded. But then I reached the mention of Intef. Intef who had given up his life to stay in the underworld. Intef who now lived in a place that was so strange I could barely comprehend it. Intef who would be horrified if he knew what I had become.

"Intef is gone," I muttered to myself. "You will never see him again."

"Perhaps you might," came a voice from behind me.

I crumpled the letter and tossed it to the floor before dashing away my tears. I turned to fix a glare on Behenu.

"You always said you wanted to come back to Egypt to make things right," she said. "Then you and Intef were going to go and make a life of your own."

"That was before Intef decided to stay with Keeper of the Lake," I said, bitterly.

"So that you could complete your quest. Don't you think he expected you to come back for him once it was done?"

I stared at her, suddenly speechless.

"It was his decision," I said, eventually, unable to think of any other reply.

"But he would not have expected it to be permanent. Do you think he would accept the situation if it was you who had stayed? Don't you think he would have done what he needed to and then gone back to retrieve you?"

"He was the price." I could barely string my words together. Emotions flashed through me. Surprise. Regret. Sadness. Hope. "Keeper of the Lake demanded a soul in exchange for letting us pass through the gate. Someone had to stay."

"But Keeper didn't say how long he had to stay," she said, very gently as if she thought her words might break me. "Maybe Intef has fulfilled what he agreed to. Maybe it is time we brought him home."

My mouth opened and closed. I had never considered that Intef's decision might not be permanent. That there might be some way he could leave that place.

"It doesn't work like that," I said. "You cannot make a bargain with a god and then find a loophole. They don't do things like that, not even a minor deity like a guardian of the gate."

"How will you know if you don't at least try to get him back?"

I had no answer to that.

"If you want to go get him, I will come with you. I think Istnofret and Renni would too."

"They probably hate me now."

"They are confused and hurt, but they don't hate you. If you ask, they will go with you."

The emotions that swirled inside of me were too big to understand.

"Leave me," I said.

FORTY-FOUR

I barely slept that night. My dreams were such a confusing mix of images that I couldn't tell which, or even if, any of them were true dreams or merely things I wanted to be. I saw Intef cradling a babe. A young girl trailing behind the leonine Keeper of the Lake. The same girl stood on the banks of the lake of fire and stared into its depths. Perhaps somebody called to her, for she suddenly looked back over her shoulder, then ran off. Intef stood in a dimly lit room with tears running down his cheeks. I saw myself sitting cross-legged opposite my shadow who was once again an independent being. I walked through a tunnel lit only by the lamp I carried. My hand trembled and I feared dropping the lamp. Someone whispered in my ear. *Be careful of the jackal. He is a trickster.* I sank down into deep water.

I woke gasping for breath and it took some time to convince myself that my lungs really weren't filled with water. I had drowned in my dream. Something tugged at the edges of my memory, suggesting it was more than just a dream, but when I tried to focus on the thought, it slid away.

Someone had spoken to me, but it was a few moments

before I could remember their words. *Be careful of the jackal. He is a trickster.* The only jackal I knew of was Anubis. My blood froze as I realised the implication. Keeper of the Lake guarded Anubis's gate. It was Keeper who demanded that one of us stay. I had believed Intef to be living in the underworld. A strange existence, yes, but an existence nevertheless. Perhaps my dream hinted that something had happened to him.

I must have eventually fallen asleep again although I was still exhausted when I next woke. I could hear somebody walking around in the main chamber. Birds chirped and the light streaming in through the window held the brightness of a morning well past dawn. I had missed the dawn worship. Why had nobody woken me?

I still used Pharaoh's chambers and instead of the image of Hathor that was positioned over the bed in my own sleeping chamber, here I stared up at Horus. The falcon-headed god, the son of Isis. Falcon eyes glittered above a falcon beak. So strange and yet oddly familiar.

Behenu heard me getting up and came to bring a bowl of washing water.

"Good morning, my lady."

Her tone was meek and she avoided looking at me, as was proper for a servant. She set the bowl down on a bench and began to leave.

"Behenu."

She froze and very slowly turned to face me.

"My lady?"

Still her eyes were averted and she didn't look at me.

"Are you afraid of me?"

There was a long pause before she answered.

"People have been punished for speaking truth to you. For

saying things that you don't want to hear. I am only trying to make sure I say nothing to offend you."

I breathed in and out, trying to find the right words.

"I have not felt like myself lately. This… this is not who I intended to be."

She looked at me finally and the relief on her face shattered my heart.

"Does that mean…"

"Yes. I intend to go after Intef. But first I need to put things right here, as I had intended all along. Send for Renni to be released and tell Istnofret she need not fear I will order her to be executed."

"Do you wish them to come to you?"

Yes, I did, but I would not order them to.

"They are free to do as they please," I said. "If they wish to leave, ensure they take their share of the gems we have left and anything else they need. They may go if they want to and I will not send anyone after them."

I bathed and dressed myself. Behenu had not yet returned and I supposed she might have gone to deliver the news directly rather than sending a messenger. She had already laid out a white linen gown for me so I put that on and brushed my hair. I didn't know how to dress my hair in the way that Behenu did and had only the vaguest idea of how to make up my face so I didn't bother with either. Let folk see me with my face bare. I didn't care. Today I would put things to rights and tomorrow I would leave to retrieve Intef, or at least to try. In the corner of my chamber, the shadowy figure of a woman waited. She was gone as soon as I turned towards her.

"Is that you Sadeh?" I asked.

I waited for her to reappear in the corner of my vision, but she didn't.

"Sadeh, if that is you, I want you to know how sorry I am. I am sorry that I let you go in my place. I should have protected you. It should not have been you who died that day."

A flicker in the corner of my eye.

"I miss you, Sadeh. It took me a long time to understand what you were to me. All those years I held myself apart, trying not to let myself feel anything. I was so lonely and I didn't realise that I had friends right here. Friends who loved me enough that they were willing to give their lives for me. I wish I had understood this before you went to the advisors that day. I wish I had been able to tell you I loved you."

I hardly dared to breathe as I waited, hoping Sadeh might make some reply. But the woman merely flickered again at the edge of my vision and then she was gone.

I straightened my gown and left my chambers. From the other end of the hallway, three figures approached. I stopped and let them come to me. Let them have one last chance to walk away if they wanted to.

Istnofret and Renni's faces both showed their hesitation. Perhaps they wondered whether Behenu's message was a cruel joke. We stood in silence, everyone waiting for someone else to speak first. Eventually I realised it would have to be me. I was the only one who needed to apologise.

"I am sorry. I have acted most appallingly and it was wrong of me. Once I let myself give in to the Eye, nothing mattered other than power. The Eye desires power. Craves it. I let myself get so swept away with what it wanted that I forgot who I was. I forgot what I wanted."

Tears trembled in Istnofret's eyes and I was surprised to find I was crying too. She leaned in to hug me fiercely.

"I knew you would come back to yourself eventually," she

whispered. "I just hoped it would be before you did something you couldn't undo."

I took a shaky breath. She deserved to know the truth about me.

"I think it wasn't just the Eye that wanted power. It was me too. There's something inside of me that wants it. And the more power I got, the more I wanted. At first, it was enough to be pharaoh, then I wanted to be a goddess as well. I wanted to be like Isis."

"You were raised with power all around you," she said. "It would be natural for you to want it for yourself, especially considering how powerless you felt when you were queen. But that isn't who you really are. You might want power, but you don't crave it. You don't threaten people to get it. That was the Eye."

"Do you forgive me?" I asked.

"Of course," she said.

Renni hugged me too, then I hugged Behenu for good measure.

"I hear you are going to get Intef," Renni said.

I had hardly dared to hope they might come with me, but my mouth suddenly didn't seem to work and I couldn't make myself ask.

"He would do the same for any of us," I said. It was what Istnofret had said when she decided we would retrieve Renni from the prison. "He would never leave one of us there."

"We will come with you," Istnofret said. "Renni and I."

"But this is the last time," Renni said, quickly. "After this, we have our own lives to live. But I would not miss retrieving Intef from that place for anything."

"Neither would I," Istnofret said.

"I am coming too," Behenu added.

I looked at my three friends. Other than Intef and my sisters, these were all the people I loved. The ones that still lived anyway.

"I don't deserve friends like you," I said.

"No," Istnofret said. "You don't, but we are here anyway."

FORTY-FIVE

There was much to do before we could leave for Crete. I released Ptahhotep and Renni personally escorted him home. I sent with him two gems as an apology to Hemetre. Renni returned with a brief message of thanks. I had thought perhaps Hemetre might come to see me one last time. After all, we had known each other for more than a decade, but I could hardly blame her for not coming. She probably thought I might change my mind again and wanted to be nowhere near me when that happened. Likely she and Ptahhotep had already left Memphis. I doubted I would ever see her again.

I released Nenwef, greatly ashamed of myself for not having done so sooner. Tuta told me that Nenwef was leaving Memphis immediately and Woser intended to go with him. Neither came to see me before they departed. I was saddened but understood that like Hemetre, they probably didn't trust my motives.

I finally remembered to ask after Mahu and was pleased to learn that Renni had indeed sent men to ensure he was freed. He had been sentenced to the slave mines and they had to track him halfway to Nubia before they caught up to the squad that was escorting three prisoners to the mines. The guards were none too pleased that only Mahu was to be released, given it meant they still had to complete their journey. Renni had sent word that Mahu shouldn't try to come to us in Memphis and didn't know where he had gone. Although I would probably never have the chance to thank Mahu personally, it pleased me to know he had been released.

There was the question of what to do with the throne. I knew that if I left without making firm arrangements for the succession, there would be a number of men vying to claim it and I had made a promise to Mutnodjmet to ensure she was queen. As much as I didn't like Horemheb, I had to admit that he was the best qualified to be Pharaoh.

I met with Horemheb privately to offer him the throne with the condition that he took Mutnodjmet as his Great Royal Wife. He couldn't agree fast enough. Neither her age nor the fact that she was likely past her childbearing years deterred him. It seemed he had wanted to marry me as little as I wanted him. He had only ever wanted the throne. My heart was heavy as I made the formal declaration announcing both my heir and my abdication. Horemheb was not the kind of man I wanted to leave on the throne, but my choices were limited and he was, if nothing else, experienced. He might make a good pharaoh. He might not. But I had achieved my goal of removing Ay. At some point I had to put Egypt back into the hands of the gods.

I sat on my throne in the audience chamber for the last time. Istnofret and Behenu waited nearby, ready to assist if I needed anything, although I had made it clear to them that they were no longer my servants. Behind me stood the two men I most trusted to guard my back: Renni and Tuta. The rest of Renni's men, including Nehi and Sabu, were arrayed around the dais.

I might have expected to be busy, but nobody came to see me.

I supposed I had done little to make anyone favourably disposed towards me and with my imminent departure, the sycophants were probably already busy making themselves known to Horemheb.

"The high priestess, Mutnodjmet," announced the guard at the door at last.

Mutnodjmet held her head high as she walked towards me, just as she always had. I wondered whether she would continue to wear the leopard skin once she was queen or whether she would pass that, and her title of high priestess, to Hemetre if she was still in Memphis. What would the people think about having a queen who was covered in the markings of a priestess?

As she reached the dais, Mutnodjmet began to lower herself to the ground.

"That is not necessary," I said, quickly. "After all, I am here for just a few more hours. The throne will be yours soon enough."

She gave me a steady look.

"You kept your end of the deal. I am surprised."

My dream flashed before my eyes. The one that showed me that either Sadeh or Mutnodjmet would take my place on the throne. I had thought that dream might come to pass when I sent Sadeh in my place to face the advisors, but Ay had ordered her killed before that ever happened. So it was Mutnodjmet who took my place and Sadeh had truly died for nothing.

I inhaled deeply, trying to keep my breath steady. The knowledge hurt. So many times I had wondered whether things might have been different if I had gone to the advisors myself. Whether Sadeh might have lived. Warm fingers wrapped around my hand, pulling me from my thoughts.

"She went willingly," Istnofret said.

How she knew I was thinking about Sadeh, I didn't know,

although I had told her once that either Sadeh or Mutnodjmet would sit on my throne. I squeezed Istnofret's hand but couldn't reply past the lump in my throat. I wanted to ask whether she too had seen a woman at the edge of her vision. I didn't know whether it was Sadeh, but I hoped it was. Whoever she was, I thought she had heard me when I told her I was sorry, for I hadn't seen her again.

"What will you do now?" Mutnodjmet asked.

I had almost forgotten she was there.

"I have a promise to keep."

An unspoken one perhaps, but a promise nonetheless. Behenu was right. If I had been the one to stay behind, Intef would have come back for me. He would do whatever he must to get me out of there.

"Do you intend to come back to Memphis?" Mutnodjmet asked.

"No. You do not need to fear that I will want the throne back. Once I leave, I will not return to Memphis again."

"I assume your friends will be going with you?"

I looked at the people around me.

"Some will," I said. "Others wish to stay here. Nehi, for instance." I gestured towards him and he gave me a brief nod of acknowledgement. "Nehi is a good man and a fine soldier. My... the former captain of my personal squad thought very highly of him. You will need a squad for your personal protection and I commend him to you."

Mutnodjmet gave Nehi a long look.

"That is a high recommendation from Ankhesenamun," she said, at last. "Can you live up to that?"

Nehi gave her a low bow.

"I will work every day to ensure that I do."

"Then you may captain my personal squad," she said. "Select

the men you wish to have. Any guard in the city is at your disposal, with the exception of those my husband-to-be chooses for his own squad."

Nehi bowed again.

"You honour me, my lady."

Mutnodjmet turned back to me. "Are there others you would recommend to me?"

"Where is Sabu?" I asked.

"I am here, my lady."

"Sabu is another good man," I said to Mutnodjmet.

Sabu cleared his throat.

"My lady, if I may?"

"You may."

"I understand you are to leave Memphis."

"I am."

"I wish to travel with you. You will need guards on your journey."

I gave him a steady look.

"You do not know where I travel to."

"I don't need to know. I only wish to serve. Intef was good to me and he would want men he can trust to guard you. Let me be one of them."

"I cannot guarantee you will ever be able to return home. I travel to a place very few mortals have ever been. Are you sure you wish to follow me?"

"I do, my lady."

I sighed. My heart was heavy and I wasn't sure this was a good idea. Sabu had no idea what he was volunteering for. But no doubt word of me had spread throughout Egypt. I had enemies, even more than I had before. If Sabu wished to come, I could hardly afford to turn down a skilled guard.

"Very well then," I said. "You may come with us."

I turned back to Mutnodjmet.

"There are other good people here. If Nenwef or Woser ever return, I commend them to you. Nehi will be able to tell you of others."

She gave me a small nod. "I shall take my leave of you then. I am sure you have other people to speak with, arrangements to make."

"Do you wish chambers to be prepared for you?" I asked. "The queen's chambers perhaps."

"Only once you have left. Tomorrow will be soon enough."

"I am not using them at present. Behenu, would you send runners to make arrangements for my old chambers to be prepared for Mutnodjmet?"

"Of course." Behenu hurried away.

Mutnodjmet watched her leave, then gave me a bemused look.

"You know what she is, yes?"

"Of course. She was my slave at one time, but I freed her. Now she is my friend."

"No, I mean what she is to her people."

"Her people?"

"She is a truth-speaker."

"I do not know what that means."

"She speaks the truth, or the truth as she sees it at any rate."

"Do you mean she has a special ability?"

Mutnodjmet shrugged.

"I suppose you could look at it that way. Do you intend to send her home? She is very important to her people."

I had long suspected Behenu was more than she seemed to be. Initially I had assumed her to be a peasant girl to have been captured as the spoils of war. But she had clearly received an education and she knew how to stitch finely. She was more than a peasant, but she had revealed little about her former life.

"She is free to leave if she wishes," I said. "She knows that. She has decided to travel with me one last time. What she does after that is her own choice. Perhaps she will choose to go home."

Mutnodjmet took her leave of me then. I waited a little longer but nobody else came to farewell me. At length, I rose and left the dais for the last time.

FORTY-SIX

I felt oddly calm as we prepared to leave Memphis. I had told Mutnodjmet the truth when I said I wouldn't return here again. I didn't know where I would live once our journey was finished. It wasn't a decision I could make until I knew whether Intef would be with me or not. Even if we somehow managed to convince Keeper of the Lake to allow him to leave, he might want nothing to do with me. He might not be able to forgive me for giving our daughter to Osiris.

My chambers were a hive of busyness as we packed up the things we would take with us to Crete. Istnofret and Behenu went through the crates of jewellery, removing the gems from larger pieces and setting aside smaller ones to take with us. I helped them for a while, but it disturbed me to see the items I used to wear every day discarded on the floor. I pulled out a pretty silver bangle inlaid with sapphires and tucked it away in my travelling pack. I didn't know whether we might encounter Osiris again on our travels or if he would even be willing to give Meketaten a gift from me, but I wanted to have something with me in case. I also set aside a necklace from which dangled an ankh amulet. Keeper of the Lake probably wasn't going to be pleased about our return, especially when they realised our purpose, but perhaps bringing a gift might help to mollify them a little.

Other items we would take with us were piled on a day bed in the main chamber. The Eye — it only seemed right that we return it to the place in which we had found it. A couple of changes of clothes for each of us, food that would travel well, blankets. Renni prepared the things we might need in the tunnels beneath the palace: lamps with oil and flint, a length of rope and several spare daggers. Long skeins of string and charcoal with which to mark the tunnel walls so we could track our turns. We would be far better prepared this time.

"Daggers?" I asked him.

"We did hear talk of a beast that lived in the tunnels," he said.

"We saw no sign of it last time."

"It doesn't hurt to be prepared."

Tuta had gone to make arrangements for a boat to take us upriver to Rhakotis. We would not be hitching a ride this time. He would seek out a captain who was willing to transport us, and only us. Sabu put together a squad of trusted men to guard us on the journey. We didn't know where Khay or Tentopet might be — there had been no word of either being seen in Memphis — but we intended to be ready for trouble this time.

That afternoon I sat in the little sitting chamber and looked out at the courtyard for the final time. The new vine was slowly growing up the wall and I was a little sorry I wouldn't be here to see its first bloom.

"Samun, we have a surprise for you," Istnofret said late that afternoon.

I had dozed off while contemplating the vine and for a

moment I felt guilty. I should have been helping with the prepa-
rations, not sitting around feeling sorry for myself. I had to
remember that once again, I was no longer queen. I would be
just one of our party of travellers.

"Come on," she urged when I didn't respond. "Come and
see."

I followed her through the chamber. A half squad waited at
the door and Renni quickly took up his position ahead of me.

"This is not necessary," I said.

"You are still queen tonight," he said.

They led me through the palace and out to my pleasure
garden. I hadn't been out here since the day I had decided I was
a goddess and the memory brought a flush of guilt to my cheeks.

Beneath the branches of the *kathal* tree lay a blanket, on which
was arranged a feast. Slices of roast duck and fowl. A salad with
crisp lettuce, cucumber and sweet onions. Cheese and breads.
Figs, dates and pomegranates. A platter of roasted *kathal* fruit.
Jugs of melon juice.

"This is perfect," I said. "Who did this?"

"Behenu made most of the arrangements," Istnofret said.

I gave Behenu a grateful smile and she ducked her head.
Mutnodjmet's words again ran through my head. *She is a truth-
speaker. She is very important to her people.* I hadn't asked Behenu
what that meant and perhaps I never would. She had made it
clear she didn't want to talk about her previous life. I would,
however, do everything I could to see that she went home.

"I thought a good meal before we left might help make the
journey a little easier," she said. "Pleasant things to think
back on."

They were all there for my farewell dinner. Istnofret, Renni,
Behenu. Tuta and Sabu, both of whom would be travelling with
us, for now at least. Tuta had been non-committal when I asked

what he intended to do next, but I didn't miss the way he kept sneaking glances at Behenu. Behenu seemed to be busy pretending not to notice.

Our party was noisy and we sat up way too late for folk who were beginning a long journey on the morrow. Once the melon juice was gone, Behenu brought out a couple of bottles of wine from Pharaoh's vineyard. It was a red wine, smooth and mellow. My heart ached at remembering how I had once promised myself I would ensure Intef drank wine from Pharaoh's vineyard with me.

"Is there any more of that wine?" I asked as Behenu filled up my mug for the second time.

"There is a whole cellar of it." She gave me a grin, her usual reticence loosened by the wine. "Did you want to raid it before we leave?"

"I would like to take a bottle with us for Intef. In case we find him."

"I will fetch one in the morning," she said, her face suddenly sombre. "And I am sure we will find him."

I nodded but didn't reply. I wasn't at all sure we would find Intef, let alone be able to retrieve him. The tunnels under the palace seemed to lead where they wished and the hole that led us into the underworld seemed to move. I didn't know whether it was the gods who controlled our access to the underworld or something else, but it was possible that whoever or whatever it was might not allow us to go back a second time. We could search the tunnels for the rest of our lives and never find the underworld again if they chose to hide it from us. We might never find Intef.

"Stop looking so morose, Samun." Istnofret bumped my shoulder with hers. "Tomorrow is a new journey. Let's just enjoy tonight while we can."

I gave her a small smile and tried to shake off my negativity.

It took me a long time to fall asleep that night. I remembered the last time I had spent what I thought would be my final night in the palace, after Ay had sentenced me to labour in the slave mines. I had lain in my bed, thinking that this was probably the last night of comfort I would ever have.

This time was different. I knew this might be my last night of comfort for a while, but not forever. I couldn't think ahead to what I would do after this final journey. It depended on whether we were able to retrieve Intef, and whether he still wanted to be with me. I suspected I already knew the answer to that, but I had to try. Behenu was right when she said that if it was me there, Intef would never give up. He would get me out of that place if it was the last thing he ever did.

When I finally fell asleep, my dreams were their usual tangled mess. The sandy shore. Sinking down into deep water. *Be careful of the jackal.* The girl who stood on the edge of the Lake of Fire.

I dreamed I ran through a tunnel. I clutched a lamp although my hand shook so much that I almost dropped it. I could hear nothing over the sound of my own heart, which drummed so loudly that the thing pursuing me could probably track me by it. My breath caught in my chest and a panicked moan escaped my lips.

"Faster," someone said. "It is catching up."

Somehow, I pushed my legs to go faster. They trembled so much that if I stopped, I would probably fall down. If I did, I would be dead.

Beside me, somebody tripped and fell.

"Don't stop."

Somebody grabbed my hand and pulled me on. I didn't look

back, but I couldn't avoid hearing the screams and the crunching of bones.

Then the dream shifted and I saw the other possible fate that lay ahead of me.

I woke, breathless and trembling, my body soaked in sweat. I would try to retrieve Intef regardless, but now I knew that whether we were successful or not, not all of us would survive the journey and it might be me who didn't.

FORTY-SEVEN

To Ankhesenamun

I write this letter secretly as my father would not be happy if he knew I was communicating with you. Your letter and your compensation were delivered by the hands of your messenger. My father is incensed. He feels that your compensation was insultingly paltry and does not come close to making up for the loss of his son and my brother, Zannanza. He has sworn that Egypt will compensate him for the loss of his son one thousand times over. He has sworn to obtain vengeance for Zannanza's death. He has sworn he will obliterate Egypt. He will make no reply to your letter, but already he prepares his army.

Your friend
  Muwatti, Princess of the Land of the Hatti, Daughter of the Great King Suppiluliumas

Ankhesenamun's journey concludes in
Book Six: *Guardian of the Underworld*

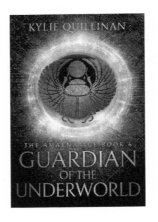

Subscribe and get THREE full length ebooks

ALSO BY KYLIE QUILLINAN

The Amarna Age Series

Book One: *Queen of Egypt*

Book Two: *Son of the Hittites*

Book Three: *Eye of Horus*

Book Four: *Gates of Anubis*

Book Five: *Lady of the Two Lands*

Book Six: *Guardian of the Underworld*

Daughter of the Sun: An Amarna Age Novella

The Amarna Princesses Series

Book One: *Outcast*

Book Two: *Catalyst*

Book Three: *Warrior*

Palace of the Ornaments Series

Book One: *Princess of Babylon*

Book Two: *Ornament of Pharaoh*

See kyliequillinan.com for more books, including exclusive collections, and newsletter sign up.

ABOUT THE AUTHOR

Kylie writes about women who defy society's expectations. Her novels are for readers who like fantasy with a basis in history or mythology. Her interests include Dr Who, jellyfish and cocktails. She needs to get fit before the zombies come.

Swan – the epilogue to the Tales of Silver Downs series – is available exclusively to her newsletter subscribers. Sign up at kyliequillinan.com.